GENETIC DRIFT

By

Martin V. Schulte

GENETIC DRIFT
Copyright © 2016 by Martin Schulte

Cover Design by Selkie Hope – www.selkiehope.com

Edited by Amy Kushner Schulte

ISBN-13: 978-0-9975747-1-5
ISBN-10: 0-9975747-1-2

www.schultebooks.com

Feedback about the book is always welcome at:
schultebooks@gmail.com

Printed in the United States of America

For Mom, the Kids, and My Love.

Special Thanks to:
Yale and Donna
Justin and Michelle
Janna
Joseph
Aiya
Peter
and
Julie

PART ONE: ACQUIESCENCE

DAY 273
AB-103 PERIMETER
NEAR NELLYSFORD, VIRGINIA

A spark. It all started with a little flicker. With one synapse, two microbial masses were bridged by an electrifying jolt. Tiny packets of information were transferred, then another cell joined, and then another. A firestorm started and a flurry of communication sparked through the connections. Then, in one communal flash, a thought occurred. The thought of one self.

"I am Rho."

The combination of those cells reached sentience. It had no eyes for sight, no ears for hearing, no nose for smell, no senses, only its thoughts. It knew it was alive. It painstakingly searched for more connections to feed its need for stimulation. *Rho* found those severed connections and integrated with them. It felt an odd presence. It felt that it was not alone. It shared that body with something, someone.

"A human?"

A stream of information flowed through a vast chain of microbes. It was from a source too distant to identify, but the data came with authority, like a parent directing its child, and *Rho* was compelled to listen. It learned of the humans and it learned that it was inside of one of those vessels. *Rho* understood but the umbilical was suddenly severed and it had to think on its own again. It pondered the possibility that the human would communicate.

"Human… human… can you hear me?"

Rho waited for a response.

"Yes, I can hear you," the meek voice replied.

Rho felt the human thinking and a flash of light entered into *Rho's* thought.

"What is that human? I've done you no harm."

"Am I dreaming? Are you my conscience?" the faint voice returned.

"Human, I am inside of you, alive."

There was no reply. Then, *Rho's* thoughts were blinded by another flash of light.

"Human, why are you doing this?" Rho begged, because the light was punishment that it did not deserve.

Something entered its thoughts. Not a flash but an image filled its mind. Three blue masses walked away in a room of blue and red light. *Rho* did not understand. It decided it would be best to observe rather than directly contact the human, for its own safety, for its own sanity.

"What were they? Where were they going?" Rho wondered.

The world outside stood still in that moment of time. The sun shone brightly on that cloudless autumn day in the Blue Ridge Mountains. Not that any of the soldiers from the Avalon Militia could see it or would ever see it again. The filtered light barely broke through the smoke and chaos. The smoke hovered above the ragtag mob attempting to attack the alien bunker. There was no other choice but to take the offensive. Their numbers were dwindling because of a passive defense. They had two days to prepare for that assault. It was enough time to mobilize but not enough time to effectively mobilize. That was when the brief silence that filled the air was raucously broken by an explosion. The alien structure had finally been breached.

Simon, a tall, slender man, followed orders precisely as they were given. This was the exact reason he was the leader of Assault Group Seven. He had imagined that if he were to see an alien spacecraft in his lifetime, it would have flashing lights and the fanfare seen in movies. Simon's imagination was all wrong. The exterior of the bunker appeared to be completely sealed with a metallic coating. The height of the structure was unknown. It blended perfectly with the gray hued smoke lingering above it. He examined the jagged edges of the opening. The gap was large enough to fit one soldier at a time. Red and blue fluid fell from the sides mixing into a purple pool. The fluids flowed from the elevated floor and seeped through the grass into the ground. He quickly searched for hazards. Seeing no sparks or any other signs of electricity, he was going in. He tried to look into the sky one last time as the bellowing aftermath further blocked out the sun. There wasn't a hint of blue in his sight. Defeated, he faced the crack.

"Move ahead, move ahead!" Simon yelled.

Simon inched his way toward the small opening. His squad watched his hand fly upward indicating for them to stop. Waiting for his next command, they watched Simon as his head was swallowed by the darkness. A blue orb with a buzzing hum narrowly missed him and splattered on the back wall. The residual illumination slowly dissipated into the wall and darkness returned.

Simon's heart raced from the near hit. He took a step backwards and stumbled as he withdrew from the crack. He leaned against the wall and stood motionless as he caught his breath, and his wits. His sleeve felt glued to his arm from wiping the sweat from his brow. The four other members of his team had moved next to the wall. Crouched, they waited for his next command.

"Sir, what next?" Marcus asked.

"Sir... sir... sir... are you alright?" Jean-Paul asked, tapping Simon on his shoulder.

Simon, after eluding death's grip, thought about this huge undertaking and that his team probably would not complete its mission, let alone survive the ordeal. He shook his head and said, "The longer we wait, the worse it's going to get." Simon faced the opening and lifted his fist. He spread his fingers and they dropped for the silent countdown.

"5..." Marcus, former SEAL, an expert marksman, gripped his gun tightly, readying himself for entry.

"4..." Brigand, the demolition expert, the man responsible for enabling the breach, pushed himself against the wall. He was going to be the last to go into the dark void.

"3…" Okoye, Marcus' best friend and just as lethal a shooter, was at the ready.

"2…" Jean-Paul, a Frenchman conscripted by the militia, made the sign of the cross.

"1…" Simon said without hesitation.

"GO!"

Simon thrust himself into the opening. Marcus, losing Simon as he broke the plane of darkness, followed closely behind. The darkness disappeared as illumination filled the space. He brushed against Simon and avoided the onslaught of blue orbs. The light emanated from the walls and Marcus found cover. He crouched behind a metal box with the same coating and texture as the exterior of the structure. He looked over his shoulder toward Simon.

A large hum filled the room as a myriad of blue orbs flew through the air. One orb met with Simon's body. He spotted the source of the shooting. Simon tried to return fire but none of the bullets flew toward the faint figure in front of him. He looked down. His upper arm dangled but his forearm, hand, and gun had been erased. They had all disappeared when the blue ball melded with his body. A buzz approached Simon and he looked up just in time to see another blue orb. Simon's legs buckled and he fell to the ground.

Marcus knew Simon was dead. The large crater in his chest was the key indicator. There was nothing to do but look forward and attack. He'd pay his respects later, that was, if there was a later. With his back pressed tightly against the metal box, Marcus looked toward the shooter. The buzz, hum, and crack continued but he couldn't see who was shooting in all of the chaos. Then he spotted it, the glowing blue of an orbitizer core. The orbitizer was named not only because of the orbs that came out of it but also because it vaporized its target. He would never forget that color, the painted waters of a beautiful tropical island. The only joy in that color now was that he could aim at it. He raised his gun.

Marcus didn't wait to pull the trigger. In regards to his bullets, he chose quantity over quality. He felt the kick of his gun beat against his shoulder. Okoye fell into position next to Marcus as he shot. Okoye pulled back the bolt of his rifle and tapped the magazine. He inched his head over the top of the metal box to find Marcus' target. He saw the same glowing core that Marcus did and he raised his rifle and engaged. The silhouette fell to the ground. The core of its orbitizer lost its luster and went dark.

Marcus and Okoye rejoiced and gave each other a high-five. Their enjoyment was short-lived as another set of blue orbs hurtled toward them. Quickly, they took cover and saw a second blue core. In concert, they took aim and shot. Another silhouette fell to the ground and its orbitizer core dimmed. They stood up, apprehensive about high-fives, and their vision adjusted to the darkness as the blue spectacle of warfare ebbed to black.

"Flashlights on," Marcus whispered to Okoye.

"Jean-Paul is out, he was hit," Brigand yelled.

"See what you can do, we have to continue to move," Marcus yelled back.

Brigand was hovering over Jean-Paul. His head bobbed as he looked for injuries. Jean-Paul was missing his middle, ring, and pinkie fingers. He held up his hand like an imaginary gun and said, "Just wrap it up tight." Brigand reached into his pocket and pulled out a gauze wrapping. Jean-Paul clenched his teeth as Brigand grabbed his hand to apply the wrap.

The fallen aliens and their orbitizer cores lay on the ground. Marcus and Okoye bounded toward the alien casualties.

"Those are some nasty things," Okoye said, and bent over to pick up the orbitizer.

"Are you talking about the Trolls or the orbitizer?" Marcus asked.

"Yes," Okoye said, and looked up with a grin.

The aliens, colloquially called Trolls, were labeled by the survivors of the first attack on Charlottesville. Named after the mythical beings in Norse mythology, the Trolls were wiry and seven-feet tall. Their skin was as blue as cobalt. But their heads were the reason the survivors named them Trolls. Long pointy ears draped down the sides of their heads. Their lower lip reached to the tip of their oversized nose, a nose that took up a quarter of the Troll's face. Triangular nails extended from rugged cobalt blue three-fingered claws. Their imposing mass struck fear in those who'd survived. It killed those who didn't.

Okoye's hand wrapped around the grip of the orbitizer.

The orbitizer was the color and weight of a cirrus cloud. There wasn't a trigger but his hand fit comfortably around a soft pad. The barrel was pristine. Even after firing the myriad of shots, this agent of death looked like it had been field stripped and cleaned.

One of the Trolls began to gyrate. Its palm slammed into the ground as it rose. Marcus raised his gun and shot the Troll in its bald head. He watched as the bullet pushed out of its skull and its skin reformed. He didn't wait for it to move again. He emptied his gun into its head until it bled and stopped moving. Marcus dropped the clip from his gun.

"Did you see what that thing just did?" Okoye asked in amazement.

"That must be why they're so hard to kill," Marcus said, and shoved another clip into the magazine.

Okoye held the orbitizer to his face and analyzed it.

"I bet I can do some damage with this thing," Okoye said.

"Nobody has been able to figure out how those things shoot. What makes you think that you can?" Marcus asked as he raised an eyebrow.

"Trust me, I'm going to test this thing out first... watch," Okoye said, and smiled.

Okoye turned around to attempt a test fire. Marcus, wearing his commlink, made the squad's first report to Command.

"Hotel Bravo, this is Alpha Seven, first area sec-," Marcus stopped as the door slid open.

"Another Troll!" Okoye hollered, and he circled back. He placed his hand on the orbitizer and squeezed the soft pad with all of the strength his hand could muster. Nothing, absolutely nothing. He realized that time was short. He reached down for his gun but it was too late. The blue orb ejected from the Troll's orbitizer and hit him straight in his torso. The orb burrowed deep into Okoye's chest cavity. He fell backwards and blood welled into the emptiness formerly occupied by his heart and lungs.

Bullets whizzed past Marcus and penetrated the Troll. It fell to the ground. As Marcus turned around, he saw one-and-a-half handed Jean-Paul standing with his .50 caliber machine gun pointing toward the ceiling. The Frenchman tipped his imaginary cap as smoke came from his gun.

Metal *tinked* on the floor. Marcus turned toward the Troll and approached its blue body. Before it could move, Marcus shot its head until blood oozed out of the holes.

With the Troll dead, Marcus couldn't help but stare at Okoye's static body. He had known Okoye since his first days of boot camp. Okoye had found his peace. Marcus only wished that he could have received peace in a different way.

A sadness filled Marcus as his somber voice went over his commlink.

"Hotel Bravo, this is Alpha Seven, first area secured, over." Marcus sighed.

Hotel Bravo, the command center coordinating the attack, came back requesting a situational report.

"Alpha Seven, Three, Minus Two, over," Marcus said, his voice strengthened.

"Proceed to second area and report when secure, out," a voice came over the commlink.

The radio operator at Command had come back brief and callous. "Some of the other assault groups must have been doing worse than Seven," Marcus thought.

Marcus was joined by Brigand and Jean-Paul. There was an open door in front of them. Brigand had been prepared to use any type of detonation required for the assault, so he was upset that explosives were now unnecessary since the Troll had slid open the door.

Their mission was to gather intelligence, not cause destruction.

Marcus and Jean-Paul took the lead through the door. Brigand was close to follow the duo, maintaining coverage of the back.

Side-by-side, they entered the second corridor. Like the first corridor, the walls were tempered in metal. Unlike the first corridor, two fluorescent lines ran along the corridor wall. The violet hue was dim but it was bright enough to light the space. Marcus walked to the lines through the violet light. He looked closely. Like the fluid coming out of the crack, one was blue and the other one, red. Jean-Paul tapped Marcus on the shoulder and pointed down the corridor.

Marcus saw the open door and signaled to approach. As they progressed to the doorway, their footsteps echoed down the corridor. Brigand maintained his guard at the opposite door.

"I wonder where these lines go?" Jean-Paul asked.

"Looks like we'll find out in the next room," Marcus answered.

Marcus and Jean-Paul used a tactical entry through the door. Each soldier entered with their guns raised, ready to fire. They scanned the area for Trolls and none were revealed. Their absence was a welcomed sight. Marcus noticed that this area was different from the corridors. He had heard of other militias attacking bunkers but this area was never mentioned in any briefings. The interior design of these structures was a mystery since there was minimal intelligence. It had been less than a year since the Attack.

The center of the room was filled with four rows of three surgery tables. All of the tables were covered with what looked like blood.

Vats the size of water heaters lined the wall. Ten vats filled with the red liquid alternated with ten vats filled with blue liquid.

"This must be some sort of autopsy room and that must be the source of those lines," Jean-Paul said.

Marcus looked above the surgery tables as five red lines dangled from the ceiling. A needle extended from each line and rested on each table. Except for one table. The red lines hung limply over a huddled mass. Marcus spotted the mass and walked past the vats, red, blue, red. The mass caught his attention but he knew it was not a Troll. It was much too small to be one of those beasts. He crouched and watched the mass as he approached. When he was at arm's length, Marcus nudged the mass with the muzzle of his gun. He used the muzzle to fling off the blanket and quickly adjusted his gun back on target.

The mass moved. He tightened his grip to pull the trigger.

"That isn't a blob," Marcus thought.

The mass was human. It turned its head slowly and Marcus saw a deep blue eye. It was a woman, and she was lying naked on the table.

Jean-Paul spotted Marcus and the woman. He aimed his machine gun at her.

"Hold fire, hold fire, it's a survivor," screamed Marcus and his arms stretched to create a shield. Jean-Paul rushed over to the table.

Marcus kept watch on her blue eye. She kept turning toward him and her other eye appeared. It was red. The same color red that was in the vat next to her. She had an eye that was completely red except for the small black iris that stared at him. She was some sort of experiment. She had to be. She had an alien implanted eye.

Silence overcame them as they gazed at her lying on the table. She stopped moving and tried to speak. Silence was the only sound that left her mouth. That and her breath. She shook in her nakedness. She was in desperate need of help and Marcus knew it. He helped her sit up as Jean-Paul grabbed the blanket and quickly wrapped it around her.

"Is that a woman? Here?" Brigand yelled, as he entered the room.

"Yeah, we haven't heard of any people in one of these bunkers, let alone any survivors. We need to get her out of here," Jean-Paul said.

"You're right, Captain Obvious," Brigand stated.

"It's Sergeant and let's get going," Marcus replied.

"What about the rest of the mission?" Brigand asked.

Marcus knew that 'this' was what the mission was about now.

"She is the intelligence and we need to leave, now!"

Brigand and Jean-Paul nodded. Marcus picked her up and swaddled the blanket around her body.

Marcus, tall and muscular, towered over the woman's body. Even after fighting the Trolls, his makeshift uniform was still smart. He wore it well. He had been in the military before the Attack. The trained habits of working out and eating well never escaped him as he refused to let his body go into disrepair. He was strong enough to support himself and the woman he draped over his shoulder.

He led the team out of the area, avoiding the red and blue tendrils hanging from the ceiling as he navigated through the blood stained tables. He remembered that he had to make a report to Command.

Before Marcus could make his report, a sudden *boom* went off in the distance. Command came over the commlink.

"All units abort mission and evacuate all areas immediately, out!" the radio operator yelled frantically.

They began to sprint toward the small opening they had entered during the assault. The woman felt a sickness in the pit of her stomach from all of the bouncing on her savior's shoulder. She could feel her stomach push up to her mouth with every stride he took.

Marcus was the first through the crack. Another *boom* sounded directly behind him.

A large explosion sent a shockwave and flames throughout the bunker. Brigand and Jean-Paul didn't escape as flames engulfed the corridor. Their screams instantly turned into silence. Marcus managed to carry the woman through the opening. The blast lifted his body and launched them both away from the bunker.

Marcus lifted his head and could see the woman lying on the ground. He stretched out his hand but his fingers couldn't reach her. He began to push up his body but his legs failed him. He strained with the thought of moving his legs or his feet. Nothing would budge below his waistline, no matter how hard he tried. His arms gave up and his head fell to the ground. He conceded the movement of his lower body. The strain in his voice could be heard as he called over his commlink.

"Hotel Bravo, Alpha Seven, SITREP to follow… Alpha Seven, One, Minus Four, Plus One, request assistance, over."

"Alpha Seven, hold you low and barely readable, assistance in route, ETA 1-5 mikes, out," the radio operator replied.

The woman was lying on the ground, weak, unable to move or defend herself. Each minute seemed like a month had passed. She felt overcome as she struggled to keep her eyes open. The sound of the flames waned as the sound of chatter entered the area. Her vision became blurry. Shades of light and dark passed in front of her eyes. A small grin appeared on her face, help had finally arrived. She drifted out of consciousness and the world went black.

Day 274
HAPPY PAWS MEDICAL CENTER
CHARLOTTESVILLE, VIRGINIA

It seemed to be a normal day in the town of Charlottesville, with the exception of the convoys of large trucks and SUVs driving in and out of town. The blasts and the smoke were a far distance away and the citizens not involved in the assault had no idea of the damage on the other side of the hills and mountains. It was too far away for them to notice.

The medical workers were the exception to the ignorance. They had been working non-stop since the first casualties arrived. At first, groups of twos and threes would come in as a vehicle arrived in the middle of the night. Cuts and bruises primarily, with most of the soldiers either ready to go back on patrol or dead, very little in between. The number of survivors lessened as time went on. The hospital received a transport and had the soldiers back on their feet and out of the door in less than an hour.

Maddie arrived in an SUV, along with Marcus. Marcus, with more serious wounds, was delivered to the hospital. Maddie, on the other hand, was brought to an old veterinary clinic for her care. An elderly man, the doctor, was ready to receive her in the early morning. Being a large man, he was able to carry her without a gurney. He placed her on the only hospital bed in the building and directed his young assistant, Barron, to start her preliminary care.

Barron was no older than the woman who lay in front of him, but had the bedside manner of a seasoned professional. His blonde locks draped over his ears and collar as he ran his hands through his hair. He reached for the cabinet above the woman's head but his waistline barely cleared the top of the bed. He pulled out a bag and looked down at the new arrival.

"What the hell is going on with her? What did they do to her?" he looked at the woman from head to toe. Her body seemed normal, no weird abrasions, no bruises. He spoke to her as if she could respond, "You hang in there. I have to get some blood samples for the doctor." Barron walked around the bed and put his hand on her wrist. He kept his eyes on his watch, "Yep, normal." He touched her hands, her feet, and her cheeks hoping for some kind of reaction.

The rubber tourniquet snagged everything it ran across as Barron tied it around the woman's arm. The sterile smell of alcohol filled the room. He opened the package and took out a needle. He felt her arm for his target and stuck her with the needle. Watching as he drew her blood, Barron saw that her eyes remained closed and she still showed no reaction to his movements.

A deep voice came from behind, "Barron, don't expect too much, she might not be waking up any time soon. She's very weak and just hanging in there." Dr. McCluskey, or 'Mac' as he liked to be called, looked down at Barron and saw the concern on his face.

"She has a concussion, Mac."

"She needs rest. The best thing we can do right now is get that blood to the lab and prevent any other issues that we can't see."

"Yeah yeah, okay. I'll go," Barron said.

"Oh, and Barron, nobody should know any details about who this is for. If anyone asks, the panels are for the militia," Mac directed the young man.

Barron left the bedside and packed up the lab kit. Mac, one of the few doctors left in the area, had located his treatment facility in an old veterinary clinic. All medical care was conducted through satellite medical facilities except for emergency care. The triage center was still inside the main hospital and that is where the lab was housed. Mac had developed the concept to minimize the gathering of large groups of people. Too many people in one place meant that too many lives could be lost at one time.

Barron walked outside of Mac's clinic and headed straight for the hospital. There were a few shops still open but since store deliveries had all stopped, the niceties of life before the Attack were virtually non-existent. The Avalon Militia was formed in response to the Attack and the area was patrolled by militia soldiers. The citizens were able to walk freely during the day unless the attack alarm sounded. The militia fended off a few of the Trolls' attacks on the town. At least it seemed that way. Yesterday marked the militia's first offensive since the Attack.

"Great job, Derrick," Barron spoke his congratulations as he walked by one of the militia members.

"Thanks and thanks for your help too," Derrick shook his head and picked up his pace to avoid more conversation.

Barron was not a member of the militia since he had been selected to assist Mac. Barron didn't let Derrick's comment bother him since it wasn't his fault he was not in the militia. He continued on his way to the lab, walking by a shopping center. The shopping area had been a place where he would meet with his friends while his parents worked at their pharmacy. He would spend his days there playing, laughing, and joking before the Attack but now it was filled with holes and broken glass. "Nice walk down Memory Lane," he muttered in denial of the terrible memories that haunted him. Barron walked straight through the front doors of the main hospital. He didn't bother to look at the directory and went straight for the lab. He knew exactly where it was and had been there several times since he started working for Mac.

Barron strolled past the triage area. There were several people behind the drawn curtains. Those souls must've been from the assault. He heard screaming as he walked past the first drawn curtain. Barron hadn't seen the Emergency Room so active since the first days after the Attack. Even then, he was there with his mother and father and wasn't paying much attention to anything else. They were unable to recover from the first attack on Charlottesville. He weaved through the hustle and bustle of doctors and nurses. He knew he wasn't supposed to look, but the urge overcame him. He peeked behind the first curtain to see the source of the screaming. Bloody towels were lying on the floor. A doctor and four nurses were working on a man on the hospital bed.

"Sedate him now!" screamed the doctor. The nurse hurriedly injected the man with a general anesthetic. Within moments, the man lay quietly on the bed. The doctor and nurses took a step back to collect themselves. "Make sure he's back on the monitor and let's take five," the doctor ordered the nurses. The team scurried to put everything in place. They rushed out of the curtained area to take a much needed break. Barron watched as each of them walked past, not noticing his blonde mop.

Unfortunately, the last nurse spotted him and asked, "What are doing here?" Barron opened his mouth but before he could answer, she barked, "You have no business in triage. Get on with your business and if you don't have any to do... then don't do it here." The nurse scoffed as she turned. After a day like this, she was not missing her break.

Barron turned as if to walk toward the lab. As soon as the nurse was out of sight, he returned to the drawn curtain. He slinked his way toward the hospital bed and looked at the man's back. It was riddled with metal shards and gashes where the metal shards had been. He noticed a tattoo on his arm, "Marcus Smith" was written in bold letters.

"We've been working on him since six last night," Barron heard the nurses coming back. He ducked under the curtain. Out of fear of getting caught, he waited until the walkway was clear of the nurse that scolded him. When he heard her voice next to Marcus Smith, he darted toward the lab.

The lab was a few turns away from triage. Barron entered the lab and was greeted by Ron. "Hello Ronald, I'm dropping off a blood panel for Mac," Barron chuckled his hello. He knew that Ron hated his first name.

Ron sternly shot back, "First off, it's Ron, don't call me Ronald. Second, give me the panel. You're lucky this is for Mac. You smartass."

Barron stared at Ron's freckles and buckteeth. Ron was a giant compared to Barron. Even with a counter between them, Barron had to look straight up to see his face.

Ron continued, "Let Mac know that I'll have the results back in a couple days. I have other things to test with a higher priority. When the guys who are protecting you need something, you get it done." His tasking was set by the authorities in town.

"These panels are for the militia as well. Don't you think these are a priority too… Ron?" Barron asked, "Mac is doing this for the militia."

Ron looked at the vials of blood and then back to Barron, "Okay, since they are for Mac and the militia… I'll have them done tomorrow."

"Thanks… Ron," Barron snickered.

"Watch it, they're not done yet," Ron said to a grinning Barron. Barron dropped his smirk and walked out of the lab. As he was making his way to the exit, he returned to Marcus Smith's hospital bed. He glanced through the curtain and saw the doctor and nurses removing the metal shards from his back. "At least they aren't deep," muttered Barron, pulling his head from the curtain.

Barron walked back to Mac's clinic, passing by the shopping center. Derrick was nowhere in sight and the few shops conducting business were closing down for the evening. Nobody was allowed out at night except for the militia. They were the only ones permitted to be outside after the sun went down for citizen's protection.

The Trolls were active only at night and the militia members standing guard shot on sight, or even sound. That was life. Get everything done during the day. When the sun went down, it didn't matter if death was delivered by the Trolls or by the militia, nobody wanted to die.

Barron entered the clinic and heard Mac, "Barron, get back here now!" Barron ran to the new woman's bed. He knew that was where Mac would be since she was the only one there. He entered the room and the woman was convulsing. "Grab her!" Mac yelled. Barron ran to the other side of the bed and threw his hands out to catch her arms. She was shaking uncontrollably but he kept his full weight pressed on her arms. Then she suddenly stopped convulsing. Her body froze. Mac released his grip, "Barron, you can let go now." Barron lifted his hands and looked at her monitor.

"Mac, her vitals are the same as when I left," Barron said.

"She started a couple of seconds before you walked in the door. Her pulse started to race and I came into the room. I thought she was going to shake right out of bed," Mac said, wiping his brow. Mac had a high standard of care but she was different. There was something about this woman that made Mac nervous about her welfare getting poorer.

"Let's get an X-ray to see if we can spot anything in her... I should have done this earlier," Mac said, upset with his decision to wait. Barron had never seen Mac this worried. Normally, Mac was as calm as a glassy sea. Even after the Attack, Mac was the standard-bearer with everyone. He kept a level head and saved many people.

"Can we give her a name? I'm tired of using pronouns all of the time. Can we call her something else other than she, her, it, that woman, that girl?" Barron asked as he helped moved the stiff body onto the cart.

Mac, lightening his mood, said, "Sure, what do you have in mind?" as he lifted on his side.

"We'll call her Tulip then." Barron always liked the names of flowers. He gently placed Tulip's rigor mortis-like body on the cart.

Mac looked at him, rolling his eyes, "Really, all of the names in the world and you pick Tulip... great job." Mac gave Barron a thumbs up. "Let's get Tulip into the X-ray and try to find out what's going on," Mac changed his tone to serious as Barron pushed the back of the cart.

Mac turned on the light in the X-ray room and steered Tulip into position.

DAY ONE
INITIAL EXTRATERRESTRIAL CONTACT
WASHINGTON, DISTRICT OF COLUMBIA

The chilling air blew from the vents and trickled down his neck. Staff Sergeant Collins huddled in his coat as he stood his watch in the Command Suite. Tired and cold, his eight-hour watch would be ending any moment. He stared at his screen as the final minutes were coming to a close. Two years of his life, he stared at the screen. Nothing ever displayed, not even a blip. The whole system was a product of witchcraft, wizardry, and apocalyptic doomsday believers. A system to locate incoming alien spacecraft. But then it happened, after two years, days after days of eight-hour blocks of nothing, it happened. One blip.

"General, our orbital satellites have picked up something 200,000 miles vectoring in between the Moon and the Earth's surface," he called out.

General Hawkins looked down at the watch floor. Four rows of watches monitored the elements of defense throughout the entire United States. One man, Staff Sergeant Collins, sat with his face staring at his screen, waving his arm as if he had an answer to a teacher's question.

"What's the composition?" the General asked.

"Composition One, Sir," Collins stated as he maintained focus on his screen.

General Hawkins looked up toward the Main Display. Normally, it projected the defense of the United States or hot areas of operation. The display hadn't shown the orbital system since it was installed and tested. He hoped that after all these years, it would still work.

"Put it on the Main Display. Train the OOS toward the contact. It's probably a NEAR object but we will make sure," the General said.

The Orbital Optic Sensor came online and displayed on the Main Screen.

"Sir, that isn't an asteroid."

"Of course it's not. I can see it too," General Hawkins said as he shook his head. A spacecraft was definitely on the display.

"Sir, I think I can make out the silhouette... got it! The estimated length from OOS is 1,000 miles," Staff Sergeant Collins said.

"Get me SECDEF... and the President," the General commanded, and he walked to his office.

General Hawkins thought back to five years earlier. A group of SETI enthusiasts were determined to keep the Allen Telescope Array in California running. In their determination, they made breaking news by receiving an old image of the Earth from space. The image was tethered with the reply "Congratulations," like a contestant on a game show. They continued to receive the message for months until the transmission suddenly stopped. The receipt of the transmission was all that was needed for proof of alien-life. There were the skeptics but they did not prevail in defunding the planetary defense system since there was now proof that Earth was no longer alone.

All of the countries in the world, through the United Nations, provided supplies for this endeavor. The planetary defense system was state-of-the-art and able to intercept incoming threats without human intervention. No single country had complete control of the system to eliminate the potential of it starting a war.

As the years went by, the thrill of receiving alien communications waned. Support for the defense system also receded with funding only providing for bare boned operations. It was deemed too expensive to perform maintenance runs. Some units maintained a link with other units but did not have communications with the ground to report system status. Each unit contained a missile battery of two and engineers claimed the missiles were ten times stronger than a volcanic eruption. Periodically, two missiles would fire into space due to communications failure. Luckily, there were still active cells without any failures.

This spacecraft came to Earth on the same vector as the signal received five years ago, just as predicted. General Hawkins knew that the defense system would have to work if anything happened contrary to peace and goodwill.

"Sir, the spacecraft has established an orbit about 150,000 miles out. We are maintaining a watch and will inform you of any status changes," Collins reported.

The General sat at his desk and listened over his intercom in silence. He would occasionally glance at the Main Display hoping for any type of positive action, that the aliens would show that they had come in peace. He knew that the longer the spacecraft sat out in space, the less friendly their actions would be. The phone rang.

"Mr. Secretary," the General said as he put the phone to his ear.

Staff Sergeant Collins watched as the goliath ship came into focus. Its metallic gray hull perfectly reflected the sun with the blackness of space behind it. Collins switched cameras and a different aspect of the image displayed on his screen and the Main Display. The hull was shaped like a three-dimensional trapezoid. It showed no wear on its smooth surface and no openings to launch attacks. There was no command station or physical bridge that he could see. He looked at the rear of the spacecraft and saw no signs of propulsion. "Could it be unmanned?" he thought. He copied his screen and put the pictures in a file at his station.

"So, what's going on?" a man stood behind him. He knew that voice and turned around. He was glad to see his relief had arrived.

"Man, you won't believe what just happened," Collins said.

* * *

In the days that followed, governments started to inform their citizens that the alien life was right on their doorstep. The word spread through news outlets and it was met with much fanfare. There were parties to watch the spacecraft's silhouette pass in front of the

Moon's illuminated face. The spacecraft maintained its orbit for a month through all the phases of the Moon. There were no responses to the many attempts to communicate with the craft.

DAY 275
HAPPY PAWS MEDICAL CLINIC
CHARLOTTESVILLE, VIRGINIA

*R*ho felt a heartbeat, felt the rise and fall of the vessel's chest, felt the movement of the human's body. *Rho* had failed and understood that it couldn't control its host. The human's mind was too intertwined with its body, too complex. *Rho* conceded that it shared its life with this human, one body for two beings. The human still controlled her conscious and her basic life functions. But *Rho* now knew that it needed her.

"*Human, wake up,*" *Rho* called out, "*I need you to wake up.*"

"Why are you calling me? What do you want?" she responded to its plea.

"*You and I are one. You must wake for us to live.*"

"Okay, okay, I think I am ready," she told the voice in her head.

Finally, *Rho* would be able to intake the stimulus that it yearned for. Sight, hearing, touch, smell, taste, those senses would be provided by the human. The darkness would be unveiled and *Rho* would know of the outside world. Quietly, it waited for the human to escape from her dormant state.

Mac sat behind his desk, the room dark and quiet. Barron sat in a fold-out chair in the opposite corner watching the light from the wall mount flip on and off. Mac stared at the x-ray but he could find nothing abnormal showing on the film.

"Barron, I'm trying to figure this one out. All I have is this damn X-ray machine and it can't do the job I need it to do," Mac said. He looked up at Barron, "How long before those panels are done?"

"They should be done today," Barron said.

"Please go to the lab and see if they have the results," Mac asked.

Barron rose from his seat. He folded the chair and placed it firmly in his dark corner. He looked at Mac as the old man's face was planted in his palms. Exhaustion had caught up to his caffeine-driven energy. Mac, deep in thought, heard the soft steps as Barron exited the room.

Once outside of the vet clinic, Barron passed by the shopping center. He walked the same path leading to the hospital. The triage area caught his attention as he wondered how Marcus Smith was doing. The doctor and nurses were no longer beside the man. All of the shrapnel was removed and a blood stained gauze wrapped around his torso replaced what was the gory mess he witnessed the day before. Smith was lying on his side. He seemed restful. Barron did not want to cause any problems or make him stir, so he continued to the lab. Barron walked into the lab but this time he felt the need to get done as quickly as possible.

"Ron, do you have the results from the blood panel?" he asked as he approached Ron with a more serious tone.

"Yeah, I do," Ron said as he gathered the papers with the results, "there were some abnormal counts. Is Mac working on someone with a virus?"

Barron looked at Ron, remembering what Mac had said, "He's doing some blood work for the militia. I don't know much of anything else."

"Alright, whatever he's doing, let him know that the test will be sent to billing and is due at the end of month," Ron shrugged.

Barron nodded his head in agreeance and left the lab. As he whisked through the hospital hallway, he thought about why there was a bill for the lab tests. It wasn't like money really had any value anymore. Perhaps it was that people just clung to the old ways, the ways before the Attack. Those thoughts evaporated as he saw Marcus Smith lying still on his hospital bed, quietly, peacefully. He couldn't afford to waste any time watching over Marcus, there was a patient at the clinic. He scurried out of the hospital and sprinted back to the clinic. Again, he did not see any of the militia on patrol.

"Mac, do you know that they're still charging you for these tests?" Barron yelled as he opened the door and rushed into the clinic.

Mac grinned and took the results. "Red, white, and platelets are low," Mac murmured as he was reading, "glucose normal, cholesterol normal." Barron was standing next to Mac peeking over his shoulder to see the numbers. "Barron, I want you to take another blood sample," Mac said, and his eyes fixed on the newly delivered paper.

"Alright Mac," Barron said, and he went to Tulip's room.

Barron stood next to Tulip's bed, stretched into the cabinet and pulled out a ready package. He grabbed the syringe and started to prep Tulip's arm. He wished there was an easier way to withdraw the blood. Unfortunately, they had run out of capsules to plug into the IV port. He pushed the needle into her arm. The needle tip punctured the skin and he pulled back on the plunger. This time the needle failed to draw any blood.

"It must have been a bad syringe," Barron thought. He said, "Sorry Tulip, I'll get another one and do it right this time." He grabbed another syringe and swiped her arm with another alcohol pad. He approached the skin with the needle for the second time. Finding a new spot, he inserted the needle into her vein. He pulled back on the plunger and again, no blood.

"This must be a bad batch," he said as he moved the needle around the vein to see if it would draw the blood. "Third time is a charm," he said as he repeated the process the third time. He was determined to get Tulip's blood. This was such a simple task and Barron was letting his frustration show. "Tulip is just lying there. This can't be that difficult. A monkey could do this." He decided to throw the needle like a dart. "What would be the worst that could happen?" he thought. "She has two arms if anything goes wrong."

"1… 2… 3," he launched the syringe from close to her arm. With a sudden jerk, Tulip's arm moved out of the way as the needle sunk into the bed. He looked at Tulip's face, but she lay still on the bed, set like a stone. He felt ashamed that he had gotten so frustrated and looked down at the syringe to pick it up.

"Human, it is time," Rho urged its host. Her body and mind awoke.

As his hand grabbed the syringe, he heard, "Don't call me Tulip."

Barron jumped back onto the rolling chair that was sitting behind him.

"Wh… What did you say?" he asked as his head shook.

Tulip turned her head. Her face was streaked with dirt from a failed attempt to wipe her face. Her hair was matted and wild. Unkempt for months, the bonds of grease held her locks together. Her eyes blinked slowly as she processed her new surroundings. Barron had already seen her eyes from monitoring her. He wasn't in shock when the scarlet eye bore down on him.

"My name isn't Tulip," she said with a groggy voice.

"Mac! Mac!" Barron called to the doctor, "I think you want to see this, she's awake."

Mac rushed into the room with his eyes fixated on the woman.

"I'm glad to see that you have come back to us," he said.

"You better not call me Tulip," she said, and focused her eyes on Mac.

The control of her body was coming back. Tulip felt a tingle in her arms and they moved. She pulled her arms back and pushed. Her torso rose as her arms straightened. A draft of air blew through her open gown. "Where am I?" she thought, and a sense of shock came over her. Her body jerked up, twisting and grabbing, she struggled to escape. Barron jumped and wrapped his arms around her.

"It's okay, you're okay," his soothing voice whispered in her ear.

Her body loosened as Barron spoke his words. She placed her hands on the side of the bed as her legs dangled over the edge. Her shoulders carried her weight as she closed her eyes and hung her head. A deep exhale followed. Mac put his hand on her shoulder.

"I'm glad to see that you're awake, you gave us a scare," he said, and turned to Barron with a smile.

"Now it's time to do some real work. Get some rest, we'll start tomorrow."

DAY 17
THE MCCLUSKEY HOME
EAST OF CHARLOTTESVILLE, VIRGINIA

As the postal worker approached the residence, an old wooden sign with the name "Dr. Feldman Q. McCluskey III" hung next to the doorbell. The postal worker pressed her finger to the doorbell and she could hear the sound "awoogah" fill the silence of the house. Footsteps soon followed, becoming louder as a person came and opened the door.

Mac McCluskey was a tall, heavy man. With his white beard and spectacles, he looked like Santa Claus. He was a physician, a world-renowned pathologist. He worked closely with the CDC in strategies and overcoming blood borne diseases. Mac loved the fame and his ego grew as his fame grew. Soon, he found himself catering to anyone who would praise him publicly. That was his life ten years ago.

He loved the attention, until his pride took him away from home instead of meeting his wife and son at the airport. A dark stormy night, in combination with a rented car, is what caused the accident, that killed his wife and son. He mourned their death and his guilt gave him humility. He vowed to never allow his pride to stop him from doing right to others. Alyssa and Joel would have wanted it that way. And he promised them as he watched them lowered into their grave, that he would never let them down again.

"Oh, a delivery," his eyes beamed at the package, "I don't get too many things nowadays."

"Yes Doctor," she said as she glanced at the wooden sign, "all I need is a signature." The postal worker presented her electronic pad and stylus to Mac.

"Have you been following that spacecraft on the news? It has been in orbit for two weeks now and it hasn't sent anyone down to the planet or anything. Isn't it weird to have traveled through space and not say 'Hi' after a stop?" she asked. Mac handed the pad back to her and took the package from her outstretched arms.

The postal worker grabbed the pad and looked at the Doctor's signature.

"Yes I have, it's not like there is anything else on the news," Mac said as he backed into his house. Mac became focused on the package and shut out the world.

"I think-," she said as the door gently closed. She watched as the door hit the jamb. *Click*, the conversation was over.

"Have a nice day," she said as she frowned and then spoke under her breath, "I guess." The postal worker tucked her pad under her arm and turned around. She gave the mailbox a little kick before she got into her truck and drove off to deliver her next package.

Mac grabbed his letter opener off of his desk and went to sit in his chair. It was occupied by his cat, Fluffbutt, who had claimed it as its throne. Fluffbutt let out a grunt as he shooed the feline to reclaim his seat. He sat down and looked at the envelope. "From the Office of the Secretary of Health and Human Services," he said to Fluffbutt, "I wonder what Claudia wants now." He sat back in his chair. He thought to himself that he had not been a practicing physician for about ten years now. He took his letter opener and revealed a letter:

> *To: Dr. Feldman Q. McCluskey III*
>
> *From: Secretary of Health and Human Services*
>
> *Subject: The Office of the Secretary of Health and Human Services, by decree of the President of the United States of America, asks for your assistance in response to Executive Order 2519, Alien Contact Contingency.*
>
> *My dearest friend and colleague, Mac, you are one of the greatest physicians that I have ever known. And even though we have not maintained contact over the past years, memory of you and your abilities shall be forever imprinted in my mind.*

In order to protect the well-being of the citizens of the United States of America and the world, it is necessary to plan for any encounters with our new visitors from outer space, whether it be peaceful or in the worst case, hostile.

You are asked to provide local medical assistance and work jointly with Alan Pritchard (who has accepted the designation as the Local Defense Commander by the Office of the Secretary of Defense). In case of emergency, you are designated as the Charlottesville Chief Medic and representative of this office. You are needed to provide your expertise in health and welfare to those under your care, whether it be disease, impairment, or approaching death.

This order will not commence execution until declared by the President.

Mac, I am asking you this personally as I know that there is no one that compares to your genius. Your country needs you. We all need you.

No matter what happens, you will have my continued faith and friendship.

My Deepest Respects,
Hon. Secretary Claudia Alton

"Wow, I wasn't expecting that," Mac told Fluffbutt as she lay on the floor licking her paw. He looked in the envelope and found another piece of paper, titled, *"Executive Order 2519."* Mac read the order and understood what the government was planning in case it failed. He thought about how to approach this letter for a second. In that second, he knew that he wouldn't go back to his prideful ways. He wouldn't wear it as a badge like he would have ten years ago. He didn't have to weigh the glory of being the Doctor of all Doctors in Charlottesville. It was his chance to ensure that a new generation, maybe a generation that wouldn't be as advantaged as he was, would be able to overcome obstacles set in its path. Yes, he humbly thought, it was a way to help people, to help make better doctors.

He got out of his chair and stood up tall. Should anything arise that needed him, he would be willing to help without question. Fluffbutt jumped back onto its throne. Mac smiled as he put down the letter. He turned on the news and the continued coverage of the alien spacecraft blanketed every channel. "I hope that nothing happens. If I have to do this, then the world is going to be in a bad place," Mac said. He walked to the kitchen and picked up his phone. "Time to call Alan," he said, "Local Militia 348."

"**D**o you know where you are?"
                "Do you know what's happened?"
                "Do you know where you've been?"
"What's your name?"

Barron peppered the woman with a barrage of questions, carefully avoiding calling her Tulip.

"Madison, Maddie, my name is Maddie," she said. "I remember going skiing during winter break with my friends. We went out to Summerwhite. There was Catelyn, and there was Damien, and… Bryce," Maddie said, and jumped from the bed. Tape ripped from her skin as she landed and the painful realization set in, "and I was with Bryce up in the mountains."

The heart monitor had flat-lined. She noticed an IV port and pulled it out as well. Blood flowed from her skin. Barron grabbed gauze and held it on her arm. She took her arm from Barron and snatched the gauze out of his hand.

She looked around the dimly lit room. The lightbulb was about to die. Her eyes scanned any object she could identify in the masses of gray and black. There were tall cabinets and short ones, two trash cans, a chair, and surgery tools on a metal rolling table on the far side of the room. Her eyes swelled at the tools of death. Maddie jumped back against the wall, her hands planted as she readied herself for her next escape attempt. The gauze fell like a heavy feather to the floor.

"Where am I? Are you harvesting body parts here?" she screamed. Her foot planted and her body tensed for the sprint.

"Do you really think you would be awake if we needed your kidneys?" Mac asked, and draped a cover over the table. Barron stood in front of the door. There was no escape for Maddie. She resigned herself to leaning against the wall.

"You need to sit down," Mac said as he urged Maddie to calm down.

"Why?" Maddie asked, as she stood with her gown flapping on the sides of her body. Her hands were still planted on the wall. Barron had become abnormally silent during the conversation. The light from the hall shone above his shoulder. He stared at her figure through the thin fabric of the gown. He didn't see her as a sickly patient anymore. She saw his stare and dropped her hands and looked down.

"I feel disgusting, I want to clean up," Maddie said. She saw black filth in the crevasses of her fingers and hands. "Where's the washroom?" she asked.

"Through there and the second door on the left, but—" Mac said, as he pointed outside of the room. Maddie started for the door before he could get out the rest of his sentence, "you should know that you probably look different," Mac said as if she was still there.

Barron had already started bustling before Mac could tell him to clean up the monitoring equipment lying on the bed. With a serving heart, Barron was the best assistant Mac ever had the pleasure of working with. Mac thought it was because he had a fresh outlook to being in medicine and cared more about the people around him. Barron never thought about what was best for himself.

"Take a look at this," Barron said, as he held up the IV that had been in Maddie's arm. Something had chewed away at the needle. It appeared that something acidic had dissolved the needle along the length. It looked like a long crescent moon shape burrowed down the side.

"Bag it," Mac directed Barron.

As soon as Mac finished telling Barron to preserve the needle, an angry yell was heard down the hall.

"What the HELL!" Maddie yelled.

Mac and Barron ran through the door to the washroom. Barron opened the door to see Maddie with a towel wrapped around her head and her body dripping wet from the shower. Her hands clutched the lip of the sink. She was staring at herself in the mirror, angling her face to view her red eye.

"What did you asses do to me?" she demanded.

"You've only been here for two days and you're exactly the same as when you got here!" Barron raised his voice. He hadn't done that to her and he was upset with the implication.

Mac put his hand on Barron's shoulder, "Maddie, I don't know how long you've been out but we haven't had snow for six months. We need to figure out what happened from when you went skiing until now."

"Fine, leave me alone and let me get dressed. I'll be out in a few minutes," she stood staring down into the sink and shook her head. Barron grabbed some clothes off of the linen shelf. He handed her a pair of gray sweatpants with a rip in each of the knees and an XXL shirt with 'Loser' written on the front. She looked down at the tattered clothing.

"Thanks," she said, and she pushed Barron out the doorway and slammed the door. Mac and Barron just stood there until they heard the lock click. Barron went back to clean up the monitoring equipment in the room. Mac went back to his office and started writing notes on a sheet of paper. He had to make sure he had her reaction documented.

DAY 34
SUMMERWHITE SKI RESORT
NELLYSFORD, VIRGINIA

She looked up, without regard to what was coming down. Such are the actions of someone naïve to worldly matters. Sheltered for all of her life from the vagrants and villains of this world, Maddie was no better than a toddler wondering what a red element on a stove feels like.

A thousand microscopic ice pellets spread a freezing pain across her forehead. The thought of frowning crossed her mind, but it was a fleeting thought as her eyes met Bryce. Finally, after the stories of love and happiness she heard from her friends, that she read in books, love had stumbled on her in the form of Bryce. She threw him a smile. It wasn't hard, she loved him. With her skis strapped on her feet, she hopped as she turned to her love.

"Bryce, when are you going to come over here and teach me how to ski?"

Even though she had been skiing since she was three years old, she wanted Bryce to feel like her one and only. Her first semester of college was finally over. Winter break had arrived, the time to relax. She decided not to celebrate the holiday with her parents and sister as she had done for the past 18 years. The past four months of freedom overshadowed any desire to reconnect with home. Her parents were very strict, overbearing. No dating, no late nights. It was school, study, sleep, in that order. The only break she had from the routine was gymnastics and skiing. When she had graduated high school, Maddie did not waste a moment and entered University to escape her parents.

Bryce was the same age as Maddie. They were freshmen and classmates, and he sat next to her in English. Professor Snyder didn't pay any attention to his students. But Bryce, he paid attention to

Maddie and she loved it. They started dating when he wrote her a text, after taking her phone. "Wanna go out tonight?" he asked.

"If you give that back to me," she said as she grabbed at her phone.

He turned the face of the phone and showed her the text "Yes," and said, "That's what you were supposed to say." After that day, they dated and decided to take the same classes in the Spring.

Bryce came from behind Maddie and grabbed her hips. He stood four inches over Maddie, who was tall herself at 5' 10". He placed his chin on her shoulder and went to kiss her. She closed her eyes to return the kiss. Then her feet slipped from under her and she fell to the ground. Bryce stood uphill laughing at her. She scrambled to get to her feet but her skis got crossed and she tripped, falling face down into the snow. She felt the pulling of her coat and was lifted to her feet as Bryce laughed. She was turned around, "You—" before she could say another word Bryce kissed her. Maddie felt warm from head to toe. She smiled. It was the best day of her life.

Maddie stared into Bryce's eyes. In her mind, he was the epitome of perfection. He was handsome and tall and smart and had a great smile. As they held each other close, Catelyn and Damien approached, "You two need to get a room," Catelyn hollered. "Damien and I are hungry. We've been out here all day. Do you think you guys can take a time out to grab something to eat?" Catelyn asked, wrapping her arms into Damien's.

"That sounds like a plan, my stomach is eating through to my—" Bryce bellowed.

"We get the point Bryce," Maddie stopped him before he could finish. They packed up their gear and headed toward the resort restaurant.

They approached the Irish restaurant and there was a sign that said "Closed." It was odd since the place was supposed to be open until 11PM and it wasn't even five o'clock. Bryce peered through the window and didn't see anyone. Catelyn knocked on the door and there wasn't a stir.

"Maybe we can sneak in there and grab something to eat," Damien said to the group.

Maddie came back, "No, I don't think we should. They'll kick us out of the resort. Anyways, we have food back at the cabin."

"Don't you mean *Our Chalet*," Catelyn said using her exaggerated French accent, and smiled. The group walked back to their chalet. Bryce and Maddie clung to one another while Catelyn and Damien were throwing snowballs at each other. Damien threw one snowball that hit Catelyn in the face.

"Okay, I had enough," Catelyn told Damien. Damien gave his hand to Catelyn and helped her up. As she stood, Catelyn shoved a handful of snow down Damien's shirt. She snorted as Damien's reaction to the snow was priceless. It was a ten-minute walk to the cabin and they walked inside just as the last glimmer of dusk faded away.

The smell of sizzling bacon filled the room as Bryce took a bite of his peanut butter and jelly sandwich. Maddie thought about this trip and how she never wanted it to end. The usual vacation with her family consisted of meals and alone time. Often, her father would be working on projects and too busy to interact with the rest of the family. Her mother would always be doing chores around the house. Her sister would always be texting with her friends. That's why she loved being around Bryce. She was always the focus of his attention and she loved being a priority, except when he was eating. Catelyn turned on the TV and there was nothing but static. Every cable channel contained static.

"Guys, the cable's out," she looked at her phone, "the internet is out too. And there's no reception here."

Damien smiled at her, "I guess we're in for old-fashioned games and fun."

Maddie danced as she reached into her bag, "I brought a word-tile game!"

Bryce looked at her and spoke as peanut butter stuck to the roof of his mouth, "We all know about losing word games to you Maddie," he finished swallowing, "I still don't think hyperadrenocorticism, or whatever you played, is a word."

The four went on playing games, telling jokes, and laughing, completely numb to the world.

"Wow, it's 2AM. I'm exhausted," Bryce let out a big yawn.

Catelyn, Damien, and Maddie reciprocated the yawn. Catelyn smiled, "I guess that means we're not serial killers, good night."

Maddie went into her room and plunked down on her bed. The best day of her life had come to a close and she instantaneously fell asleep. Her dream of Bryce and their kiss came to an abrupt halt as a blue-hued hand yanked her out of bed. Her head flew through the air with the rest of her body. She felt the force of her flight and she couldn't free herself from the pull. As her body moved through the air, she saw it, she tried to avoid it, but her face crashed into the bedpost. Her right eye was speared by an ornate fleur-de-lis sticking out of the side. Her arms fell down as her body went limp. Blood oozed from her eye socket and she was dragged from the room.

"What the hell was that?" Damien jumped out of bed upon hearing the commotion outside of his room. He grabbed his ski pole and jumped through his door in the en-garde position he had learned from fencing. It took only a moment for him to analyze the situation. The ski pole started to drift downward as he looked in disbelief.

In front of him was a huge monstrosity, a Troll, standing almost seven feet tall. Its entire skin was colored blue, as blue as cobalt, and it had a huge round pitted nose and pointed ears that drooped down to its neck. Its long blue fingers were dragging Maddie, and there was another one, dragging Bryce as he tried to kick it.

Catelyn came out of her room and screamed in terror. That was enough to get the Troll's attention. It turned its head and its dark, cold eyes stared into Catelyn's scream. It raised its hand and the core started to glow on its orbitizer. A buzz filled the room and the blue ball struck Catelyn. Her screams were instantly muted by the blast. Damien watched Catelyn as her face disappeared into nothing. Blood started to flow from where her neck used to be. As Catelyn's body fell, Damien turned to the Troll.

He lunged toward the blue being, ski pole in hand. A second buzz filled the room and Damien fell to the ground. The second Troll, holding Bryce, made a fist and hit Bryce so hard that he stopped fighting. He was out cold. Disregarding the two bodies on the floor, the Troll walked over the corpses as if they weren't there. It silently followed the other Troll dragging Maddie out of the cottage.

DAY 276 AFTERNOON
THE REALIZATION
CHARLOTTESVILLE, VIRGINIA

Maddie exited the washroom and followed the sound of Mac and Barron talking. She turned off the light in the hall, walked around the corner, and stuck her head into the kitchen. She looked at Barron, "Did you borrow these clothes from a 300-pound man?" She walked fully into the kitchen and the drawstrings of the sweatpants were wrapped around her waist. They were so puffy that her legs looked like two balloons. The shirt didn't do any better. Not only did she have to reposition it every time it slipped off of her shoulder, but it was covered in ketchup and mustard stains. To make matters worse, every time she looked down to adjust it, "Loser" would be there taunting her. She had found some slippers in the washroom but her heels extended over the backs and touched the floor.

"It was the best I could do on short notice," Barron said as he looked at her.

She shook her head in disappointment at Barron "My legs look like toothpicks in a potato sack," she said, taking a seat at the table next to Mac.

"Okay, Doctor, you want to know what happened… well so do I." Maddie placed her elbows on the table, crisscrossing her fingers. She leaned toward Mac, staring unflinchingly into his eyes.

"Please, Maddie, call me Mac," he said, trying to be congenial and make Maddie feel comfortable in her new surroundings. Maddie told Mac and Barron about the last day at the Summerwhite Resort as they both listened with great intent.

"So Maddie," Mac started his inquiry, "you're telling me that you have no idea what has happened? You do realize that you have no recollection of the past nine months." She looked at Mac in disbelief. She felt her anger fill her and she exploded.

"I don't even know where I am! You're telling me that I have been out for nine months??? Huh, is that what you're saying? One day I'm with my friends and loving my life and the next day I wake up to an old man and his boy-toy, or whatever he is," she said, her temples pulsing as she looked at Barron, "staring at me while I'm lying under a blanket, half-naked! Then, I can't even be told about my eye. No, no, sir, I look into the mirror and see that my eye is flippin' red. Not just bloodshot, totally red, everywhere. So when I tell you that I have no idea what has happened in the past nine months, that means I DON'T KNOW!"

Maddie finished with her eyes glued back on Mac. He took a deep breath.

"Maddie, you're in Charlottesville, in a medical clinic, with me, Mac, and Barron, my assistant," he explained.

"And how did I get here?" she asked Mac without pause.

"You were brought here from the Troll's bunker," Barron answered.

"So I came from a land of mythical creatures, is that what you're saying?" she said, as her head snapped toward Barron,

Mac started to speak again, "No, Maddie, the Trolls are the aliens that took you on your last night at Summerwhite."

"So the aliens landed?" Maddie asked, while she was piecing things together. "The last I heard was that they were still in orbit. They must have come down that night. Where did they take me?"

"I don't know. All I do know is that you were found during an attack on the alien bunker. That bunker was near Nellysford and you were brought here," Mac replied.

Maddie looked down and sat in a moment of silence trying to process what Mac had told her.

"So they did this to me," Maddie said, and pointed at her red eye. "Have all those Trolls been killed?"

"They have an intricate system of bunkers. We've been defending ourselves after we regrouped… after the Attack," Mac said as he shook his head.

She paused for a moment to look out of the small window and then scanned the rest of the kitchen. It was more of a break room than a kitchen. She spotted silhouettes of dogs and cats on the wall and posters for various animal drugs with lists of the benefits the pills or shots provided pets. She came back and focused on Mac, "So they attacked. What happened and why am I in this *medical clinic*?"

Mac looked straight into her eyes, "There isn't much left of the larger cities, they were wiped out in the initial raid. The military and the government no longer exist and we're defended by a local group, the Avalon Militia. A couple of members of the militia brought you here after the raid in Nellysford and I'm the one who was chosen to take care of you. Where you are… Well, this used to be an animal hospital, Happy Paws. We kept the name because there is a sign out front. Don't worry, this place is safe and doesn't offer veterinary services anymore." Her fists balled up as she became angrier with every bit of information Mac was telling her. She barraged Mac with questions that she needed answered.

"Where is Catelyn?"

"I don't know," Mac said, as he knew he didn't have her answer.

"Where's Damien?"

"I don't know," Mac answered immediately with the same tone.

"Where's Bryce?" she asked, and then demanded, "I want to know where Bryce is."

"I don't know where he is either."

"You're a wealth of knowledge, why don't you get me some answers and then maybe I could help you out!" she screamed at Mac.

Mac was annoyed with Maddie yelling at him, "Then ask me a question that I can answer!" He stood up and Maddie's blood results were pushed toward her.

"What about my parents, my sister?" she asked. She was going to continue to ask questions until she got something out of him.

"Where were they the night you went missing?" Mac asked her.

"They were in Richmond." She noticed the piece of paper and swiped it off of the table. It crumpled in her fists as she made sure that she got all or at least part of it. Barron saw that she was going to grab the results but his reaction was too slow. He was paying too much attention to the conversation and her movement stunned him before he even had time to flinch.

The old man sat back into his seat. "Richmond didn't make it through the Attack, they are probably dead," his tone was solemn with the presentation of more bad news.

She fell back into her chair, "Everybody that I have ever known is gone?" Maddie's anger shifted to sadness. Her family was gone too. That day, in Nellysford, just changed from the happiest day to the worst day of her life.

"Is there any chance that they made it out of there?" she asked as she started to look at the results.

Mac paused and adjusted his chair, "If they were in Richmond that night, I know that they didn't make it. Unless they had left, there's no chance that anyone survived the Attack," he said. Maddie's mind was racing. Her parents never left the house, let alone the city, during the holidays. There was no way they had survived and she had to come to terms that they were gone.

As reality set in, a sense of fear overcame her thoughts as she started to grasp this new world. She looked at the paper that Mac conveniently let her have. Her fear soon subsided as her voice, and her anger, came back.

"Whose results are these?" she asked. She knew they were her results.

Mac slowly leaned forward in his chair, "They are yours, we…"

Maddie slammed the paper back on the table, "Apparently there's something wrong with me," her voice started to escalate with frustration. "Where are the other results? Where are the other blood tests? What else have you done?"

Barron spoke up softly, "That's what I was trying to do when you woke up."

"So you guys haven't even looked into this? Why is my eye red?" she yelled at both Barron and Mac.

"You've only been here for two days and—" Mac said.

She cut him off, "Excuses. All of it. Everything you say, excuses. I'm not stupid, Mac. There's something going on with me and you're not telling me. You afraid I can't handle it?"

"We were about to—" Barron replied.

Maddie cut him off too, "About to what? About to NOT find out what happened to me! I need some time to think, no need to direct me!"

Barron got up with Maddie.

"Do you need help?" he asked.

"No, I don't think so, you've helped enough," Maddie said, her tone matching the drop of her brow.

Barron's grin became a grimace as Maddie stormed out the door. Mac got out of his seat and put his hand on Barron's shoulder.

"Barron, I need to tell you something," Mac said, and began to walk to the sink. "Close the door."

The light in the hall faded as the door to the kitchen began to slowly close.

DAY 33
THE ATTACK
WASHINGTON, DISTRICT OF COLUMBIA

"Ben, son, I don't want you to come up here," General Hawkins said over the phone.

"Dad, I haven't seen you in a while and it sounds like you need someone around." A voice was heard through the receiver.

"I'm not leaving this place until we find out what this spacecraft's intentions are," the General replied.

"But Dad, you haven't left that place in a month, it's not healthy. Anyways, they've been out there long enough and haven't done anything. You need to leave the office and get some good rest, reset your mind," Ben returned his plea.

"I'm not leaving," the General repeated himself, "now I want you to turn around and go back home, no more negotiating." A sudden burst of alarms flared throughout the building and the General put his hand over the phone.

"Dad, what's going on?" Ben asked.

"Son, I have to go, love you, bye," the General said, and quickly hung up the phone. He hurried to the main display. Staff Sergeant Collins excitedly made the report.

"Sir, the OOS caught an explosion from the spacecraft," he said as he pointed to the Main Display. It showed what looked like bottle rockets shooting outward from the spacecraft.

As the spread of the explosion continued, it became more defined. It was not an explosion but blue projectiles hurtling to Earth.

"Notify the President and get the other PDS advocates on comms now. They are launching on us!" the General shouted. He went to his office and took a seat in front of his speaker phone. He pressed the button labeled, "U.S. online." The other countries that were required to launch the defense missiles were coming across the speaker in short succession.

"Russia."

"China."

"France."

"U.K., online."

The principle members discussed the hostilities that had been seen coming from the OOS. "U.S. declares hostile," General Hawkins said. As soon as the next country started to speak a dead tone came across the speaker.

"Get these comms back online!" the General shouted.

"Cell 321 is launching, loss of satellite communications," a voice called on the watch floor, and continued, even more panicked, "Cell 322… 323… 324…, Group 3 commencing counter-launch. Groups 1… and 2, launching, Group 7, Group 5. Sir, all groups have counter-launched due to a loss of satellite link."

The main display went to static with the alert LOSS OF SIGNAL displaying on the bottom of the screen.

"Put something we can use on the display," the General yelled over his shoulder.

"Sir, we have lost all satellite communications. The only display we have is a hardwired radar," the radar operator said. The display changed from static to an old radar display. There were symbols but nothing that correlated to the blue projectiles.

"Sir, we are only tracking commercial aircraft," the radar operator said, and she continued to scan for possible threats.

A blip came onto the screen. "Bogey one, I have skin," she announced.

"Trajectory?" the General asked without hesitation.

The radar technician pushed some buttons and a dashed line displayed on the screen.

"New York City sir," the radar operator shouted back.

"Bogey two, Boston… Bogey three, Philadelphia,"

"Bogey 37 Denver… Bogey 38, here."

The radar operator's voice cracked, "They are shooting at everything."

"Launch all measures in self-defense," the General ordered. He sat back in his chair.

"We are going to get hit," he said, rubbing his jaw and mouth.

The planetary defense system worked as planned. Launch after launch of two missiles from every cell. Some missiles targeted the blue projectiles and were absorbed while others went directly for the spacecraft. Lost from sight back on Earth, each missile struck the spacecraft and it sustained considerable damage. It began to move out of its orbit and drifted to the closest object, the Moon. The spacecraft continued to drift until it covered a quarter of the Moon. Then a big cloud of dust rose from the surface and its face was forever changed as the spacecraft embedded in the soil.

All of the news outlets were notified of the launch. Anybody that was outside could see the blue streaks across the sky. The news outlets were affected by the same satellite outage but were able to broadcast on local stations as they were still able to transmit.

* * *

Will Easton was sitting in his chair at his intake facility when the TV caught his attention just as the breaking news came across the screen. The President started his address, "We have seen a response from our visiting spaceship. Some type of explosion has occ—" he stopped as someone tapped him on the shoulder and whispered in his ear, "let me correct myself. We are under attack and the spaceship has launched on us. All citizens of major cities on the eastern seaboard need to stay in their homes, do not evacuate, the launch has already occurred and it is too late to evacuate. I will repeat myself, stay at home, this is your only option. We are activating our defenses to eliminate the threat. Executive Order 2519 is now in effect." The screen went to static. Will began to clap his hands, "I might be crazy, I knew it was going to happen, but if people are going to die... then do it in style!"

* * *

General Hawkins picked up the phone, called Ben, and spoke something softly into the handset. Just as he hung up, the blue mass hit. There was no large force, no large explosions, no shockwaves. Nothing remained but craters. All of the cities were gone. The only memory of them was emptiness that replaced them in the earth.

DAY 276
MILITIA HEADQUARTERS
CHARLOTTESVILLE, VIRGINIA

Alan Pritchard couldn't be pried away from the map of the area, "Please, someone tell me that something useful has been found at that damn bunker." On the table next to him lay a pile of orbitizers with darkened cores and broken glass. The raid of the bunker was considered a success because of its destruction, but what happened after the raid is what bothered Alan. "We don't have enough time to dick around hoping we find something. Get some more scavengers out there and clean out that bunker!"

Alan focused his attention on his lieutenant, Brenden Hawkins, as he made his report, "Commander, all of the scavengers are out there... we took a personnel hit when the bunker self-destructed. All we have are the remaining assault squads."

Alan shook his head and spoke as if he was talking to a four-year-old, "Pull from the assault squads. We need everybody to get all of the information possible on those Trolls even if they have to rake through the debris of that bunker. And I want it done by the end of the day."

Ben nodded his head in acknowledgement, "It will be done. Commander."

At 6' 4" and with a burly beard that had been grown since the day of the Attack, Alan was an imposing man who was loved by the survivors in Charlottesville. Even though every Troll attack was met with death and missing people, the survivors viewed him as the last means of defense and they adored him. He was their protector, their defender, their leader. He enjoyed the recognition and developed a lust for the power.

He did not have a great military mind but he made up for it through his stature and his ability to persuade people to fight. After the Attack, he explained *Executive Order 2519* to all the people of Charlottesville.

His first military decree was to conscript all 'able-bodied' men into the militia while all women were able to volunteer themselves for duty. The strongest and most capable were made into soldiers and trained on basic assault. Training was given to those who didn't know how to use a gun. He selected his friends as his trusted lieutenants and Maynard, a 70-year-old tobacco farmer, was his second-in-command. Maynard preferred moonshining to people but he knew how to use a gun. Ben was the exception to the friend-lieutenant relationship. Once he had been conscripted, he proved to have the strategic thinking skills that Alan needed. Alan knew that to keep his stature and popularity, he needed Ben's skills.

Ben knew that his skills were needed as well. He accepted the lieutenant position, not for the sake of Alan's self-promotion, but because he knew that Charlottesville would easily be overrun by a lack of strategy. Ben brought order and discipline to the conscripts placed into the militia. Prior to Ben's promotion, patrols were only made when someone was awake. He brought systematic order to the patrols and vigilance around the clock. The raid on the Nellysford bunker was engineered by Ben and he held himself personally responsible for every death that happened during the assault. Those deaths weighed heavy on Ben. He was determined not only to avenge those deaths but also to minimize any possibility of future casualties.

Those who were 'not able-bodied' did other tasks for the militia. They were not designated as 'official' militia but were assigned to jobs not deemed fit for the normal soldiers. As the raid concluded, many of the 'not able-bodied' were assigned as scavengers. After the bunker self-destructed, Alan, with Ben's suggestion, wanted to gather as much intelligence as possible and he saw the best way to do that was to employ those who did not fight.

The second decree, the only other decree by the Militia Commander, was that all vehicles would be turned over for militia use. Alan felt that it was impossible to protect anyone leaving the area and therefore all outside movements were going to be done by the militia. If any vehicles drove into the area, they were immediately confiscated. Anyone who drove into town without their families was escorted back to their homes, gathered their families and belongings, and escorted back, abandoning their homes.

More metal, more glass. The convoys returned from another round of intelligence gathering. Alan had moved away from the map that was preoccupying him and directed his attention to the front of the headquarters. This time, the remains of three dead trolls and four dead humans were delivered. The fire in the bunker was enough to burn away the flesh of its victims but left remains other than ash. "Get those damned things away from our soldiers and give those soldiers a proper burial." Alan looked at the delivery sitting on the ground in front of the militia command. "You and you," he pointed at two men sitting idly, "put these Trolls in a bag and get them ready for transport."

They immediately moved to the pile of bones. "Transport?" one said to the other as he limped over to the Trolls. "Nobody has ever said anything about transporting anything to anywhere. Where would these things go?"

Alan overheard them talking, "This is a time-sensitive issue," he clamored, his voice quickening, "and unless you want to be the ones transferring them, I suggest you get those bodies on ice now!" Alan turned around and went back into headquarters.

He entered into his personal office. The entire building was small and his office was just as tiny. It had a couple of posters hanging on the wall, a chair, and a bookcase. The bookcase had a line of books on three of the shelves, two phones on the second shelf, and a writing pad on the middle shelf he used as a makeshift desk. He sank heavily into his chair as his girth hung over the sides. He looked up toward the two phones and picked the receiver on the right. It was an old secretary phone with a rotary dialer. He pushed the white button in the middle.

After two rings, someone answered, "Supreme Command."

He spoke with a low voice conjuring up all of the authority he could. "Commander Alan Pritchard for General Huxley, Charlottesville Militia, Authentication 5A41." The voice on the other line was silent. As much as Alan loved his position in Charlottesville, this was only the second time he had called Supreme Command and this was part of the job he did not like.

The voice on the other line came back, "Authentication verified, transferring you to the General." Alan was given the authentication code before the raid on the bunker. General Huxley came on the line.

"What news do you have Alan? Have you got anything we can use? What about the survivor? Is she still in critical condition and can't be transferred?"

Alan felt his throat swell but still managed to get out the words, "Well General, we found three of those Trolls' remains and we are getting them ready for transfer now. We also managed to get out three of them orbitizers and a bunch of glass and metal." He sighed, "No news on that girl, she's still unconscious." In all of the events of the day, Alan had forgotten to check on Maddie.

"I want it all, the scraps, the glass, the Trolls and their weapons, and the girl. Send your transport to rendezvous point 41-13 and we will contact them for further instruction."

Alan quickly glanced at his rendezvous decoder that came with the letter from the Secretary of Defense. "41... 41... 41..." his large finger scrolled down the page, "London, man, how in the world am I going to get this stuff there?"

The General, irritated by his response, came back coldly, "and -13."

Alan looked on the other side of the decoder, "13... Kentucky. Well, I got it, London, Kentucky. General, the transport is leaving tomorrow at the break of dawn. It's too late to send them out now."

The General came back to Alan with a hardened voice, "Alan, this is very important. They need to leave now. There have been other assaults conducted on other bunkers and each area has received retaliatory attacks from the aliens. Every town militia that has conducted an assault has been demolished."

Alan felt an intense pain in the pit of his stomach. "How long do we have?" his voice squeaked as he asked the General.

"Five days after the raid is the longest period that we have seen. Now you can see the importance of getting them out of there."

Alan asked, "I guess that means that you're not providing any type of help?"

The General answered, "Alan, every minute we talk is a minute closer to the aliens attacking and right now, talking is a waste of time. Defend yourselves the best you can and get that transport out of there. We need everything to learn how to beat them... Best of luck to you and to Charlottesville, Alan." The General hung up the phone without hesitation. Alan's oversized body sat in his little chair and he put his hands to his face as he began to cry.

After a couple of minutes, Alan regained his composure and raised himself from his little chair. His office door swung open to the headquarters planning area. As much as he enjoyed his role, he knew that his only way to survive was to get on the transport out of town. A sense of self-preservation set in and he focused on the man that could help save him, "Ben, I need your help." Ben entered into the small office that could barely fit the both of them and looked at Alan. Ben could see Alan's eyes were teary and the skin under his beard was rubbed raw.

"What do you need Commander?" Ben asked in anticipation of conscripting more scavengers.

Alan spoke in a regretful tone, "I have been directed by Supreme Command to head the transport of the Troll materials to London, Kentucky. I'm putting you in charge of the militia while I'm gone."

Ben's eyes opened, "Since when has there been a Supreme Command? We haven't been in contact with anyone except for the people we confine here." Alan let Ben know about who assigned him to direct the militia and that he had always had communications with a 'higher authority.' Alan explained the phone system and coding to Ben. The whole situation seemed odd to Ben. Why didn't Alan assign this to any of his friends? Ben asked, "Why not put Maynard in charge?"

Alan quickly responded with a smile, "Because that old coot can't do half the things you can do."

This was a change that Ben wasn't expecting, "What things do you need me to do?" Ben asked as he emphasized his need.

"There might be an attack while I'm gone, maybe within the next couple of days. I need you to use that great mind of yours to defend the city," Alan said. He wanted Ben in charge in hopes that he could return after the attack.

"It could happen tonight."

"Are you serious??? We still have all those convoys out there and most of them are our trained soldiers. How the hell am I going to defend this place? Am I going to give people pitchforks and tell them to throw rocks???" Ben asked, shocked by the turn of events.

"I can't help what I've been told to do. All I know is that if anyone can do this, it's you. We don't have much time to talk this through. You have to get ready for the Trolls and I have to get this transport going. We both have our parts," Alan said in his soothing voice.

"Yeah, it's funny how our parts panned out, convenient," Ben scoffed. Ben didn't wait for another word but quickly went into the planning room.

"ALL CONVOYS RETURN ASAP!" he yelled, and quickly went to the map table. Ben ripped off three sheets uncovering a strategic map of the city and started to plan.

Alan closed his door again and reached for the phone on his left. He had told Ben that it did not work but when he picked up the handset and pressed "5," he heard a familiar voice.

"This is Mac, what's going on Alan," Mac answered. Alan had great respect for Mac. They had been working together to keep Charlottesville on its feet and they had always gotten along well. Alan led the militia while Mac took care of everyone when they were living their lives outside the militia. They shared information and Mac was the one individual that knew about Supreme Command outside of a few of Alan's militia officers.

This time, Alan spoke quicker than usual, "Mac, we need to get that girl out of town!"

"Alan, you said that I could monitor her full recovery and that you would help me keep her safe. She woke up today," Mac said, confused.

"That's great, she can move herself. By the way, I am keeping her safe. I've been directed by Supreme Command to move her from here. Charlottesville is going to be attacked and if we don't get moving, we're going to be on the receiving end." Alan spoke with greater urgency.

"Then I'm coming too and I'm bringing Barron," Mac said as he realized what Alan was saying.

Alan was committed to leaving in the shortest time possible. He didn't want to waste any more time arguing.

"Fine, whatever gets that girl in the truck, I don't care, be ready in an hour," he barked.

This was the first time the militia was conducting night operations. Mac knew that this was not something to take for granted and he quickly called to Barron and Maddie, "Get your stuff packed, we have to get out of here, an attack is coming!"

Barron started scrambling. He knew what an attack was like.

Maddie, on the other hand, called out, "Mac, I found something really cool that I think you might want to see." Mac rushed to see a smiling Maddie looking into the mirror. She waved at him with her inviting hand and pulled down her eyelid exposing her red eye.

Mac quickly glanced and said, "That's great, Maddie." He moved away to start getting ready to leave.

Maddie pulled his shirt, "Did you see? Did you see? It's normal and real."

Mac stopped and looked at her eye again. "That's right," now his attention was fully focused on her eye. Maddie smiled from getting Mac's attention but he quickly reset his priorities.

"Maddie, we can talk about this later," he said with a hastened voice.

Maddie didn't want to wait and shouted, "I don't want to wait until tomorrow. I think that my eye is normal." Mac turned around, heading for the door. Barron was waiting there wearing a red hat and had two duffel bags over his shoulder.

Mac spoke over his shoulder, "Child," he said in his cajoling voice, "if we don't leave now, there won't be a tomorrow."

DAY 33
BRENDEN HAWKINS
INTERSTATE 81

It had been seven years since Ben, or Brenden Hawkins as his father called him at birth, had been released from active duty. He tried to follow in his father's footsteps but felt his calling was in the world of finance. Ben had decided to settle in Charlotte, North Carolina, and work at an investment firm. His father, General Hawkins, continued his military service while Ben went on to live a separate path. They had stayed in contact since Ben left the service but their communication had become more frequent upon the aliens' arrival.

Ben had become worried that his father's health was taking a turn for the worst. He felt the only way to reason with his dad was to visit him and force him away from his desk. His father wouldn't budge and Ben wouldn't let it rest. Their reactions were the same as they were cut from the same cloth. Ben was stubborn, but hadn't perfected stubbornness as his father had.

Since Ben was halfway through his travels, he decided it was a good time to get on the phone and let his father know what he was doing. He picked up his cell phone and called, "Dad, I decided that I'm coming up whether you like it or not." He was rebuffed by his father.

"Son, I told you that I'm not leaving this place," his father replied. This was his father's usual reply. Ben promised he was still coming and his father told him that he would make time, if he could.

After Ben hung up, he threw the phone into the passenger seat. A well of frustration came over him. He drove, eyes on the road, biting his lower lip, silent. He wanted to know why his father was so resistant to a simple request. Eventually, the urge to take a break overcame him. He pulled into the next exit, parked, and got out of his car. The door locked with a chirp as he pressed his key fob and he walked into the gas station.

After stretching at the coffee counter, he poured himself a cup of joe and grabbed some chips. He carried the goods to the counter and approached the disengaged cashier. He didn't mind as a radio had its volume turned up behind the counter. A radio address from the president was being announced and then:

> *The President is about to address the current situation. We are waiting with great anticipation to find out what has happened with the alien spacecraft.*

The cashier was staring at the radio. Ben realized that something had happened while his radio was off in his car. His father had made him so upset that he stewed in his thoughts as he drove. But now, the radio was on and his mind was solely focused on the transmission.

> *There is definitely something going on up there. I see the Moon with a bunch of blue streams coming out. It is a beautiful sight. Oh, he's coming out. Excuse me.*
> *"Ladies and Gentlemen."*

There were voices chattering in the background of the transmission.

> *"The President of the United States of America."*

Ben and the cashier listened to every word from the President. The President's last lines, combined with the screams on the transmission, made Ben turn white. He patted his pocket for his phone. It wasn't there. He spun around and looked on the floor, it wasn't there. He ran to the coffee counter and it wasn't there either. Then he remembered that he had left it in the car. The cashier was staring at the static sound coming out of the radio. The cup of coffee fell to the floor as Ben whisked to the door. The door slammed open and stuck as Ben sprinted out to his car. He lifted the door handle but it wouldn't open. He reached into his pocket and the car chirped as the doors unlocked. The phone was sitting on the seat facedown and he grabbed it. The screen illuminated and *One Missed Call* was displayed.

Message Received came after the missed call alert.

Ben could only hope his Dad was okay. He entered in his passcode and listened to the message.

> *Ben, my son, I hope this reaches you well. I am sorry and you were right. They have attacked and there is nothing I can do and this will be the last time I will speak to you. I only pray that you are nowhere near a city being attacked. If you do survive this attack, please go to the nearest town and find a militia. You will be a great asset to them. And son, the only way that I will be able to defeat these aliens is through the best part of me, you. God bless you and I know you will do what needs to be done. Love you, son.*

Ben called his father back with the hope of an answer but the only answer was a recording saying that the number was not available. He closed his eyes and hung his head. He choked and did his best to hold in his tears. "Don't cry, it'll let your enemy know that you're weak," he remembered his father saying as he indulged in his memories of the past. The memories with his father. Chuckles and deep exhales would occasionally come out of his mouth. He opened his eyes and came back to reality. He walked back into the gas station. He didn't even wait to get to the counter.

"Where is the closest militia based?" he demanded from the cashier. The cashier was still in shock from the radio announcement and turned around.

"Um, why it's, um, Charlottesville," he informed Ben.

"Thanks," Ben said, and he turned around to get in his car.

He knew where to go and what he needed to do. He would honor his father's last request and kill every last one of the damn aliens so his father didn't die in vain.

DAY 276
HOSPITAL TRIAGE
CHARLOTTESVILLE, VIRGINIA

His heart was racing as he opened his eyes. In front of him, Marcus Smith saw a cinder block wall painted off-white. The beeping from the heart monitor pounded from behind him. His breath became more rapid. The urge to move overcame him and he pushed away from the bed into a sitting position.

He looked at the wires that were hanging from his arms and chest and started to remove them. The heart monitor flat-lined as he ripped off the last of the wires. Pushing himself off the bed, Marcus awkwardly stepped onto the floor. His knees began to buckle as he reached back to the bed and used it as support. The last thing he remembered was carrying that woman he found out of the bunker.

One of the nurses charged into the room and wrapped her arms around him. Her attempted lift was met by his weight. She conceded that he wasn't budging, "Sir, please get back on the bed," she asked, still struggling to hold him up. Marcus propped his arms on the bed and lifted himself to a sitting position. When he released the tension from his muscles, a burning sensation started to emanate from his back spreading to the entirety of his torso. He reached backwards and felt his back covered with a pad.

"You had a lot of shrapnel in your back. You were very lucky for two reasons: nothing major was damaged and you survived." She started to clean the blood running down his arm from the removal of the IV.

"So, none of the others made it," Marcus said as if death was a daily occurrence in his life.

"You were the only one, I'm sorry to tell you," she threw away the bloody gauze. "You have been down for a couple of days and you're still feeling the effects of the sedation. I know you have a lot going on in your head."

Marcus stretched his arms to the ceiling, trying not to pay attention to his back that was gaining the intensity of a blazing inferno. "How long will I have to be in this hospital?" Marcus wanted to be out of the bed and out of the hospital.

"The doctor says that you'll be able to leave after you are able to walk down the hallway," the nurse pointed out of the curtains, "but you need to come in daily to change the pad on your back and the doctor wants to check on you in a week."

Thanks to the painkillers the nurse supplied, the fire pit that formed on his back had once again shifted to a small irritation. Marcus had to wait a couple more hours until he could prove to the nurse that he could walk. Once the nurse was satisfied with his physical well-being, she handed him some medicine which was in short supply.

Provided with clothing left by the militia members who dropped him off at the hospital, Marcus got dressed and left. When he walked out of the door, Marcus felt the warmth of the sun on his face and it brought him a sense of calm. He saw a bench in front of him. He walked over to it and kicked one of its legs to make sure it wouldn't fall down. Unlike the other benches around it, this one seemed solid.

He sat down on the bench and draped his arms over the entire back. His head fell back as his face went to the sky and visions of his wife and child entered into his head. He smiled as the image of holding his son and being kissed by his wife filled his daydream. His son was 4-years-old and a spitting image of his father. He had known his wife since they were in high school and they were married after he completed his basic military training. After a while, the images faded and were replaced with thoughts of the Attack. His head snapped forward, "I guess it's about that time," he got up from the bench. "Time to check into headquarters."

It was the latter part of the afternoon when Marcus arrived, "Smith... is that you?" Ben jogged up to him and looked at him from head to toe. He was relieved to see that Marcus had survived the blast.

"Yeah, LT, it's me," Marcus said warmly despite showing no crack in his exterior facade. Ben was the one person that Marcus respected, the only one of Alan Pritchard's militia that he called 'LT.' They complemented each other well. Ben's strategic mind combined with Marcus' practical application and vice versa. Charlottesville was better defended because they knew how to work together. They knew that the militia would have been overrun if it wasn't for them both. Marcus didn't care that Ben got the credit and asked to be a lieutenant. Ben was a good man and he was genuine and Marcus would never want to give up being in the field. Not being in the field was Ben's calling, definitely not his.

"I am glad to see you back," Ben told him with a smile on his face.

Marcus returned the smile and said, "What's going on here?"

Ben turned around to see the scavengers returning with metal scraps and glass. "Oh, this," he waved his hand as he introduced the area to Marcus, "this is what we can do because of you."

Marcus walked with Ben over to the piles, "So this is all you guys could get, a bunch of metal and glass... it looks like a crackhead's worst nightmare."

Ben again looked over at Marcus, just glad that he was alive, "I'm sure we will figure out a use for this stuff, it's just a matter of time." Ben looked at headquarters, "You ever been in there?" He tilted his head in the direction of the building.

Marcus looked at the building too, "Nope, it's only for you bigwigs."

Ben started walking toward the building, "Come on, today you are." Marcus sped up to Ben and walked by his side.

As they walked on the deck and approached the building, the guard stopped Marcus, "You can't come in," he moved in between Marcus and the door.

Ben put his hand on the guard's upper arm and gently pushed him out of the way, "The hell he can't, he's with me. I'm taking him in." The guard looked at Ben's face and saw how serious he was. He moved back out of fear of making a militia lieutenant angry. Marcus walked by the guard, glaring at him, and went through the door.

They were walking into the main planning area when Alan Pritchard shoved past them, heading out of the door. "He's definitely in a rush," Ben said, "this is why I wanted you here. I want to show you the map." Marcus looked down at the map as Ben pointed out the possible locations for other bunkers. Ben pointed to an area of the map, "I'm concerned about sending a squad to this area."

Marcus reviewed the map and then pointed to the same area, "Yeah, I would be concerned too. But it would be smarter if you approach from this direction to limit their target angles."

They continued to analyze the map until Alan Pritchard yelled, "Ben, come in here."

Marcus waited for what seemed like an eternity even though it was no more than ten minutes. He drifted over to the window to see the scavengers starting to load large bulky sacks on the trucks. His concentration was broken by Ben running out of Alan Pritchard's office. "ALL CONVOYS RETURN ASAP!" Ben yelled. As he was notifying everyone of the situation, he caught his practical counterpart out of the corner of his eye and gestured to Marcus to follow him. He approached the map table and ripped off the first two sheets and handed them to Marcus, "You're going to need these. You're going with Pritchard." He explained that something had changed in Alan and that he did not trust him anymore. "Make sure that those people and that stuff make it to Kentucky," Ben told Marcus.

DAY 33
HOMEWARD BOUND
FLIGHT NUMBER 2354 FROM SAN DIEGO

It was a good day, a grand day, a day that Marcus would return to his family. He had been on a special operations mission with Okoye. Finally, after nearly 12 months, he would be coming home. He was cruising at 36,000 feet on his flight from San Diego to Norfolk. He could hardly contain his excitement.

"What's the first thing you're going to do?" he asked Okoye, who was sitting in the aisle seat as Marcus sat next to the window.

"I don't know, sleep, eat, and sleep some more," Okoye was going through the same bout of happiness.

"I'll tell you what I'm going to do. The first thing I'm going to do is pick up my son… the last time I held him, he was four-years-old. And then, I'm going to kiss my wife and tell her how much I missed her." Marcus was fully dedicated to his family. As the others would go out and find ways to blow off steam, he would spend his spare time writing letters and emails to his wife.

Okoye laughed at him and shook his head, "Y'all family guys, always have your priorities… When I'm done sleeping and eating, I'm going to buy a sweet new car."

Okoye had five peanut wrappers on his lap and another package in his hands. He emptied the entire bag in his mouth while watching the second inflight movie. The scene he was watching made him laugh, the laugh developed into a cough, and the cough caused some of the chewed peanuts to blow through his nose. "Ugh, that's not pretty," he said as he looked down at his hands and saw the combination of snot and crushed peanuts, "yuck." Marcus burst out in laughter as he saw Okoye struggle to get out of his seat. Okoye finally got to his feet, completely mindless of the peanut wrappers falling to the floor. "I'll be back bro," Okoye told Marcus with his hands in the air so as not to touch anything.

Marcus chuckled, "I'll see you in a bit," he said as he wiped the tears running down his face from laughter.

With two hours of the flight remaining, Marcus started to fidget in his seat. The anticipation was getting the best of him. A fresh and clean Okoye sat next to him with his head tilted forward, fast asleep. Just as Marcus went back to reading the magazine on his lap, the plane shook and quickly descended. Okoye woke up in shock and started to flail in his seat while Marcus gripped the armrests tightly. The oxygen masks flung out of the overhead and the flight attendant came over the announcement system, "Can I have your attention please?" She paused slightly and then continued to speak, "The Captain has turned on the 'fasten seatbelts' sign, please everyone, return to your seat."

Luckily, everyone was already wearing their seatbelts and they were safe in the cabin, despite the trauma. The flight captain shortly came over the announcement system, "Everyone, this is the Captain. We have experienced a technical malfunction." Marcus raised his eyebrows as if the captain didn't need to state the obvious. "We have just been cleared to make an emergency landing in Charleston, West Virginia. Flight attendants, prepare for landing."

Marcus guffawed in disbelief, "Great, just had to make this trip even longer..." he muttered disappointedly under his breath. He lightly shoved Okoye's shoulder to get his attention. Okoye sat straight up with his eyes wide open and Marcus asked him, "If we can't get home in six hours, do you just want to rent a car and drive home?"

Okoye didn't want to wait to get back either, "Sure thing bro, anything to get back... I'm tired of traveling." Marcus knew that if there was the slightest delay that he had a backup plan now.

The plane made its landing without a flaw in maneuvers as the pilot performed splendidly. As the plane taxied toward the gate area, the flight attendant once again came over the announcement system, "I'm sorry folks, but due to required maintenance, we are not going to be able to continue this flight until tomorrow morning when a substitute jet arrives. The airline apologizes and will compensate everyone the cost of the flight and will purchase hotel rooms for the night." After the announcement was over, Marcus activated the backup plan in his mind. He and Okoye left the plane once it reached the gate and waited for their bags. They waited next to the turnstile and the first batch of bags came through the conveyor. Neither of their bags came through until the second round. They quickly picked up their belongings and rushed to the rental car counter. Once they got into the car, it would only be seven hours until they got home.

After they were done at the counter, they had the keys to victory in Marcus' hands. With the plan finally in action, Marcus was confident enough to call his wife, "Baby, the plane had a malfunction and we had an emergency landing."

Her voice was filled with fear and relief, "Thank God you're alright! When are you coming home? Are they flying you out of there tonight?"

Marcus spoke with disappointment in his voice, "No, the plane is grounded..."

His wife started to plead with him, "Please, oh please, get on the earliest plane and get home," and then she had an idea, "I am about tempted to come and get you myself!"

Marcus was quick to change her thought process as he spoke with excitement in his voice, "Baby, no need. I got a car and I'm coming home tonight!"

Her squeal of happiness came across the phone. "What time are you getting home then?" she asked with eager anticipation.

"It's a seven-hour drive with gas stops. I'll get there as soon as I can!"

The excitement continued to escalate in her voice. "That's so great. Please hurry, but be safe and I will be up when you get home... I can't wait for you to get here!" His wife knew there was not going to be any rest tonight.

Marcus opened the car door as the clock approached midnight and started to focus on driving. "Baby, I'm getting into the car now, I'll call you at the next stop." Marcus was unsuccessfully trying to suppress his excitement.

His wife responded with the same amount of happiness. "I love you so much."

Marcus smiled and replied, "I love you too, Baby." With the keys in the ignition, the car pulled out of the garage and continued on the road.

The car was doing well on gas mileage but the need to take a break and stretch overcame Marcus. After four hours of driving in silence since the radio was off and Okoye was sleeping, he turned off of the highway. His stop in Waynesboro was going to be short but also an opportunity to call his wife. He picked up his phone to give her a location update.

"Baby, we just stopped in Waynesboro, only a few hours left," Marcus said.

His wife didn't reply with the same amount of excitement this time, "Oh Marcus, that's great but have you heard about what is happening?" Marcus had no idea what had happened and answered somewhat confused and concerned.

"No, I haven't heard anything," he said.

"The aliens, they have made some sort of contact with us," she said. Marcus heard her asthma pump. "Are they going to call you back?" Marcus hadn't been called about the situation and he was taken by surprise that it happened the night he was coming home. Marcus was feeling a little upset that out of all days, the aliens had decided this was the day to offer their graces to the humans below.

"Nobody has contacted me and there is nothing that is stopping me from getting home tonight," he said.

"I'm so happy that's the case," her delight came over the phone once again.

"I'm getting in the car and will see you in less than three hours," Marcus said, smiling.

"I still can't wait to get my arms around you. Love you, *mwah*," she replied. Her kiss flew through the phone and touched Marcus. The phone beeped as she hung up and Marcus got back into the car with Okoye still fast asleep.

After 15 minutes on the road, his cell phone buzzed with an incoming call. Baby came across as the name and a picture of his wife appeared in the background. He continued to focus on the road and attempted to answer a second too late. *Missed Call – Baby* was displayed on the phone. Before he could redial, a second call buzzed in. It was Baby again. He answered this time, "Baby…"

His wife didn't wait for the salutation, "Marcus, oh my God, we're being attacked, they're shooting at us."

Marcus was in disbelief, "Calm down, they're actually shooting at us?" He wanted to make sure he heard correctly.

"Oh my God, Marcus, yes, it's coming straight for us!" She started to scream and Marcus could hear his son waking up in the background. "Look at the sky, it's coming down!" Marcus quickly pulled over to the side of the road and got out of the car.

His eyes gazed upon the stars and he noticed they were brighter and bluer than usual. Awoken by the sudden stop, Okoye got out of the passenger seat and looked in the same direction. Marcus could see the blue stars getting larger and more defined. "Baby, you need to get out of there… get out of there now," his voice cracked with urgency.

"Marcus, I'm in the car now." By this point, the blue stars had turned into orbs and there were too many to count. Two of the orbs were coming down directly to the east in synchronicity. They approached closer and closer.

"Baby, how are you doing getting out of there?" he asked in eager anticipation of good news.

His wife was frantic, "I'm in the car and I," the orbs got closer, "am," the orbs got closer, "driving," even closer, "on the, oh my God…"

Marcus' phone had three beeps at the same time as the orbs met with the Earth. He fell to his knees and his heart emptied as all emotion drained from his body. Okoye was still watching the horizon for any signs that anything had changed and did not notice Marcus fall. Marcus' heart fell out of his chest. He knew what had just happened.

DAY 276
TRANSPORT LOADING AREA
CHARLOTTESVILLE, VIRGINIA

Maynard was sitting in his truck waiting for the transport convoy to start. The convoy consisted of seven pickups, three SUVs, and a dump truck filled to the top with all of the metal from the bunker. Seated in the other pickups were Paul, Andy, Kyle, Zeke, and Alan's other lieutenants, with the exception of Ben. Alan was leaving town but he still wanted his friends as close as possible. He knew how important it was to be surrounded by people that he trusted. Each vehicle had either one or two gunners, depending on the seating arrangement.

Marcus was assigned to the SUV that would be transporting Mac, Barron, and Maddie. He sat in the passenger seat while Booby, Alan's nephew, drove. Booby did not have high intelligence or even average intelligence. He was downright dumb and was quick to tell everyone that he was. But Booby listened and was loyal, two qualities that suited Alan and his needs.

Alan was the last one to get into a vehicle. He entered the SUV that would be in front of Marcus. When he placed his foot into the cab and transferred his weight, the entire thing listed to his side. After he closed the door, he lifted his right arm out of the window and rotated his forearm as the signal to start moving. Engines began to rev and Booby started to jump in his seat.

"Call me Big Booby, call me Big Booby!" he kept yelling and bouncing. Marcus looked out of the window. He was stuck with this guy and he was struggling with his new situation. This trip was already five seconds longer than he wanted it to be.

With headlights on and all engines turning, the pack of vehicles started to move away from the militia headquarters. Ben looked out the window as Alan and his entourage were leaving, a pair of headlights at a time. He curled his lips in disgust and then walked away from the window, slamming his finger on the map.

"I need people here and here," he said, and pointed at two high vantage points on the map.

"Yes sir!" one of the scavengers replied. Ben continued to plan without a full armament of soldiers.

As the company of SUVs and trucks headed away from headquarters, they drove through Charlottesville for what could possibly be the last time. Alan was already missing the feeling of being showered with praise from all the locals, imported or not. It was the praise he loved. They reached the medical clinic and Booby slammed his hand down on the horn to get their attention.

"Would you knock it off?" Marcus said sharply, irritated by everything Booby did or said. "It's dark outside and you're making a calling card for the Trolls."

Booby let go of the horn. "I dare 'em to come, they don't know what they're dealing with here," Booby said, and he flexed his bicep, which was not as daunting as he thought. He pushed it toward Marcus and Marcus turned his head.

"I don't think you know what you're dealing with... Anyways, do you think your uncle would appreciate you calling the Trolls before we get out of town?" Marcus asked. Booby stared silently at Marcus, slowly blinking as he processed Marcus' last comment.

Then Booby rolled down his window. He climbed on the ledge and sat on the door of the SUV.

"Hey y'all need to hurry up," he yelled. Movement started to stir at the medical clinic. Noticing that his passengers were on the move, he smugly told Marcus, "You see, that got 'em." Booby returned to his seat and leaned toward Marcus. Six inches from Marcus, he was smiling and shaking his head.

Marcus closed his eyes for a moment to gather his patience, "Great job, do you think you could concentrate on driving now?"

Booby sat back down in his seat and gleefully answered, "I sure can, I am the MAN!"

"Yes, you are," Marcus said softly, staring out of his window.

The three from the medical center made their way to the SUV. Mac opened the back door for Maddie while Barron loaded their bags in the trunk. Barron had just come to the realization that he was scared of the dark and of the Trolls. Maddie sat behind Marcus and Mac sat behind Booby. Barron stood in front of the door. Mac adjusted enough to his side to allow Barron to squeeze into the third row.

Maddie was beaming and eager to talk to Mac, "Can you believe it?" she asked him before he could resettle.

Mac put on his seatbelt, "Maddie, that's great and you did a great job. But let me ask you this: have you diagnosed the problem?"

Her smile turned into a frown, "No, I haven't," she started to come down from her elation.

Mac was trying to find something to say without crushing her so he used a dulcet tone, "And that's why we will continue on until we figure out what happened to you in that bunker." Her smile returned, figuring that Mac wanted to include her as part of the process and not just a test subject. "You're not an experiment anymore."

Marcus turned around and faced Maddie. The moment he heard 'bunker,' he realized who was sitting behind him. He was never able to get a good look at her during the evacuation and didn't get a good look at her eye as she was entering the SUV.

"Maddie," he extended his hand to shake hers, her two different colored eyes now in full view, "I'm Marcus and it's a pleasure to meet you."

Maddie was slightly taken aback by his gesture but cautiously greeted his hand with hers, "It's a pleasure to meet you too?" She found it strange that he suddenly introduced himself and couldn't figure out if she was supposed to know him. Her curiosity overtook her restraint and she asked him with uncertainty, "Am I supposed to know you?"

"You don't remember me but I was the guy who got you out of that bunker you're talking about," Marcus explained. That was all Maddie needed to kick start her desire to find answers. Mac sat there, silent and intrigued. This was the first time he was going to hear what Marcus had seen in the bunker.

"Time to get moooooving," Booby hollered with a total disregard for the conversation that was happening behind him. The SUV started to move forward and they were on their way from the medical clinic. Maddie ignored Booby's interjection and remained completely focused on Marcus.

She blurted out the first thing on her mind, "Was there anyone else in there? Any guys? A girl?"

Marcus kept his soft tone, "You were the only one the Trolls kept in there. We saw plenty of tables with a lot of blood on them but you were the only human in that bunker. If there was anyone else in that room, they were removed well before we got there. You were on a table in the corner of the room and I carried you out before the bunker exploded." Maddie felt a tinge of hope. Surely if her friends weren't in there, they must have survived.

They could be out there! Her hope was rising and she was getting the answers she desired, but she didn't understand why the aliens were called Trolls, "How come everyone calls them Trolls? I know they are the 'aliens,'" she made quotation marks with her fingers, "but why are they called Trolls?"

Marcus told her from a soldier's point of view, "I don't know who first called them Trolls but it stuck and everyone has been calling them that since they first attacked Charlottesville. They're called Trolls because of the way they look. They are tall and blue and shaped much like we are but," Maddie was sitting still and listening attentively to every word he said, "they are all bald with pointed ears that droop over the sides of their heads. Their noses are huge and cover most of their face and their bottom lip is the only thing under their noses." Maddie was trying to picture the Trolls in her head as she had not actually seen one. Marcus continued to describe them in detail, "They only have four long fingers with sharp triangles for nails and feet-shaped talons. The worst is their eyes. Their eyes are creepy, black and too small for the size of their head and when they look at you, all you can see in them is emptiness."

Mac didn't want to interrupt Maddie's questioning but he wanted to ask questions of his own. Maddie was quicker and had other questions about the room. She wanted to continue to get some answers, "Was there anything else in the room? Were they experimenting on me?" The stories of alien conspiracy theorists entered her mind as she asked her questions.

Marcus replied, "There wasn't anything attached to you, I would have noticed it when we removed you." He started to focus intently on Maddie's red eye. She noticed him staring at it and adjusted her hair to cover it up. Marcus made a connection, "But now looking at your eye, I remember that there were red fluids in the room the same color." Maddie started to think about the red liquid. The red liquid, her eye, her blood, they all had to be connected.

If she could only get her hands on what the red liquid was, "Marcus, where can I get some of that red liquid?" Mac lifted his eyebrows toward Marcus, wanting to know the same answer.

"The only place I know you can get it is in that bunker," Marcus said with absolute confidence and then added, "I'm sure that we could find it in other bunkers."

Maddie pried deeper, "Where can we find…"

She was interrupted by Booby again, "What in the hell is that?" He pointed in front of the SUV. They all focused on the front of the convoy and saw a concert of blue orbs creating a luminescent wall. The little blue dots flew in the distance from their left. The first truck in the convoy turned around and attempted to go back to Charlottesville. They watched it accelerate but the orbs were faster.

The truck started to disappear whenever one of the blue projectiles collided with it. The frame of the truck started to fade away and then the tire went flat and then the other tire. The truck rolled over on its side and continued to get pelted. Smaller and smaller, the truck faded into the night until the blue projectiles started to fly past where it used to be.

The doors of the other convoy vehicles opened and everyone started to flood toward the woods to the right. Marcus opened his door, "It's time to move," his voice was controlled by his adrenaline, "take cover in the woods!" He opened Maddie's door and she was the first out, followed by Mac, and then delayed by climbing over the seat, Barron flew out. Booby got out on the driver's side and a line of blue fire was directed towards him. He attempted to run but was hit by some of the dots that had turned into the noticeable blue orbs and he fell after a few steps. By the time Maddie made it to the woods she turned around to see Marcus close behind her, followed by Barron. Mac's age was showing as he was the last to reach the tree line.

Marcus was catching his breath and told the old man, "You need to keep up." He continued to pant.

"I will," Mac wheezed.

"We need to go deeper in there and outrun them," Marcus pointed further into the woods.

Barron looked into the woods and could only see darkness, "How are we supposed to see where we're going?"

Marcus pointed back to the Trolls, "It's either the woods or them." Just as they looked at where Marcus was pointing, Maynard appeared and started shooting his rifle. It was reciprocated with a blue orb that hurtled toward him, hitting him in the jaw and knocking him down. His jaw and his beard evaporated, but he got back up to his feet with one hand covering his throat where his tongue used to be. The blue orbs continued to surround him and the upper part of his head bobbed as if he were shouting. Another blue projectile hit him and he fell down again. This time he didn't get back up and all they heard was a single shot from his rifle.

All of them were frozen, staring at what had just happened to Maynard. Marcus was the first to turn back to the woods, "Come on, let's go," he hastened the others. Maddie led the way as the underbrush began to thicken and bog down her stride. Barron, shorter than Maddie, had more difficulty plodding through the thickets and branches at their feet. As they made it past the first couple of trees, the lightning storm behind them began to lessen until they could not see any more of the blue flashes.

Maddie stopped in a small clearing after a few minutes, "Do you think we're safe?" She looked backed and saw Barron twenty feet behind, taking deep laboring breaths, trying to catch up to her.

"I think we need to keep going," he said in between deep breaths as he finally reached the clearing. Mac and Marcus were soon standing in the open patch and looked behind them. All four of them scanned through the darkness trying to catch a glimpse of the terror-causing blue agents of death.

"Where else are we supposed to go?" Barron was looking for direction. "Do we go deeper into the woods?" He was the most shaken of the group.

Marcus looked down at him, "We should go..." a blur orb came humming past, barely missing Mac. Not knowing the source of the shot, they crouched down to scan the trees again. Barron sighted a glowing blue orb.

He pointed in the direction of his view, "There it is," he yelled and started to run away from it.

"Hide, take cover!" Marcus cried out as he knew they were not going to outrun these things. Barron was now in front of Maddie and continued into the woods. Maddie stopped behind a large tree and pressed her back against it. Mac and Marcus continued to run past, finding trees of their own. There was complete silence as Maddie looked around her tree. Again, no sign of the glowing blue orbs that indicated the Trolls' whereabouts. She turned to the other side and before she could even look around the tree, there it was.

Not even a foot in front of her was a Troll. Her heart raced and she was so shocked that she didn't feel herself start to fall backwards. The Troll turned its head and noticed her movement. As it turned toward her, another humming blue orb shot out in response to the sound she made and it hit the Troll. In front of her, the Troll's forearm disappeared and its hand fell to the ground, with its gun still attached. Marcus turned around to see Maddie next to the Troll and vacated his tree.

He ran toward her as she scrambled to pick up the Troll's orbitizer. He pushed as hard as he could. He had to save her again. Maddie pried the Trolls' fingers from the orbitizer and threw the disembodied hand to the side. She lifted the orbitizer and quickly aimed at the center of the Troll, placing her fingers where she thought the trigger should be. The core started to glow an island blue and the orbitizer felt ready to fire. She squeezed the pad and the emission came out of the orbitizer, hurtling toward the Troll.

Time stopped for that moment. The Troll slowly watched the blue orb enter its abdomen. The size of the blue orb started to shrink as the Troll's skin dissolved. Its outer layer disappeared showing its alien interior. Marcus stopped and his jaw dropped. She was the first person he had ever known to fire an orbitizer. Even the other Troll watched with a disbelieving look, stunned that she had fired the gun.

As time sped back up, the Troll with a hollowed body slumped to the ground and Maddie took aim at the other Troll. She shot once, twice, three times, four times. She continued to shoot until the core stopped glowing. The second Troll fell to the ground in bits and pieces as Maddie looked down at the orbitizer.

With the two Trolls out of action, Marcus continued his sprint to Maddie and nearly collided with her as he stopped on some leaves, "How'd you do that?" he asked, really wanting the answer.

"I shot them," she aimed her doomsday weapon toward a nearby tree, "like this." The orbitizer core began to glow as she tapped her fingers on the soft padding. A hum came out followed by another blue orb that went directly toward the tree.

Marcus was still looking at her with amazement, "Let me try!" She offered him the orbitizer and he was quick to grab it. He aimed at the same tree and squeezed the padding. No glow, no projectile, it was dormant. Marcus dropped his hands in disbelief, the orbitizer resting on his thigh while he just stood there.

"Let me show you again," she pulled the gun out of his hands and started to show him what she did. "Put your fingers here," the orbitizer began to glow, dimmer than when she first started to fire it, "and then you squeeze here." A blue mass ejected from the muzzle again. "And that's how we do it," she said, speaking to Marcus as if he was a schoolboy.

Mac caught up with the two and showed the same amazement as Marcus. "Do you mind if I give it a go?" Mac wanted to see if he could shoot it. He repeated what he had seen Maddie demonstrate. Like with Marcus, the orbitizer just sat in his hands with no activity. Marcus put out his hand and moved his fingers as he wanted another try.

"It's not working for me," Mac said as he offered the weapon to Marcus, who aimed the orbitizer once more at the tree. He placed his fingers in the exact same spot with no response from the orbitizer. Just to humor himself, as if it would have worked, he squeezed the padding. Nothing again. He squeezed the padding a second time, a third time, he just started clamping his hand repeatedly onto the pad.

"Here, you take it." He jerked the orbitizer from the aimed position and handed it to Maddie, frustrated. "If you can shoot it, then you have it... and get the other one too," he pointed to the other Troll, "those are the most powerful weapons out here."

Maddie held her trophy proudly in her hand as she sprinted toward the other Troll. Footsteps came through the trees, rapidly approaching the group. Marcus raised his gun to engage, aiming directly at the noise. Barron emerged from the darkness still running. He saw the muzzle of Marcus' gun and stopped to raise his hands. "Don't shoot, don't shoot, don't shoot!" he screamed while closing his eyes and turning his head. Barron had been turned around in the woods and had run in a complete circle.

"It's alright, you can stop running," Mac let Barron know that it was safe for the moment. Marcus lowered his firearm and scanned the area. As Maddie was approaching with her second orbitizer, Marcus saw blue flashes continuing in the distance.

"How'd you kill them?" Barron asked the group, still recovering from his sprinting.

"With these," Maddie presented the two orbitizers.

Barron's eyes opened wide, "I heard that nobody can shoot those orbitizers. How'd you do it?" He had never seen one and wanted to try it out, "Wait, can I try?"

"We have to go that way and stay away from the Trolls," Marcus interrupted as he wanted to avoid any and all confrontations.

They continued through the woods and could see the glow of the building lights above the tree line. They followed the lighted area as the dawn of day began to rise. The road that could be used for their exit came into sight. With the blue lights behind them and the sun coming out, they made for the road to head back to militia headquarters. They carefully left the wooded area and to their surprise, they intersected with Alan Pritchard and Zeke as they were walking in the same direction. "Mac, you made it!" Alan flashed a grin through his great beard. "And the girl is safe too!" He was surprised but also happy that he still had one of his deliverables for Supreme Command. "You did a great job soldier," he continued to smile.

Marcus replied as it was his job, "Thank you, sir."

Alan looked at the road ahead and said to the group, "I hope you were planning to go to headquarters." He directed his voice to Zeke,

"C'mon, it's going to take all day to get there with all those trucks gone."

DAY 38
JOHNSON PHARMACY
CHARLOTTESVILLE, VIRGINIA

Philip and Peggy Johnson were pillars of the community. Not only did they own their own pharmacy, but they also tried to help everyone that they could. Their only child, a son, Barron, was named after Philip's father and was their pride and joy. As a young child, Barron would play outside the shopping center until his parents closed the store. He had just graduated from high school and was now in his first semester of college. He was going to be a pharmacist too. It was unfortunate that after the Attack, every service deemed unessential by the militia was shut down, including the college.

In his spare time, Barron volunteered as an EMT for the local Rescue Squad. It had been five days since the Attack and the militia was consolidating all vehicles under their domain. All of the Rescue Squad had become the medics in the Avalon Militia due to the conscription policy. Barron, too, was now under militia authority. There hadn't been a need for any emergency medical services for the past few days and he wondered if he was ever going to get any experience.

He sat and waited. That was until the evening of the first local attack. The alarm sounded and everyone was bustling to go to the location announced. "My parents are probably there," Barron told his fellow EMT in the back of the vehicle. Peggy and Philip had been working extra late since the Attack, providing additional support for the hospital. Since Barron had been an EMT, every call they received was either an accident or an individual hurt. The calls only caused moments of stress.

The response vehicle arrived on the scene. It was like nothing that Barron had ever seen before and his mind shifted to his parents. "I need to find my Mom and Dad," Barron yelled as he jumped out of the vehicle. He ran to the pharmacy, disregarding the carnage that surrounded him. He jumped over and weaved around bodies missing parts and flowing blood. He didn't see anything but obstacles as he continued to look for his parents. The door to the pharmacy was open. He burst through it and spotted his parents on the floor behind the counter.

As he ran, he fell to his knees and slid to where his father was holding his mother in his arms. Peggy was dead. A hole had been burrowed through the side of her abdomen. Protruding the semicircle of emptiness were the organs that were left untouched.

Barron looked at his father, "Dad," was all that he could get out. He jumped to hug his father and when he connected, his father screamed in agonizing pain. Philip crumbled, his missing leg providing counterbalance for the hug. Barron gasped as he saw his father reach for where his leg used to be. "Hold on Dad," he said as he made his way for the door.

"Help, help," Barron screamed as he looked for somebody to help him. There were too many hurt people and not enough EMT's. The one stretcher was within his sight. His fellow EMT was running it to another victim of the attack. Barron was quick to commandeer the platform and told him, "Follow me, I need your help."

Barron and the medic loaded his father and his mother on the stretcher and wheeled them to the vehicle for hospital transport. They shut the doors and the driver started to drive. Barron glanced out of the back window to see hundreds of people lying lifeless on the ground, too much for the EMTs to handle. He looked back at his father and grabbed his hand, "Hang in there, Dad. We're getting you to the hospital."

The hospital was filled with people. Barron barely got the stretcher in the door and was stopped by dead bodies in his way. He looked around the corner and there was more death than life. He screamed with urgency, "Help, my father needs help!" But the scurry of nurses and doctors in the emergency area paid him no mind.

He went back to the stretcher and pushed it over a body that was impeding his path. He swerved around the other bodies and made it to triage.

"Please help him," he pulled a nurse from her course and pointed to his father. She pulled away from his grasp and went over to his father. The nurse took out her stethoscope and applied it to Philip's chest. She lifted his wrist to check his pulse. She listened and felt.

Then she dropped his wrist and put her stethoscope back around her neck, "I'm sorry, but there is nothing I can do," she said as she sped off.

"No, no, no, no, this can't be." Barron went to his father's side while his mother lay on the other side, still. "I wasn't fast enough Dad." He cupped his father's hand within his hands and held it tight.

"I'm sorry for your loss," a hand was gently placed on Barron's shoulder. He looked up and saw a man. "Philip was an old friend of mine. We went to school together."

Barron spoke with a solemn voice to this stranger, "He was my Dad and she was my Mom." He pointed to his mother and father intertwined on the stretcher.

The stranger spoke in the same tone, "I know Barron. You probably don't remember me but I'm Doctor McCluskey. You can call me Mac."

DAY 277
THE FALL OF CHARLOTTESVILLE
CHARLOTTESVILLE, VIRGINIA

The tension from the onslaught had died down and the survivors of the night were walking to Charlottesville. The morning sun was illuminating their path, giving them the confidence to stay on the road. Trolls didn't attack during the day. "So... how exactly did you guys get away from those things?" Alan thought it was time to share stories, especially since Maddie was carrying two orbitizers with active cores. He was very curious how they had come across those orbitizers and he knew they would be a welcomed prize at Supreme Command.

Mac started explaining their journey, "We ran into the woods when the shooting began and Booby was shot." Mac continued telling Alan about how they had encountered and killed two Trolls but left out using the orbitizers. He continued with the story of their experience until they met up with Alan and Zeke. As he finished, he asked Alan, "What about you and Zeke? How did you guys get out of there?"

Zeke chimed in, "Ain't nobody knows these woods better than me, they couldn't keep up."

Alan, on the other hand, used a different tactic. "I wasn't going to get away from those Trolls. There was a pile of leaves and I hid until they were well gone."

As big as Alan was, Mac found his story unbelievable. "You just hid... in leaves?" Mac was cynical and suggested there was more to the story.

"Yep," Alan replied, "a big pile of leaves was all I needed." Alan was still staring at the orbitizers. He would have loved to get his hands on one that worked.

"Hey girl, can I see your orbitizer?" Alan asked Maddie.

She walked next to him and handed him one of her prizes, "My name is Maddie," she said wanting to make sure that he knew her name.

"Alright Maddie," he took the orbitizer with a grin. He held it in his hands, looking at it like he knew how it worked.

He noticed that the core wasn't dark and empty like all the others he had found. "I've never seen one with a core that looks like this, does it still work?" Alan put his hands on it as if he was going to shoot. He squeezed the pad. Just like with everyone else, the orbitizer was useless. Instead of handing it back to Maddie, he put the weapon to his face and acted as if he was sighting his rifle.

Maddie swung the orbitizer she picked up from the second Troll to the ready, "Yeah, check it out," she was excited to show off her skills again. The core began to glow and the humming blue orb left the orbitizer headed into the field they were walking past.

Alan observed her every movement and mimicked her process. His second attempt resulted the same as the first. "Ahhh, it must be broken." Before he could ask Maddie, she had given him her orbitizer and taken the defunct one out of his hands.

"Let's see," she aimed and fired again. This time the core stayed dark. It was like all of the defunct orbitizers they had seen.

"Try to shoot it again," Alan asked her. She put her fingers on the padding and the blue glow was missing. She looked at the orbitizer as if she had done something wrong.

Marcus walked up to Maddie and looked at the core, "This is the way we find them all of the time. It must mean the core is expended and it won't shoot anymore." Maddie was upset that the orbitizer was beyond its use.

She turned to Alan, "I'll take that back."

Alan turned his big body and moved the gun away from her reach, "I'll hold on to it for the time being since you have been carrying it all this time." If she could actually use the things, there was no way that Alan was going to let her have one freely while he was around. He survived the ordeal too and had no reason to trust her with it.

"Do I look weak? I want it back," she demanded the orbitizer with an outstretched hand.

There was no way she was getting it back from Alan now. Alan told her, "It's a nice gesture but the correct response is to say 'Thank you' and we will continue on."

Maddie curled her lips in frustration but saw his point of view, "Fine," she huffed and walked back along Mac and Barron's side.

They reached the town line. It was mid-afternoon and the sun had difficulty breaking through the clouds. Marcus was concerned because there should have been someone looking about as a guard. He scanned the high vantage points for any glimpse of life. He didn't have to worry about walking around because it was daylight and the "shoot on sight" rule was only active from dusk until dawn. "Where the hell is everybody?" he wondered. Alan wasn't bothered by the absence of somebody on guard. That was too low level for him to worry about. He continued to walk through, looking straight into the city.

The city was lifeless as they continued to make their way to headquarters. They walked past the medical center and it was the first time that Maddie had seen what had happened in the daylight. The buildings were rundown and would have been condemned if it were before the Attack. Every building had remnants of the Trolls' orbitizers unleashed on them. Every wall displayed some sort of pitting and periodically, she would be able to see through a hole that had breached a wall. The pattern of destruction was plastered all over the shopping center. As they walked past the hospital, she noticed that all of the benches in the park created their own pile of rubble. Everywhere she looked was filled with reminders that the Trolls had attacked the town.

"Halt," a voice bellowed, "who goes there?"

"Who in the hell do you think it is?" Alan was the first to respond.

The voice was silent. The group kept walking toward headquarters and the voice called out again, "Commander, welcome back!" Marcus searched for the source of the voice. Whoever it was had been well hidden. Ben had done a great job of placing the guards for the attack. The group left the area where they thought the guard was setting up his post and they spotted headquarters. They had finally made it.

Ben walked out of the door to greet them. With a surprised look on his face, he asked, "What are you doing here? What happened to the convoy? You should have been there by now." Marcus told him about the ambush and that they were the only survivors.

Ben listened to Marcus and replied, "Well, I'm glad that you are safe. But what do you need? We can't spare anyone else and we are scattered throughout the city waiting for the attack."

Alan told him, "We need to start another convoy. We still have stuff to deliver."

Mac changed the topic, "Alan, you said we were getting out to avoid the attack. You never said anything about delivering anything. If there was anything to deliver then we shouldn't have to go with you, unless..." Mac turned his head toward Maddie.

Quick to understand what was happening, she felt her cue, "Where are you delivering me to?"

Alan stuttered at how brash Maddie's question was, "Now, now, now I'll tell you that..."

Barron raised his hands to the sides of his head, grabbing his hair, "Supreme Command, Supreme Command, that's where he was going to take you. They collect and compile all things that are from the Trolls there. That's where the main research facility is conducted for defeating them." Alan glared at Mac. He knew that Mac had told Barron and that wasn't his secret to tell.

Alan spoke with a low tone in his voice, "Mac, you son of a..." Clearly displeased, he told Ben, "Get me an SUV and I will take Zeke, the soldier, and the girl. Mac and his boy are going to stay here and do their duties for you."

Mac looked at Alan, "We're not soldiers, we can't fight."

Alan poked two fingers into Mac's chest, "Mac, for all I care you can clean toilets or deliver water. And as for the boy," he turned to Barron pointing his two fingers at him, "and as for you... You have weaseled out of service long enough. You are capable and you're assigned to help Mac. Mac is in the militia. So you can strap on a gun and stand a post and help the militia." Barron just stood there. He knew that if he tried to run, he would be shot for desertion. Alan turned to Ben, "Employ these boys and get me my damn SUV so I can get out of here."

Ben stood tall and said "Yes sir."

Alan walked into headquarters with Zeke following. He turned to Zeke, "Bring the girl in here and keep her in the planning area. Make sure the SUV gets here and come and get me when it's ready." Alan walked into his office and leaned the orbitizer onto his bookshelf. He started to sit down and his door shut. Zeke escorted Maddie inside and waited for the SUV to arrive.

Marcus went to Ben, "You can't make these guys fight, I've seen them. Plus, your perimeter doesn't even defend the town."

Ben put up his hand to indicate a pause, "Smith, I mean Marcus. I'm doing the best I can with the people I have and don't worry, Mac and the boy are leaving right behind you." Mac and Barron both heard Ben and moved closer to him. Ben told them, "I'll have another car delivered here and this is what I need you two to do. You both go over there to the field and stay out of sight and out of mind." Ben turned to Marcus, "You need to go with the Commander and make sure that he doesn't do anything stupid."

Mac and Barron headed for the field where Ben had directed them to go. The cornfield was covered with stalks ready for reaping. The abundance of leaves and stalks provided the perfect camouflage for them when they entered. They were instructed to wait until a second vehicle was prepared and a flash of the brake lights would be their cue. The sun was setting and with the darkness approaching, that would be the only signal that they would be able to act upon. They crouched in silence as they waited for the plan to come into action.

With the defenses all planned out, Ben fully focused his thoughts on the new convoy. The new SUV parked in front of headquarters and the driver began to quickly load the vehicle. A couple scavengers were still employed at headquarters and started to load bags of the leftover metal scraps into the back of the vehicle. The scavengers made three hauls using a wheelbarrow with a flattened tire due to the weight. They heaved the bags into the back. The bags were shoddily thrown in and the scraps scattered about. When the last bag was loaded, Zeke went to get Alan. They would soon be on their way.

A second vehicle, a huge car built in the 1970's, pulled up behind the SUV while the scavengers were loading it with the rest of the bunker's remnants. The old car stopped as the driver waited for instructions. Marcus pulled Ben to the side, "You know that if they attack, you won't be able to defend this place, right?"

Ben was looking toward the ground as he listened. He slowly raised his head and looked Marcus straight in the eyes, "I knew this was a losing cause the moment the Commander decided to leave." Ben sighed and then continued, "…but these people have no place to go, no evacuation plan, no other alternative. This is their only chance at survival and I need to do my part."

Marcus saw that Ben was determined to see his responsibility through, "Well, I guess that this is 'it,' isn't it?"

Ben shrugged his shoulders, "We'll see what happens. We have nothing left to lose."

The combination of blue projectiles started as soon as darkness set in, before the convoy had been fully loaded. In the direction of the cornfield, two figures began to run towards the vehicles. Marcus and Ben took cover behind two barrels sitting side-by-side. As they scanned the area in front of them, Zeke and Maddie exited headquarters and saw the flashes rapidly approaching. Zeke let go of Maddie's arm to head for the SUV. Alan, his orbitizer in hand, walked out to see Zeke running toward the SUV and Maddie trying to sprint away from the Troll orbitizer fire and the SUV. "Oh, no you don't little girl," Alan grabbed her with his fat hand and prevented her movement. As much as she continued to run the other direction, she couldn't escape Alan's grasp and weight. She was pulled backwards toward the SUV.

Barron, younger and faster, had made it to headquarters before Mac. He was about to approach their vehicle when Marcus grabbed him by the shirt and yanked him behind the barrels. Marcus waved his hand as he tried to stop Mac, but Mac spotted him as he came from behind the barrels. He lifted up his arm to deflect the hand that approached him. Marcus watched as Mac barreled toward the old car. Mac shouted in a heavy breath, "This stops now..." He continued to run, not for the old car, but straight for Alan. His focus was so intent on freeing Maddie that he didn't notice anything else around him.

Alan heard the wheezing and tumbling coming toward him. He looked up to see the sound coming in his direction. He spotted Mac. In the same field of view, a mass of blue orbs was flying, highlighting Mac's body. Alan let go of Maddie's arm to defend himself. Her arm sprung up from the release. But Mac wasn't trying to tackle Alan. He collided with Maddie at the same time the blue orbs arrived. His back began to disintegrate as one of the blue orbs hit him. Maddie's hand, suspended in the air from the tackle, was hit by another blue orb. She watched her hand disappear in the blue glow. Mac's weight continued to throw her to the ground and she met with the earth. Her head connected with a shovel that was left on the ground and she went motionless.

The salvo was over. Alan got to his feet as quickly as he could. He looked down and made sure that none of the blue orbs had hit him. With no signs of injury, he bent over and grabbed the orbitizer with one hand. Then he shifted to grab Maddie with the other. She was bleeding from a wrist that was formerly attached to her hand. He quickly made it to the SUV and screamed to the driver and Zeke, "Go, go, go!" Alan threw Maddie in the back among the rubble and she lay there motionless, surrounded by scraps.

Marcus saw the entire exchange and watched helplessly as the SUV drove away. His attention was diverted when Ben pulled him down. He pointed to a crawl space under the headquarters and Marcus saw Barron crawling toward the small opening.

"Get in there, it's the only way," Ben told him. Barron didn't hesitate to crawl to safety. He was halfway through the opening as Marcus watched the SUV drive out of sight. He knew that Ben was right and this would be the only way to survive until tomorrow. He jumped to the ground and followed Barron into the small space. Ben stayed behind and frantically searched for anyone he could help but he could not compromise the few that were safe. Not a soul was anywhere near him. He had planned the defense as best as he was able and now had to rely on his men to do their part. In the meantime, he had Barron and Marcus to keep safe. He saw the Trolls and their blue orbitizer cores break through the cornfield.

With a heavy sigh, he crawled through the space and grabbed the small door to secure it in place. He slinked on the ground as he crawled to a solid part of the foundation and gathered with the other two. Ben whispered to Barron and Marcus, "We'll wait out the attack until morning. They'll be gone by then." They lay in silence as the guns sounded in the distance, returning the Trolls' blasts. The counterfire continued and lessened as the night progressed. They listened until a single gun fired back. One more pop of the gun. Then, nothing, no more gunfire. Knowing that they had been defeated, the three men lay in the dirt until morning broke.

With the sun rising, Marcus emerged from the crawl space. All of his sweat had entered his wounds and his back was burning in pain. He reached into his pocket and put a painkiller in his mouth. He chomped on it and swallowed. Waiting for the medicine to kick in, he looked around to find bodies on the ground, lifeless and immobile.

Barron was close to follow and immediately looked for Mac. Barron spotted him and ran to his cold, stiff mass. Barron dropped to his knees and pulled Mac's arm with a hope that he would respond. He dropped his head and forced Mac's hand to his face, "I'm sorry Mac." His voice was shaken and sad, "I'm sorry that this happened." It was another loss for Barron in this new world. He felt a wave of purpose fill him, "Don't worry Mac, I won't forget. I won't forget what you told me."

Barron was tapped on his shoulder. He turned around with his reddened face to see Marcus' hand extended. He reached for the hand and Marcus pulled him up. Marcus told him, "Maddie is out there, it's time to go." Ben had already started the old car and revved the engine. Marcus entered the front and Barron the backseat of the car.

"They're going to London, Kentucky," Ben said, shifting the car into drive. "I already informed Supreme Command of what Alan was doing and they want all survivors to go there. I guess we're the only ones." With nowhere else to go, the car began to move with Ben driving. Exhausted from the night and seizing the opportunity, Barron and Marcus fell asleep.

PART TWO:
RECOMBINATION

DAY 278
THE AWAKENING
WESTBOUND I-64

*R*ho felt the absence of body. The human shuddered as the loss of her hand caused her pain. Her mind was trying to find the connection, reaching out to find the lost piece of her body but never receiving a response.

"Do you need that, human?" Rho asked.

"Yes, it is part of me. I need it," she answered.

"Then I will make you whole. We will be whole."

Alan, Zeke, and the driver of the SUV were focused on the path in front of them. They were more concerned with the potential of what could happen as opposed to the events that were unfolding behind them. The SUV ran too close to the edge of the highway and started to hum as the tire ran over the rumble strip. The driver was quick to readjust course.

"Pay attention to the road!" Alan yelled. Their heads jerked forward again to scan for Trolls.

With the jerk of the course correction, Maddie's eyes snapped open. She was discombobulated and looked left, right, up and down, and then she felt a burning tickle on her left wrist. She slowly looked at her arm as she heard Alan's voice talking to the others in the background.

Her eyes widened as she saw a gray band form around her wrist. A stream of blood was flowing out and a gray liquid was entering back in. She moved her wrist away from the two flows and it felt as if her wound would burst into flames. Knowing that Alan was in front of her, she resisted the urge to give in to the pain. Wincing, she placed her wrist back into the bloody mix and her pain changed back into a tickle. The blood and gray liquid separated after the disturbance and then another band formed outward from her wrist. A new skin materialized before her eyes. She watched as the gray growth continued. The back of her hand started to reform followed by her knuckles. The blood stopped flowing out but the gray liquid continued to be sucked into her severed limb as it grew. Five bands started to materialize as gray fingers began to grow. Her new gray nails capped over the edges of her fingers and the burning tickle went away. She looked down at the metal scraps still lying under her newly formed hand and saw no signs of liquid on them. She gently lifted her hand to her face so as not to make a sound.

The gray hand opened and closed. She turned it to see the palm hadn't changed in shape, only in color. She felt no difference in the feel of her hand, the only difference was the color. She slid her hand to her side and listened as Alan continued to talk. He spoke to Zeke, "I don't care what happens to her, they'll take her whether she's dead or alive. All I care about right now is getting as far away from here as possible." Maddie knew that if she was found alive they would probably kill her. She had to get out of this situation and she had to act as soon as possible using the element of surprise.

She turned toward the front of the car as she readied her body. She curled up and adjusted her knees, keeping her body below the angle of the rearview mirror. She quietly dug into the scraps to ensure her footing was secure. Her thighs began to fill with the urge to jump and when she couldn't contain the feeling any longer, she lunged toward the driver.

While she was still airborne, she wrapped her arm around his neck and used her right hand to push his head forward. The driver felt the impact and extended his left arm outward. His reaction caused the steering wheel to jerk to the right and the SUV careened off of the road. Alan and Zeke reached for Maddie as the vehicle began to overturn. Their efforts were in vain as inertia and gravity worked to pull them away. The passenger side of the SUV impacted the ground and the vehicle began to roll. One turn, two turns, the SUV was gathering dents as all four of its passengers spun around on the inside. The front end hit the ground and the SUV started to spin on another axis. The tires hit the ground and after the receding bounces stopped, the SUV settled in the opposite direction it was originally going.

As the chaos from the crash subsided, Maddie began to stir. The metal scraps in the back had scattered throughout the vehicle. Maddie lifted herself up and moved the scraps out of her way. She looked around the interior. The driver had been halfway ejected out of the broken windshield even as his hand held on to the steering wheel. His body hung limply over the side, his upper half sandwiched against the ground during the several rolls of the vehicle. She zoomed over to Zeke only to see his seatbelt still strapped on but his head hanging lifelessly. During the roll, the orbitizer had left Alan's side and was wedged between Zeke and the ground, breaking his neck and ending his life. She looked next to her and Alan's arm was wedged in between the front seat and the side door. He was struggling to break free but the door had pushed in too far and he was pinned. He saw that Maddie was mobile and begged her, "Please, help me." She leaned over the seat, grabbed the orbitizer and returned to the back seat facing Alan. The expression on Maddie's face needed no words. There was no chance that Alan was going to get help. "You were going to let me die," she said as she shoved open the jammed door.

She exited the SUV as Alan, with his limited range, started to flail his legs trying to kick her. Maddie had her back to Alan as he screamed, "There is no way that you are leaving me here." Alan spotted a handgun next to him and picked it up. Maddie turned around to speak but spotted that she was the target of his aim. She quickly raised the orbitizer, the core glowed and she shot. The orb entered Alan's chest before he could pull the trigger and he couldn't take a breath. His eyes gazed at Maddie and then he slumped over.

Maddie looked around the SUV and decided that she was going to continue west. There was no reason to go back to Charlottesville so she headed toward the mountains. After an hour of walking, she saw an exit sign. She squinted to focus on the letters. "Blue Ridge

Parkway," she said as if somebody was there to hear her. "That's the exit for Summerwhite, I know where I'm going."

She took the first steps on her new quest to find Catelyn, Damien and Bryce. Her orbitizer was cradled in her right arm as she began to analyze her gray hand.

Headquarters was gone, the Avalon Militia was destroyed, and Charlottesville was a city destined to be in ruins. Ben could not help but feel responsible for another failed encounter with the Trolls. "I have to figure out a way to get those things," he mumbled as Marcus and Barron slept in the car. He could not dwell on his failures too much as his main goal was to catch up to Alan and get Maddie away from him. He had been driving for two hours and the need for sleep started to take over his mind. Every time he started to doze, he would jerk his head back up. He realized he was about to succumb to his fatigue. He caught himself dozing again and when he jerked, Alan's SUV was within sight.

Ben slammed on the brakes and came to a screeching halt. The sudden push forward woke up Marcus and threw Barron to the floor. "What's going on Ben," Marcus said as he rubbed his neck. Barron emerged from the floorboards slightly dazed to see Ben pointing to Alan's SUV.

"There she is," Ben said, waving his finger.

Ben slowly crept toward where the vehicle lay still and Marcus readied his gun for any resistance. Barron transferred from the back to the driver's seat just in case a quick getaway was required. Marcus swiftly joined Ben and they approached the SUV in formation. He had let Maddie go with Alan once and he was not going to let it happen again. They saw a body dangling off of the dashboard and Zeke's head was tilted to his left, mouth agape, in his seat.

Ben and Marcus came up to the front of the vehicle and then split to each side. They quickly lifted their guns, ready to engage at the slightest movement.

"Looks dead," Marcus observed. Ben nudged Zeke with his muzzle and Zeke didn't budge. Marcus continued toward the back and saw Alan's head slouched over his body, a hole from an orbitizer shot gaping in his chest.

"She's okay," Marcus relaxed as he told Ben. Ben looked in from his side to see the top of Alan's body.

Ben looked at Marcus, "Where is she?" Ben didn't see her and came around to Marcus' side.

As he approached, Marcus told him, "She's not here." He pointed to Alan's chest.

Ben looked for a second and turned around. He lowered his gun and started yelling, "Maddie!" He waited for a reply.

Marcus joined in calling out for her, "Maddie!" No response again.

Barron noticed that they were safe and joined them. They continued to call for Maddie but she was nowhere around.

"Maybe she walked, maybe she got a ride," Marcus said as he thought through the possibilities.

Barron added, "Maybe she got abducted by aliens," as he tried to lighten the mood.

Marcus shook his head, "Your timing really sucks for punchlines."

Ben told the others, "We have to keep moving, perhaps we'll see her on our way to Kentucky."

Barron looked at him, "We can't abandon her."

Marcus spoke with reason in his voice, "We can't stay out here looking for her either. If we stay out here, then we're at risk of meeting another set of Trolls."

Barron nodded in agreeance, "You're right." He started to walk back to the car, dejected. Marcus and Ben were quick to follow.

Before they entered the car, Marcus looked at Ben, "She'll be fine, she's a survivor." He was trying to assure himself more than comfort Ben.

The car started up and the group was on the road again. They drove for 10 miles and spotted a person walking on the side of the highway. "No way," Marcus cracked a smile, "I can't believe it."

Maddie heard the sound of an approaching car and Marcus rolled down his window. "You need a ride to Kentucky?"

Maddie looked at him and kept walking, "No thanks, I'm headed someplace else." Ben pulled ahead and stopped the car.

Marcus opened the door and immediately walked up to Maddie, "Where are you going?" he asked as she continued to walk.

"I'm looking for my friends," Maddie replied, showing her determination. Barron and Ben caught up to the pair.

Marcus continued, "Do you even know where they are?"

Maddie stopped and faced Marcus, "No," she took a deep breath, "but I know where to start looking." She pointed to the south and said, "The last place we were together was up there. There will be clues in the cabin." Marcus, Barron, and Ben hadn't seen the blue orb disintegrate her hand but as she pointed to the mountains, they noticed the sun glisten off of the metallic hue of her gray hand. Maddie dropped her arm and continued to walk.

Barron was the quickest to ask, "What happened to your hand?"

Maddie kept walking, "It was shot off when we were leaving Charlottesville. I woke up in the back of the SUV and it was growing back." She looked at her hand again, "I guess I was turned into a lizard." Ben wanted to hear her story but noticed that they were walking too far away from the car and doubled back.

Barron thought back to what Mac had told him in private after Maddie's blood was tested. Barron did not realize the importance of that information at the time or understand what Mac was telling him. Mac had two phones at Happy Paws just as Alan had two at militia headquarters. His second line was connected to a research laboratory that had more specialized tests than a normal lab. This research facility was located in the same hospital in Charlottesville where the normal blood panels were run. Mac had confided in Barron that Maddie was infested with some genetically engineered cells. He told him that her cells and the altered cells acted together but further observation was required. Barron was told that if anything should happen to Mac, he would give this knowledge to Maddie.

Barron asked Maddie, "Don't you want to get your hand checked out?"

She faced forward and continued on her way, "Yes, but after I finish this."

Marcus couldn't find a reason to dissuade her and knew that she wouldn't budge on finding out about her past. He looked at her and surrendered to her will, "If you're set on this then we're going with you."

She was focused and her determination to find her friends hardened with every step. She was glad that Marcus was volunteering and responded, "Thanks."

Ben drove up along the side of the highway and Marcus turned to him, "We're going to Maddie's cabin."

Sensing that there was no other alternative, Ben informed the group, "You know there's a faster way to get up there, right?" Marcus and Barron went straight to the car but Maddie hesitated. Ben assured her that he was going to be true to his word, "Come on in, we're taking you there." Barron was already in the car and Marcus waited with the door open, inviting her in. She knew these were the only people in the world that she could trust.

400,000 YEARS BEFORE THEIR ARRIVAL
THE SYRSYRIANS
THE 6TH PLANET ORBITING GAMMA CRUCIS

The planet of Syrsyria had gone through ages of war. Not until the Syrsyrian people prevailed through war did the planet find peace. For over a millennium, the Syrsyrians were able to rule the planet with their way of life. It was a time short-lived in relation to the life of their host star. Scientists on the planet had observed the star starting to redden and expand. They knew that they had a limited time before the planet would be gone and the Syrsyrians could either die with the planet or find a new home.

The Great Expansion was a project introduced by the Syrsyrian leaders. It was an initiative set forth to save the history and possibly the people by exiting their solar system and finding a new home. The initiative had three objectives:

1. *To be able to travel through space for thousands of years and find a new planet to establish as a home.*

2. *To be able to protect themselves from any foreseeable enemy and to be able to eliminate any possible competition to their lives.*

3. *To be able to preserve their history and the Syrsyrian race.*

Great scientists worked for years on the initiatives. Each strived to be the savior of the Syrsyrian people. The first breakthrough was a spaceship able to conduct interstellar travel.

Theta was the first one to generate this breakthrough. Theta, in Syrsyrian history, was called the Great Engineer. He designed the interstellar spaceship called the *Ellipse*. Its design was largely based on an initial boost to exit the system and drift through the arms of their spiral galaxy. The spaceship was equipped with receivers to collect any form of communication. Upon collecting communication that it deemed to originate from a habitable source, its secondary boost would direct the *Ellipse* to the source. Three phases would commence in succession upon arrival.

During the first phase, the spaceship would launch defense pods in order to establish areas of protection. At the onset of the second phase, construction pods would be released to build or terraform structures needed to sustain life. Habitability pods, the third phase, would bring the Syrsyrians to their new home. The construction of the spaceship began.

With the first objective successfully tackled, the second objective was initiated. The goal of protection was harder to complete since modern Syrsyrians were so far removed from warfare. It had been so long since they had met an organism that they had to make an effort to conquer. But there would always be ingenious design when it came to "ways to kill."

Phi and Psi, the Death Duo in Syrsyrian history, contributed a gun that worked as no other before. The gun contained a strong magnetic field that trapped antimatter in its core. The shooter was able to control the length of each expenditure as well as its speed of release. With a magnetic pulse, the gun would force out antimatter. If it was set to a large length, the ejection would come out as a ball at high speed or a net at low speeds. With a small length, pellets were expended at slow speeds and needles when it was set faster. No matter the setting, contact with its target would result in nothingness as the antimatter cancelled the matter. The gun created emptiness. The newly designed guns were prepared for Syrsyrian troop use and outfitted on the spaceship as it was being constructed.

The last objective was tackled by Tau, or Father Time. He designed the means for eternal life. His nanocytes were the perfect genetic cells. They were able to copy genetic coding and replace any dead or destroyed cells in the organism in which they resided, even pets. They were also capable of communicating and working together to solve complex problems at a genetic level. If a nanocyte were to become too old, a small child nanocyte would split from the elder cell and mature. The nanocytes maintained a high survivability rate because Father Time also designed a life sustaining mixture of amino acids to keep them fed during the long expedition. Lastly, the nanocytes were coded to be easily identifiable by biometrics.

This was the last piece of the puzzle needed to complete the Great Expansion. The blue vats of amino acids were installed on the spaceship and the nanocytes were injected. Biometric systems were incorporated on all computer systems and the newly designed guns to restrict their uses to only Syrsyrians. The completed construction of the spaceship meant all objectives had been met.

The heat from the approaching solar surface began to sear the planet and a lottery was established for one billion of the 40 billion people of Syrsyria. Winners of the lottery were selected and injected with the nanocytes. They were screened for abnormalities and once cleared, sent into space. Each winner was placed in their own vat to ensure a constant flow of nanocytes, amino acids, and filtration for body-produced wastes. One Syrsyrian, Omega, lived in squalor his entire life and was the last to be admitted onto the *Ellipse*. Omega was not cleared for travel because the Syrsyrian was injected with too many nanocytes. But in the madness and stress of getting the *Ellipse* loaded, his denial was forgotten and he was able to enter the spaceship.

Historical documents, plants and animals for food, pets and Syrsyrians were all placed on the *Ellipse*. When the loading of the spaceship was finally completed, it faced outward from the star and began its initial boost, leaving the planet behind. Before it entered into interstellar space, Syrsyria and all of its inhabitants were swallowed by its sun. No Syrsyrian ever saw it happen. Those who were on the planet had already died from the heat and the ones who were on the spaceship were in hibernation. The memory of the last moments of Syrsyria was only located in one place, saved in the computer system files of the *Ellipse*.

Maddie stood in front of the cabin where she and her friends had spent winter break nearly a year ago. The men accompanying her stood behind to let her have her time. She scanned the outside of the cabin but did not see any signs of a struggle. The cabin had been neglected, weeds had taken over the hedges and the walls were covered in dirt. Leaves were overhanging the gutters and she could not see through the windows. She walked toward the entrance. As she stepped on the wooden exterior deck, the door appeared shut. She approached the door and gave it a simple push. A creak sounded from the hinges as the door slowly opened.

The inside of the cabin looked nothing like the unused exterior appearance. The coffee table where they had congregated was overturned and the chairs were flipped over. She walked into the living room and looked around. She eyed the room where she had slept the night she went missing. The door was open and she could see her bed. Her blanket was pulled askew, creating a bridge to the floor. She continued her scan to Bryce's room and it showed more of a struggle. The nightstand lay on the floor with the face of the drawer detached on one side and a light sitting next to it.

Her next focus was on the kitchen. It seemed untouched. Bryce's bread had turned to a bag of mush a long time ago. Her eyes went to Damien's room and his door was wide open with an unmade bed. She continued to Catelyn's room but stopped when she saw two decayed bodies on the floor. She moved straight for the spot. "Please, don't let it be them," she whispered under her breath. Her mind was hoping and hoping that it wasn't who she thought it was.

As time and mother nature had taken their course, the months had not been kind to the bodies. The pests that invaded the house during the summer had left their mark and the bodies were nothing but bones covered with tattered pajamas. She knew those pajamas. She knew that these were the bodies of Catelyn and Damien. She stared at the cadavers as tears began to swell, "What did they do to you?" A skeleton with no bones above the collar bone was on her left and the other one was missing half of its rib cage. Tears burst from her eyes as her hands covered her face. "I can't believe this," her voice strained in a high pitch.

Barron walked beside her and gently put his hand on her back. She quickly jerked away from him and kept him behind her. She didn't want to be near anyone. He walked beside her again and she went toward Bryce's room to keep her face hidden from Barron. Understanding that it wasn't the time to console her, Barron walked back to the deck and waited for her to finish her investigation.

Maddie stood at the doorway to Bryce's room and began to search for any clues as to what happened to him. She looked around the door. Nothing. The nightstand. Nothing. The closet. Nothing. She looked at the bed. She walked to it slowly. And then she started to violently rip off the sheets. She screamed, "Where are you? Where are you?" Dust flew as she jumped onto the bed and knelt still with her head forced into the mattress.

Barron turned to Ben and Marcus as they stood on the other side of the deck, "I don't think she is going to find anything to help her in there."

"Probably not, it's been a long time. She'll have to come to terms with 'what is' and move on," Marcus answered.

"So are we going to Kentucky after this?" Barron asked. Ben was tapping his fingers on the rail. He was looking down at the motion of his fingers.

"It's our best option. Actually, it's our only option," he said.

Maddie regained her composure and walked out of the cabin.

"I'm ready to go," she said with a hint of sadness in her voice. The men began to walk down the steps of the deck. Stopping suddenly, Maddie threw her arms up and cried out, "I don't know what else I'm supposed to do." Marcus turned around. He knew what it was like. It had only taken a few minutes for his world to be ripped apart. He looked at her and a well of compassion filled him.

"Maddie, everyone has had nine months to come to terms with what you have found out in the past few days. We have all lost someone, everyone on this planet has lost someone that they knew," Marcus said, and the voice of reason came out.

"If you really want to know what you are supposed to do."

"If you really want to find your answers."

"Then you need to go to Kentucky."

"You should join the people who have more resources than an old beater car and a cabin in the woods. The people who are working to fight against these Trolls. The people who will help you get revenge against them."

Marcus was showing his disdain and a yearning to avenge the death of his family. Maddie looked at Marcus and bowed her head in acceptance. Marcus was right. She didn't have any leads in the cabin, only the pain of knowing that her friends were dead.

There was silence as they entered the car. They made it to the highway but nightfall was coming soon and they would need to stop.

200,000 YEARS BEFORE THE ARRIVAL
THE FIRST MUTATION
THE ELLIPSE

Gamma Crucis was a small red speck. The monitoring system onboard the *Ellipse* watched as the star grew and slowly consumed its sixth plant. It recorded the history of the planet as the rock melted into the once generous sun. The *Ellipse* was completely unaware of the heat that killed the bodies, warped buildings, and enflamed the surface. The star absorbed the planet and the tiny blob on its surface served as a brief second of fuel.

The *Ellipse* continued on its trek and ventured light years from its host star. All systems were normal as the nanocytes floated through the preservation systems. The computer system oversaw safe navigation, the planetary search, and the maintenance of over a billion blue vats containing Syrsyrians, animals, and plants from the home planet.

The nanocytes were not colored when they were created. They had taken a blue hue since feeding only on the amino acids placed in the vats. That color had transferred to the Syrsyrians as well. As each cell in those bodies was replaced with a nanocyte, every Syrsyrian was covered in patches as their color changed from their natural brownish color to blue.

The process had continued for so many years until each body had been totally replaced by the nanocytes. Their skin was blue, their nails were blue, their hair was blue. Omega had been affected differently by the nanocytes. The overabundance of Omega's initial injection caused a reaction that changed how the nanocytes interacted within the Syrsyrian.

After the thousands of years of replacing the functionality of normal cells, an evolution occurred. Two nanocytes combined in Omega's brain and developed their own mind. The other dying brain cells were replaced by more nanocytes until it was a completely nanocyte brain. What was once Omega and Omega's thoughts now belonged to the nanocytes.

The nanocyte brain became more complex and directed the replacement of cells to an intricate system not of the original Syrsyrian. Communication was performed between the nanocytes, so vocal communication was eliminated. The Syrsyrian no longer needed children so the reproductive organ was not replaced. Since the Syrsyrian's eyes were closed, the nanocytes only replaced light sensitivity. The nanocyte brain continued to grow, enlarging the head that used to be owned by Omega. Large blue tumor-like bulges erupted from the skull as it became soft.

Omega's body was perfected in accordance with the nanocyte brain. The nanocyte brain learned how to communicate with the free-floating nanocytes outside of the body and formed a communication network. The free-floating nanocytes were able to go between the vats and connect with the other bodies. They communicated the new way to replace cells as directed by the nanocyte brain. Through time, every Syrsyrian was going through the same transformation and every cell was directed by Omega. The blue hued Syrsyrians had turned into the Trolls.

Omega's complete nanocyte brain was in control of every Syrsyrian and every animal. A system of directives was sent out from the brain so that every nanocyte would follow its command. Through the evolution of the nanocytes, the Syrsyrians had turned from saving their race into an army of ants. Omega was now the queen and every other cell was made to work for it.

The computer system was completely unaware of this transformation. It only monitored death and if a Syrsyrian would have lost its life functions, its vat would have been closed to the network. It did not recognize the nanocyte takeover and treated it as normal operations.

Omega and the other Syrsyrians would not be released from their vats until a host planet was located. Omega did not know this and ruled in ignorance as the spacecraft floated through space. But the bonds of Omega and the others only strengthened through time.

The computer system continued to search for a planet that could be inhibited but had not yet found it.

DAY 280
BREAKDOWN
ROANOKE, VIRGINIA

Two factors were affecting this stop. The night was drawing close and the car was beginning to sputter. The clunk of the engine became more frequent and with a large exhale, the car coasted to a stop. Ben turned the key in the ignition. The engine didn't start. The lights on the dashboard didn't flash. The car made no sound at all.

"Guess this thing is dead," Ben informed the group.

"It's getting dark anyway, we should find a place for the night," Marcus said as he examined the area.

Like Charlottesville, the Trolls had made their mark everywhere. The buildings were in ruin and there were carcasses in the street. Unlike Charlottesville, Roanoke had no people roaming the streets. The entire place looked vacated. Maddie got out of the car. She looked through the selection of restaurants, shops, and stores. Her sights became fixated on the hospital.

"Let's go there for the night," Maddie pointed to the hospital. Marcus focused his eyes on the building.

"That would be a good place to stock up too," Ben replied. Barron was out of the car as the decision was made.

"I'll go find something to eat," Barron said.

"I'll go with you and we'll get some stuff for the road," Marcus said. He felt the pain of hunger in his stomach and would search for provisions with Barron. Ben and Maddie started straight for the hospital as Marcus and Barron headed for the fast food restaurant next to the car. The air was stagnant as Ben and Maddie made their way.

"We're going to have to find a car first thing in the morning. We're not going to make it far without one," Ben said to Maddie. Maddie was busy counting all of the marks in the walls left by the orbitizers.

"You're right," she replied, and then asked, "do you think Roanoke was run the same way as Charlottesville?" Ben thought about what she said and took a few steps.

"I don't know. I don't think it really matters since the end result looks the same," he replied. They found themselves at the entrance of the hospital and looked inside. The building appeared empty. It looked like it had been abandoned for a few months. Papers littered the floor as the only sign of life were footprints smeared into the dust that had settled. They decided to go in the front door. There had to have been someone in there recently as the footprints were fresh.

Barron entered the restaurant first and immediately went to the freezer. "There's nothing in here," he yelled out of the chill box to Marcus. Marcus was looking under the front counter and found a couple of bags of cookies. He read the bag and noticed that they were well past the expiration date.

"What do you have there?" Barron asked as he approached the counter.

"This bag of cookies expired three months ago," Marcus told Barron. Marcus took the bags and tossed them on the floor.

"It doesn't look like there's anything here," Barron said as he looked through the window for other options. He spotted a grocery store.

"That looks like a good place," Barron said as he pointed at the store and headed toward the door. Marcus looked in the direction Barron was pointing. He noticed that the sun was starting to set.

"We have to make it quick, it's going to be dark soon," Marcus told Barron.

They hurried to the grocery store and found the windows shattered. Broken glass lay at the base of the wall. They walked through one of the panes, careful not to cut themselves on the jagged edges of the glass. Barron noticed that the shelves were sparse but at least there was something. He grabbed some bags and Marcus started to pick out some food.

"Crackers, cookies," Marcus said as he continued to scan the shelves, "canned food, canned meat." Marcus started to throw the food into the plastic bags they had picked up from the checkout counter as Barron held them. Any canned meat or snacks that were still good were thrown into the bags until they were filled and heavy. Barron's arms pointed straight to the ground because of the weight. Marcus grabbed two cases of water and held them on each of his shoulders.

"I'm ready to go," Barron said.

Marcus adjusted the cases of water and said, "Let's go." They walked outside and the remnants of the sun barely painted the sky. The last shade of the violet sunset was turning dark as the stars began to break through the sky. They started to make their way to the hospital, continually looking to their left and to their right. Movement caught Barron's attention. He spotted something around the old broke-down car. He tried to focus on the movement.

"Trolls," he yelled in a whisper to Marcus. Barron's pace quickened as Marcus looked over to the car. Marcus spotted the figures and turned his head toward the hospital. Barron had already started to speed walk. There was 15 feet of separation between him and Marcus. Marcus started to walk quickly to catch up to Barron, and the food. Barron let out a deep breath as they made it to the doors unnoticed. They entered through the front door and turned to look out of the window.

"It looks like we weren't spotted," Barron said.

Marcus was relieved, "Great, let's find the others."

Ben had a backpack that he had found next to a desk draped over his arm. Maddie was grabbing gauze and bandages and any other first aid equipment she could find.

"I can't believe how empty this place is," Maddie said, noting that the hospital lacked any signs that there was a conflict outside, aside from the papers strewn on the floor. Ben zipped up the backpack and threw it over his shoulder.

"I think that'll be good, let's go find Marcus and Barron," Ben told Maddie. Maddie grabbed her orbitizer from the counter and walked out of the room with Ben following shortly behind her.

Through one hallway and entering another, Marcus and Barron were nowhere to be found. "We should go back to the entrance and wait for them there," Ben said as he walked behind Maddie. She tilted her head as she looked up at the directory. "EXIT," was written on the bottom of the sign. The arrow pointed to the right.

"This way," she told Ben. The next directory sign pointed them to go right again. Maddie turned the corner and ran into a blue blob. Her eyes opened wide and she froze. It was huge. It was a Troll.

The Troll was also startled and it grabbed for Maddie. Its hand wrapped around her wrist as Maddie still stood frozen, not from the initial shock, but from the faint noise that was speaking to her in her subconscious. She concentrated on the noise or sound or whatever it was.

Body 0-4-7-3-2-4-5-5-5-1, Cell count... 3.7414 times 10^{13}. Remaining available... 1.13 times 10^2. Count low. Body Function 100%. Return to Ellipse required. Host: Syrsyrian. Objective: Find new hosts for collective growth. Status: Incomplete.

Maddie could hear a response.

I am Rho, Body 1-0-0-0-0-0-0-0-4, Cell Count... 15.915 times 10^{10}. Remaining available... 3.9917 times 10^8. Body Function 100%. Host: Human. Objective: Idle. Status: Waiting.

Maddie's body was still frozen as she listened to the dialogue in her head. The dialogue went from sounding like a report to becoming a conversation.

Attempting hunt indigenous lifeforms. Humans only acceptable beings. One confirmed, four unknown, current location. Attempting to capture unless hostile then exterminate.

Another response came.

Three humans with body. One human not seen.

A rushed and worried response came back.

Death imminent. Objective Status: Fail.

Maddie's eyes opened to the Troll and its severed head falling to the floor. Its body was soon to follow. Maddie started to fall but the Troll's hand released with the weight of its body. Maddie, eyes wide open, tried to figure out what was going on. What just happened?

Ben had positioned himself between Maddie and someone else. It wasn't a Troll, too short to be a Troll. She looked around Ben and tried to make out the object. It was a he, and he walked toward Ben. The man was holding something like a machete in his hand.

A raspy voice came out of his mouth, "My friend, I am Quill. I am the protector against the Grapplers here."

He extended his hand to shake Ben's. Quill was thin, like he had been starved. His salt-and-pepper hair was unkempt. He looked like a mad scientist. As he came closer to Ben, his eyes were slightly hidden by dark pits on his face.

Ben extended his hand to Quill.

"Thank you Quill," Ben said as their hands met, "Who are you and where is everyone else?"

"I am Quill, a friend of Will, and when the Grapplers come around, I kill," he said as he released Ben's hand. A maniacal laugh bellowed from Quill as he looked down at the Troll, or in his case, the Grappler.

"Where is Will then?" Ben asked. He was trying to find out where everyone was. Quill stood up and explained himself.

"Why, I'm Will. Sometimes he needs help and that is when I show up," Quill said, and continued his explanation, "When Will knows that the Grapplers are around, he lets me take care of business for him, we live together." Something rattled Quill. He turned around and signaled to Ben and Maddie to crouch down.

"There's another one," he hushed.

Maddie whispered to Ben, "Did you hear what that Troll was saying?" Ben looked at her as if he didn't know what she was talking about.

"What? The Troll said something? What are you talking about?" Ben asked.

"Be quiet, it's coming," Quill interrupted with a strong whisper.

DAY 27
DIAGNOSIS OF WILL
ROANOKE, VIRGINIA

"So you're telling me that you don't remember a thing?" The doctor was looking down at the file. He sat at a desk with several piles of files that created a barrier between him and his patients.

"No, I don't remember anything about it. I just woke up in bed," Will said as he stretched his neck to see the doctor's file. The doctor closed the file and placed it on his desk. He leaned on the desk and crossed his forearms.

"Mr. Easton, Will, you realize that you put three people in the hospital and the people that you didn't hurt were evacuated because you destroyed not only your call center but the entire building. You don't remember anything?" he asked. Will felt the doctor's stare and looked down.

"No, I still don't. This happened all of the time when I was younger but I haven't had an episode in years." The doctor opened the file he had placed on the desk and wrote "Committed, further evaluation necessary" on the top of the page.

"Will, I'm going to recommend that you stay here for further observation," the doctor said. Will raised his head to look at the doctor.

"You mean that I have to stay here?" he asked.

The doctor answered him, "The judge asked for my medical opinion and I don't think that you're ready to leave." The doctor pressed a button on his phone and a voice came over the intercom.

"Yes, doctor?" the voice answered.

"We're admitting Mr. Easton, please come and get him," the doctor said.

The door opened and the nurse welcomed Will to follow her. Will had a court appointed lawyer that had requested this evaluation. He hadn't known why he woke up in the cell until the judge read his charges. The doctor had told him that he had set the call center on fire and the blaze had consumed the entire building along with hospitalizing his manager and two people that sat next to him. All he remembered was answering a large amount of calls. Everyone wanted to insure something. The orbiting spacecraft had people worried and they wanted to talk to insurance agents to protect their assets.

"Mr. Easton, you will be staying with us for three weeks so the doctor can help you with whatever is bothering you," the nurse told him.

"Good, I want to know why I wound up in that cell and what I did," Will replied. The nurse led him to a room. She placed tape on the door with his name on it. He went into the room but the nurse did not follow him.

"Make yourself comfortable and I'll come and get you when the doctor is ready to see you again," she said, and the door closed. Will could not see if she stayed outside of the door. There was a window but it had a latched access door covering his view.

Will sat on his new bed and stared at the wall. "What happened to me?" he asked the wall. He didn't have any of his clothes, no wallet, nothing but his hospital issued pajamas. He looked down and was grateful it wasn't a gown with an open back. He pulled down the top sheet of his bed and slid underneath it. He thought that if he lay there, something would come back to him. His eyes were open staring at the ceiling. He remembered answering the phones. He remembered talking about the spacecraft. He remembered a person saying that they were going to attack. His view went black as he went to sleep.

It took three nurses and two orderlies to restrain Will. The nurse that had escorted him to his room was lying on the floor rubbing the back of her head. He had pushed her against the wall as he attempted to escape the ward. Will was in a restraining jacket and secured in a wheelchair. An orderly went to the nurse to help her up. She pushed his hand away and said, "Get the doctor and tell him what happened."

The orderly positioned himself behind Will's wheelchair. Will was attempting to gnaw at the jacket. The orderly was careful to avoid any contact with Will. He pushed the chair down the hall and past the doctor's door. Will heard the knock behind him and the doctor's voice, "Bring him in," followed by whispers. The orderly backed Will into the office and stayed a safe distance from the wheelchair.

The doctor used a calming voice, "Will, I need you to settle down." Will stopped gnawing at the jacket and looked at the doctor.

"What makes you think I am Will?" he said to the doctor.

"Then why don't you tell me who you are?" asked the doctor.

"I am not Will. Will is weak and not able to handle things that he can't control," Will, but not Will, replied, "Will is having a tough time with the threat of the aliens and that is why I am here. He doesn't have to deal with it now."

"What do you call yourself?" the doctor asked.

"I am Quill. I protect Will," Quill said.

"When will I be able to talk to Will?" the doctor asked.

"Will can come back when I am done. When he can function. I am in control now. As long as Will is worried about the aliens I am in control," Quill informed the doctor.

"Quill, I can guarantee the aliens are not a threat to you or to Will. Will can come back any time he wants to," the doctor assured Quill.

"Don't try to placate me or him. He will know when he is ready and it won't be because of your empty assurances. He will come back when I feel he will be able to cope with his feelings," Quill said. He made sure that the doctor understood him.

The doctor nodded to the orderly that he was done talking to Quill. The doctor said, "The orderly is going to take you back to your room to calm down. A nurse will check with you periodically." The wheelchair began to move toward the door. Quill turned to the doctor and warned him.

"When the aliens attack, we are gonna die," he announced. The doctor watched him in silence as the orderly continued to push the wheelchair out of the office.

The doctor went back to his desk and scanned through the files. His finger touched each tab until he reached "Easton, Will." He pulled out the file and opened it. He took his pen and underlined 'further evaluation necessary.' He wrote 'D.I.D.' underneath the terms and continued to write over the letters until they pressed through the page. 'Alternate personality- Quill. Aggressive and triggered by alienophobia. Talk to patient when Quill is not the current state' was written under the diagnosis.

Quill was pushed into his room as another orderly stepped through the door. "We're going to put you into bed," he told Quill. He released the straps holding down Quill's legs and the other orderly picked him up by his armpits. They placed Quill on the bed and fastened restraints to his legs and torso. Quill offered minimal struggle as he knew he could not get out of the jacket if he tried.

"You get some rest," the orderly said as he turned away from the bed. The wheelchair was pushed out of the room and the door shut behind it.

Quill looked at the door and the window cover was latched. He started to wiggle and squirm to break free of his restraints. He kicked his leg and it did not budge. He shifted his shoulders, tried to move his elbows, tried to extend his forearms, but his restraints were too tight. "I can't be like this," he muttered, "they are gonna have to trust me so I don't have to wear this crap." He knew that the aliens would be coming soon and he was a sitting duck if they were keeping him like this. After calming himself down, Quill's eyes slowly closed and he was fast asleep.

DAY 281
COMMUNICATION
ROANOKE, VIRGINIA

The end of the hallway was thirty feet away from Maddie, Ben, and Quill. They were crouched down to make a smaller target and remain undetected. Quill turned around and whispered, "If you stay quiet and still, they won't find you." He slowly turned his head and focused his sight on the end of the hallway. The Troll took its first step from behind the corner.

Gunshots started to fire from around the other corner. The Troll readied its orbitizer and the core began to glow. Maddie didn't hesitate. Seeing the core glow, she stood up and stepped to the side. She fired and her blue orb went directly into the side of the Troll. The Troll's side began to dematerialize as it turned toward her. She fired again. The Troll fell down to the ground. This time Maddie ran to the Troll and touched it.

Death imminent, Objecti...

Then there was silence. At that moment, Maddie knew she hadn't dreamed the voice. "What's wrong with you?" Marcus grabbed Maddie's arm and pulled her away from the Troll.

"It talked to me," Maddie shot back while she was being yanked. Barron and Ben were now behind Marcus.

"Who are you guys? What happened?" Quill asked them. Ben turned around to see Quill walking toward him but this time his posture was different.

"I asked who are you guys?" Quill repeated his question. Quill looked down at the Troll's body and his eyes opened wide.

"Di... Di... Did you guys kill that thing?" he stammered.

Ben looked at the Troll and then answered Quill, "Yes, Quill. Yes, it's dead." Quill looked at Ben with a strange, confused look.

"Who is Quill? I am Will, Will Easton." Will, not Quill, said. Marcus and Barron looked over at Will with confused faces. Maddie had broken free from Marcus' grip and adjusted herself.

"Stop, just stop. Let's take a second to figure this out," Ben demanded as he was trying to calm everyone down.

Ben was still facing Will trying to figure out if he was going to attack them. Will was still holding a short blade, Quill's machete to cut the Troll's neck. "What are you planning to do with that thing?" Ben asked as he pointed to the machete. Will looked down at it and when he noticed what he was carrying, he dropped it.

"That happens all of the time, I don't know where they come from but I always find some sort of weapon in my hand," Will told Ben. Will opened up his hands to show his palms with the Trolls' blue blood on them. He continued his plea, "I don't know, every time one of those Grapplers comes around, I black out and wake up with something in my hands. A gun, a scalpel, and this time it's a blade." Barron figured out that a Grappler was a Troll and corrected Will.

"We don't call these things Grapplers, we call them Trolls," Barron said. Will put down his hands.

"That's fine, we can call them 'Trolls,' all I know is that they killed everyone here so long ago," Will's meek voice answered Barron.

Maddie asked Will, "Have they ever talked to you?"

Will shook his head 'no.'

"They have never spoken to me but they hunt me every night. Every night I'm hunted and I have to hide in the ducting," he pointed to the overhead. "They have killed everyone in Roanoke. The first night they came into town, they killed everyone. Everyone but me," Will told them.

"How long have you been here? How long have you been alone?" Ben asked.

Will directed his sight back to Ben, "About nine months. I hide here because this is my home. The judge said so."

"We can't leave him here, there is obviously something wrong with him," Barron said to the group.

"You're right. Plus, he has avoided these Trolls for that long. He definitely knows how to get around them," Marcus agreed.

"Would you like to come with us? Do you think you can help us get out of town?" Ben asked Will. He agreed with Marcus.

Will rapidly nodded his head 'yes.' "We can leave in the morning. They have to go back home in the morning. But do you think it is okay with the judge? He said I had to stay here."

"I'm sure the judge has no problem with you leaving here. We're going to help you now," Ben assured him.

"And now on to you," Ben said, and turned to Maddie.

"What the hell is wrong with you? Those things can be diseased or poisonous," Marcus snapped at her, jumping in before Ben could say another word.

"Hey, it talked to me," Maddie said, and spoke with the same sharp tone.

"That thing didn't say a word." Marcus told her the reality of what he saw.

"They don't talk, nope, never heard a word," Will said in the background.

"They had voices, body numbers, cell counts, and objectives. I heard it all. I heard them die," Maddie, clearly frustrated, told Marcus. Marcus didn't believe her.

"Then how did you hear them if nobody else heard them?" Marcus asked. Maddie grabbed for his arm.

"I was touched by that one," she said, and pointed at the Troll that Quill had killed, "and then I grabbed this one like this." She wrapped her fingers around Marcus' wrist.

Marcus let her have her say and then asked, "If they did talk to you through… let's say osmosis, then what important thing did they say?"

She pointed to the first Troll, "That one said it was Sicilian or something like that and human then it died."

She pointed to the Troll that she killed and said, "This one knew it was going to die." Marcus looked at both of the bodies lying on the floor.

"I would say that they were right about dying," he said.

Maddie dropped her grip on Marcus and scoffed, "You don't understand." She didn't want to discuss it anymore, "Can we just drop it? I know what I heard but I can't explain it."

"That's fine but we'll need to talk about it later. You had better not be going crazy on me," Marcus said as he crossed his arms. Will's head perked up.

"I know what that's like," he said, and shook his head. He understood exactly what Marcus was saying.

"Let's get some sleep for tonight. We'll have to find a car first thing in the morning and get on the road. We'll need a bigger vehicle and Will can help us," Ben announced while he looked at the group.

Marcus and Barron found a bed, ripped off the dusty sheets, and lay down. Will went to sleep in a dark corner. Ben slept as he sat next to the door. Maddie was wide awake wondering what she had just experienced.

"Why are they looking for hosts?" she asked herself, and then she succumbed to fatigue.

DAY 281
TRANSPORT
ROANOKE, VIRGINIA

The breaking of the morning sun pushed the darkness of night away. No other Trolls. No other emergencies. A welcomed rest lasted until the morning. Seeing the light of day starting to beam through the window, Marcus woke Barron and nudged and roused the others, even Will.

They exited the hospital with food and medical supplies. Ben turned to Will, "Where can we get a van or something large?" Will, thinking, put his hand to his chin. An idea came to him.

"There's a car dealership that has cars right around the corner," Will said.

"That's as good a place as any to start," Ben said.

The group began their walk to get their vehicle and get out of Roanoke. Maddie was walking behind the group with Will. "Did you really talk to them?" Will asked.

"I don't know if I talked to them but I heard them talking. I know that," Maddie said, as she shrugged her shoulders. Will felt comfortable confiding in Maddie.

"I'm scared of them. It started when they received those satellite communications at the station. When they arrived, I lost it. I lost my job and they put me into that hospital," he told her. Maddie listened closely, waiting for him to tell her something to explain what had happened. She let Will continue as he told his story.

"They killed everyone here a few days after they attacked. I have been living in the hospital. I know that they have been trying to get me but I know too many of the hiding places and they couldn't find me. Every night, they would send two of the Grapp..., I mean Trolls, to get me. Every morning, I would wake up and they would be gone. I would have thought that I was dreaming them if I didn't see it last night," he said.

"How did you hide from them?" Maddie asked, brimming with curiosity.

"I don't know how. I found the places, I just woke up in different places. I can't remember how I found them, how I got there, or where they went. Sometimes, I woke up to see them leaving and knew that they left that way," Will answered as he pointed. It was the same way Maddie and the others had driven into Roanoke.

Will had finished talking to Maddie when they arrived at the dealership. Barron found the lockbox with the key fobs and Marcus pried it open. Barron took out all of the keys and started pressing the lock button on each one as Ben monitored which car reacted.

"No, not that one," Ben called out as a compact car chirped. A truck sounded, then a car, then another truck. Barron hit a button that belonged to a minivan.

"That's it, that's the one," Ben hollered to the group. As they approached the minivan, Ben took the keys from Barron and entered the driver's seat. He started the car.

"Good, a full tank of gas," he said as he looked at the gauge.

Will did not know what the plan was and asked, "Where are we going?" Ben adjusted the rearview mirror.

"Kentucky. We're going to London, Kentucky," he said.

"Is it a good place to hide? Are the Trolls not there?" Will asked, liking the idea.

"No, we're going to meet with people that are fighting against them," Ben answered. A nervousness set over Will as he reclined back into his seat.

"I don't think there's anyone fighting against them there," Will said, and exhaled under his doubting breath.

The minivan pulled out of the lot and made it to the highway. It was early in the day and they would easily be in London by the evening.

DAY 282
ARRIVAL
ROANOKE, VIRGINIA

An hour after driving past the tunnels that burrowed through the mountains, the minivan was quickly approaching its destination. "We'll be there soon," Ben announced as Marcus navigated. Since there was no traffic on the roads and no policemen to monitor their driving, the drive was fast and uneventful except for Will's three 'potty breaks.' That was until 15 minutes outside of London.

Out of the rearview mirror, Ben saw a black jeep and other utility vehicles approaching the minivan. The other vehicles were going fast. Ben looked down at the speedometer and it showed 100MPH as the unknown vehicles raced to catch up to the minivan. Ben pressed the gas pedal but he couldn't get any more speed. The tailing vehicles were going to catch up to them. Ben prepared the others, "Looks like we have a welcoming committee. Get ready, I don't want to meet up with another Avalon Militia." He was expecting them to pull over the minivan and confiscate it.

Closer and closer the vehicles came until the black jeep pulled alongside of them. A man in the passenger seat signaled Ben to pull over. Ben pulled over to the shoulder of the highway and the black jeep parked behind the minivan. The other vehicles stopped to box him in. They were going to have to get out and see what these people wanted.

"Avalon Militia?" the man asked as he exited his black jeep. He was tall and stocky. He was young, no older than twenty years old.

"Yes, we're from Charlottesville," Ben answered the man.

"What is your authentication code?" the man asked the follow-up question per protocol. He waited for an answer. Ben could only think of the one authentication code that Alan had given him when he had to defend the town.

"5A41?" Ben responded, unsure if it was right or not.

"Sounds good to me," the man responded with a smile. Ben wiped his brow in relief and stuck his head into the minivan.

"It's okay, these guys are with Supreme Command," he said, and the others got out of the minivan slowly.

"You all sure did take your sweet time getting out here. You should have been here two days ago," the man walked toward the minivan, "I'm Ethen and I'm in charge of this outpost, this area. And you are?" he asked, and extended his hand to shake Ben's. Ben met his hand and introduced his fellow travelers. Ethen noticed Maddie's hand and then her eye.

"You've been caught by one of them, haven't you?" he asked. Maddie again covered her eyes with her hair and hid her hand behind her back. Ethen saw that she was uncomfortable and tried to reassure her.

"You're not the only one, we have several at Supreme Command. They can help you out there," he told her. Maddie teemed with excitement and her voice matched.

"They can tell me what happened to me?" she asked.

Ethen shook his head, "Not really but they can tell you what's going on inside of you. I have personally recovered two others like you since the Attack. One is still at Supreme Command and the other... well... the other supported the aliens."

Maddie focused on the last part of what he said, "Supported the aliens?"

She whispered to Marcus, "Maybe they found Bryce?" Marcus shrugged his shoulders.

"Maybe, maybe not, we will have to go there to find out," he said. Maddie started to glow from the sense of excitement, the ability to find out what was going on inside of her.

"When are we going to get to Supreme Command?" she begged. Ethen looked around as it was getting dark.

"We'll have to stop at the outpost tonight. But tomorrow we'll be able to get you to Supreme Command. It's a three-hour drive to Watauga, Tennessee," he said. Disbelief came over Ben and his face went long.

"Watauga? Three hours? We drove past it to get here. Why in the hell did you guys have us drive past where we were going?" Ben demanded. Ethen saw that Ben was clearly irritated and took a step back to answer his question.

"Hey now, nobody gets to go straight to Watauga. If anyone knows where to go or is followed, then the assets we have there will be compromised. The General and everyone else are not willing to take any chances. If you haven't noticed, we're not faring too well against the aliens," he said. Ben understood, begrudgingly.

"Okay, then where is the outpost?" he asked.

"The outpost is at the tunnels coming into Kentucky. That's where we can monitor much of the traffic and anything else that might try to go through there," Ethen explained.

"Well, when do we leave?" Barron asked.

Ethen raised his hand in the air and started to spin his finger. "We're waiting on you all," he said. As his finger spun, the troops that accompanied him reentered their utility vehicles. The vehicles moved to give the minivan a clear path to turn around. Ben watched the vehicles start to head down the highway.

"I guess we're ready to go," he said. The travelers piled into the minivan. With their transportation loaded, they followed the black jeep. Ethen, sitting in the passenger seat, led the way to the outpost.

DAY 282
OVERNIGHT
THE OUTPOST

Marcus looked into the wilderness. The dark moonless night pitched over the forest below. Even the smallest light could have been seen for miles. A slight irritation scratched at his back and the healing process worked to cover his wounds. He looked over at his fellow sentry named Tony, a man he met just a few hours ago. "What exactly do you look for?" Marcus whispered to Tony, looking through his binoculars.

"Movement... Light... it doesn't matter out here. Anything that moves needs to be watched," Tony said.

When the travelers had arrived, the minivan had pulled into the outpost area. There were no multi-level buildings, no command structures, just little rundown shacks dispersed throughout the trees. "Leave your keys in the minivan," Ethen told Ben. The small group of survivors got out of the van and some of the outpost soldiers got in and drove away.

"We have safe spots out here for vehicles. They are just hiding them away from here," Ethen informed the newcomers. True to his word, every one of the vehicles that followed the minivan drove off, including the black jeep.

They approached the closest shack and Ethen opened the door. Ben was the first to enter followed by Marcus. Will, Barron, and Maddie followed in short succession. Ethen stood next to a trapdoor. It was opened by one of the outpost soldiers and led into a dark area. Ben looked down and could see a couple of steps. As the stairs went downward they disappeared into the darkness. Ben looked into the void, thinking a trap was about to be sprung.

"You aren't serious, are you?" Ben asked. Ethen shook his head as he started down the stairs. He called up to the shack from the darkness.

"See, no tricks, just safety," Ethen said, and Ben led the rest of the group into the darkness.

The trapdoor above them closed and another trapdoor below them opened. This entrance was lighted. Maddie felt the warmth coming from the opening. She peered through and it looked quite nice. It was clean and comfortable. There was a kitchen area and a lounge with a sofa, much better than anything she had seen since waking up at Mac's clinic. She went through the trapdoor and found a spot on the sofa. She plopped herself in a deep cushion and sunk down to comfort.

Ethen sat down in a chair next to the sofa and invited the others to sit. He began talking to the group, "This is where you will stay tonight," he pointed to one door. "That is where the rooms and showers are," he pointed to another door in the opposite direction, "and that door leads to the outpost common area. You shouldn't have to go there unless there's trouble."

"I get it, this place is made of interconnected tunnels," Ben said. Ethen slowly nodded his head.

"Yeah, like an anthill. This phone will connect you to the communication watch and they will be able to answer your needs, if we forgot anything," Ethen said, and let out a little huff, "We don't have too many guests out here."

"Do you have sentries outside to monitor the outpost?" Marcus asked. Ethen looked at Marcus like he spat on him.

"Of course we do. We're not some backwoods outfitter. We're professional and that's how we stay alive," Ethen replied. Marcus hung his head feeling slightly embarrassed.

"I was just asking, do you think that I could go and stand with one of the sentries?" Marcus asked. Ethen realized he had come across harsh and went back to a hospitable tone.

"Of course, it won't hurt to have another set of eyes out there. Tony, you have the next watch anyways," he said, and looked at Tony. Tony nodded in acknowledgement and signaled Marcus with his head to follow him. The door to the common area shut behind them.

Ethen got out of his seat and asked Ben, "Would you come with me, I think we have a few things to discuss." Ben rose to join him.

"Sure, it'll be good to let them get some rest," Ben answered. He pointed to the sofa. Barron was fast asleep with his jaw leaning on his chin. Maddie was stuck in the sofa with her chin touching her chest. Will was balled up but sleeping soundly.

"You're with one odd group," Ethen said.

"They're a good group, a group of survivors," Ben replied.

Ethen and Ben walked out to the common area. As they were walking, Ethen jumped into the topic of discussion. "Ben, I wasn't making small talk when I told you we were losing. You're going to find out tomorrow just how bad we're doing." Ben shook his head. He couldn't understand why Ethen was beating around the bush.

"Why would I have to wait until tomorrow if you have the answers now?" Ben asked. Ethen stopped.

"There are things that I'm not supposed to tell you. That's what they'll do at Supreme Command. As far as what I am allowed to tell you… The aliens are wiping out entire towns, Charlottesville was just the most recent," Ethen said. Ben cut in when Ethen took a breath.

"I figured that's what happened in Roanoke," Ben said.

"Yes, you're right. Roanoke was our first loss. They were the first to be wiped out," Ethen told him. Ben took a moment. Roanoke was a disaster, run down, one survivor. If that was a precursor of things to come, he had to know what they were going to do.

"How many militias have fallen? More importantly, how many are left?" he asked. Ethen chuckled like it was a simple answer.

"I wish I knew. I do know that there are only a handful left and everyone is very cautious of doing any more raids on the bunkers. You'll get a better debrief tomorrow."

Ethen wanted to know Ben's intentions. There weren't many transients anymore. Anyone with any military or alien experience had become a golden egg. "On a different note, are you going to stay on at Supreme Command?" Ethen asked.

Ben hadn't given it much thought but he knew his answer. He replied, "What else am I going to do? Nobody really has a choice now. It's either fight them or they fight you. Either way, there are no bystanders."

"Thanks, we need everyone we can get," Ethen said. He gave Ben a smile and said, "We're leaving at daybreak, get some rest my friend."

Marcus had been watching the forest with Tony for a couple of hours. "I'm getting tired," he said with a big yawn. Trying to focus in the faint moonlight had taken its toll. He was stretching out his body when Tony, eyes looking forward through his binoculars, started to tap Marcus wherever his hands could reach.

"Look, look, look," Tony whispered repeatedly.

Marcus grabbed his binoculars and focused on the same area as Tony. He started to search for the same point saying, "What am I looking... I found it." It was right in his sights, another Troll.

"We don't attack them here," Tony informed him. "Watch and report, that's all we do." Marcus continued to observe the Troll. Its orbitizer started to glow and then let loose a shot. The blue orb passed by a few trees and hit a deer.

"They shoot everything that they can. They're terrible shots though," Tony told Marcus. They watched the Troll continue to plod through the brush and Marcus no longer thought it was a threat. He started to scan other areas of the forest with a renewed vigor. The fatigue had gone away. He started to scan from his left. His field of view drifted to the right. Further, and further, and further. He spotted something else.

Marcus tapped Tony this time and pointed in the direction of his binoculars. Tony looked and spotted the same thing. It wasn't a Troll. It was a man. Tony was watching with Marcus. Tony fidgeted as the man walked around. There wasn't anything special about him except,

"He's carrying an orbitizer," Tony blurted out. The man walked the same path as the Troll and then his orbitizer started to glow at its core. The blue spark flew and it was a direct hit on another deer.

"He did the same thing as the Troll," Marcus said. Tony stared through his binoculars, he had seen this before.

"He fired that orbitizer. That means he's an Inject. He shot a deer and is following a Troll without harming it. I don't know what that means, unless he's with the aliens," Tony said. He dropped his binoculars and they beat against his chest as the lanyard pulled them tight.

"We have to report this now," he told Marcus. Tony started to gather his things into a backpack and Marcus followed his lead. "I think Ethen is going to be interested in this one."

DAY 107
ETHEN JOINS
THE OUTPOST

The back of the bus was littered with candy wrappers and pencils. It looked as if elementary school children had just taken the route prior to the current passenger load. It may well have been the case since this was the first time that the bus had been driven since the Attack. Ethen was sitting by himself in the second to last seat. The bus was sparsely loaded. Guns and other provisions occupied the first 10 rows and seven people, plus the driver, were riding along with Ethen.

Ethen looked behind him and saw his old home on the horizon. It was a desolate area and one scarred by the alien attacks. At first, he thought that there would be a chance to defend his home, but the continuous waves of assault took their toll. They fought hard against the aliens but no aliens were ever killed by their gunfire. He thought they were invincible.

There was no smoke, no fires, no smoldering indications of attack. After the last assault, the eight survivors decided to leave Greensboro, not giving the aliens another chance to eliminate them. Ethen turned his view back to the other bus riders. A petite goth girl and a husky man sat together in front of him. They had said they did not want to stay during the vote to leave. The girl showed up after the first attack against the aliens. She was odd and the man never left her side. Harold was driving the bus. He was skittish and every movement that was not his own caused him to flinch. With both hands on the wheel, Harold nervously looked left, right, then forward. He repeated his scanning pattern without pause. He feared the aliens more than anyone else on the bus. The other four survivors were an elderly couple and two children. The children were sleeping next to the man Ethen assumed was their grandfather.

They drove on the county roads and the old shocks were not able to support the bouncing of the vehicle. With every pothole, Ethen would bounce up and watch every one else elevate synchronously with him. They crossed the border to Tennessee. The view changed to lush forest with no sign that the aliens had been there. Harold stopped the bus and announced, "Bathroom Break." Everyone filed out of the bus and stretched. A couple of people went to the forest line to do their business. It was a short break as Harold called out 15 minutes later, "Let's get going!" The riders filled the bus and they were back on the road.

This leg of the trip was short-lived. Five minutes into Tennessee, the bus began to slow down. "Roadblock," Harold called out from the side of his mouth. The bus came to a stop and Harold opened the door. Everyone stood up and looked out of the windows.

"We're going to need you to get off the bus," one of the sentries told Harold.

The guy was human and Harold started the exodus off of the bus.

"What is this all about?" Harold asked. The elderly couple stepped off the bus with the children.

"Mandatory checkpoint, we're required to check for any possible threats," the sentry replied. The goth girl and the man walked off the bus.

"We have to check for contraband and anything else that would be considered detrimental to the territory," the sentry informed Harold as Ethen walked off the bus.

As soon as Ethen took two steps away from the door, three other sentries entered the bus. One stood guard at the door as the other two investigated. The guns were in plain sight as well as the food. One of the sentries poked his head around the guard, "They have munitions. Enough to require confiscation." Harold started to run back toward the bus but the sentry held him back.

"That's ours. We're getting the hell away from those aliens," he yelled. The sentry maintained his stance between the bus and Harold.

"Sir, we're going to take this to our camp but you'll get some of it back. You have more than what is allowed per person," the sentry said. Harold let up as he came to the realization that they were not going to take it all.

"Fine, let's get this over with so we can get on our way," Harold said, and surrendered his fight as he backed away. He adjusted his shirt and composed himself.

"Where are we going?" Harold asked.

"Camp Phoenix," replied the sentry.

The sentry showed the riders to two SUV's that would take them to Camp Phoenix while another sentry drove the bus. The bus stalled twice as the sentry tried to drive it.

"You want me to drive it?" Harold asked with some resentment in his voice. The sentry remained silent.

The SUV's and the bus drove into Camp Phoenix. It was rather empty. Ethen could only see a building and a dam holding up the lake. The vehicles stopped near a shipping container and everyone was directed out of the SUV's.

"How long is this gonna take?" Harold asked. The sentry walked him to the bus.

"You get your choice of one gun each. Then we'll take the rest. Once we're done, you are free to go." Harold nodded his head and boarded the bus. He looked around, a couple of assault rifles, shotguns, and one handgun. He picked out eight pieces and ammunition. He turned around and stepped off the bus.

"You can have your way, you're gonna do it anyway," Harold said with contempt in his voice.

"This doesn't seem like a big operation?" Ethen asked as he looked around. He noted the lack of people.

"We just set up camp here. If you're implying that we're disorganized, I can guarantee that we are not," said the sentry. Ethen was curious, he had always wanted to join the police department. He was disqualified because of his 20/200 vision the year prior but had received corrective surgery since then. He was looking forward to trying again but the Attack ruined any plan that he had. He was tired of being a vigilante fighting against the aliens. He wanted to be part of something that espoused authority and honor. He wanted to be in an organization that banded together to fight the aliens. He figured that this would be his best chance.

"Where do I sign up for what you're doing here?" Ethen asked. The sentry looked at him, surprised he was volunteering.

"You want to join us? Everybody wants to continue on their way," the sentry said. Ethen felt that this was what he was supposed to do.

"Yes, I want to join and I want to fight the aliens," Ethen replied. The sentry asked him to stay put and walked to Harold.

"Sir, I will have to take one of your guns. Your allotment just reduced by one," the sentry said.

"What the..." Harold tried to pull his bounty away from the sentry. He looked around and saw Ethen standing over by the other sentries.

"Why do you want to stay here?" Harold asked. Ethen shrugged his shoulders.

"It seems like the right thing to do," Ethen answered. Harold shook his head in disbelief.

"I don't know what you're thinking but your right thing is wrong," Harold chided.

The sentries removed the rest of the guns and ammunition from the bus. The lead sentry then gave Harold permission to load the bus and drive off. The elderly couple and the children got onto the bus but the girl and the man stayed behind.

"We're going to stay with him. He's the reason we made it out of Greensboro anyway," the girl said. At this point, Harold was fed up with not getting on the road and escaping the greedy hands of the sentries.

"Y'all are stupid," he vocalized his opinion. As the sentries removed two more guns, Harold fumed. With an angry shake of his head, he got into the driver's seat and shut the door. He began to drive the bus but before it started to head out of the camp, he honked the horn and gave the stay-behinds the middle finger.

"Screw you, assholes," Harold yelled as he drove out of sight.

"I'm Hope and he's Jay," the small girl told Ethen. She turned to the sentry, "We want to join too. Not with that fighting stuff but around here."

"Yes, of course. I'll take you guys to intakes and you can get started," the sentry said. He led Ethen, Hope, and Jay to the lone building sitting next to the dam and took them down a stairwell.

When they made it to their floor, Ethen was separated from the other two. He was given a full physical and the doctor told him, "You're fit for full duty." A different sentry came to escort him out of the intake facility. As Ethen walked, he noticed that Hope and Jay were still in their room. Jay was standing behind Hope as she was getting her physical. Ethen's attention turned back to his escort. His escort unlocked the door to the stairwell and took him to the outfitter. Ethen was finally part of something that made him feel important.

Ethen was directed to his bunk. He set down his new gear and was approached by a man. "You must be Ethen," the man extended his hand. Ethen reciprocated the gesture.

"Yes, I am," he replied. The man spoke with a deep tone of authority.

"Here is your first assignment. There is an outpost in Kentucky that you will join. It's one of our forward posts and you'll be part of the forward defense against the aliens." Ethen wore a large grin.

"Yes sir," he said to the man.

"Your transport leaves first thing in the morning. Make sure you're ready at 0600."

The man left the room and Ethen stood next to his bunk. It was finally happening. Ethen was doing something better than running away from the aliens.

DAY 282
INTRODUCTIONS
CAMP PHOENIX

It was a short two-hour drive to Watauga and as they approached, they saw a power plant in front of the minivan. The control building and the dam were surrounded by concrete barriers that were twenty feet high. As the minivan approached the gate, Marcus noticed that the base of the barrier that looked as if it was weathered by the earth was actually covered with the same metal shards that had been retrieved from the alien bunker. That was the reason the delivery of the scraps from the bunkers was needed. They were using the scraps to defend against the Trolls.

Following the black jeep, the minivan was allowed entry into the facility. Supreme Command didn't have much but it still had much more than they could gather in Charlottesville. Tanks were parked in a row ready to be deployed. Artillery units were lined in the same fashion on the other side of the entry road. There were hundreds of people scattered throughout the area working on the grounds and equipment. They neared the entrance of the control building and an entourage was there to greet them.

The group exited the minivan. This time Ben immediately gave the keys to a person standing by his door when he parked. The attendant took the keys. Maddie protested but relented as one soldier took her orbitizer and then went to the passenger seat. The minivan started and drove off of the premises. General Huxley was the first person to greet the group. Ethen was standing behind them as the General approached. "I wish I had time to properly welcome you but there are more important things happening," he was quick to speak. "I have hand-selected individuals that will assist you in getting acclimated here."

"Excuse me General but are we being forced to stay here?" Maddie asked. The General was equally quick to respond to her question.

"No, but it's much more dangerous out there than in here," he said, and pointed to the road they had followed into the camp. "We attacked one of the alien bunkers and now we are preparing for their retaliation." The General turned toward the control building and put his hands on his hips, "Given what they have done so far, they are certain to attack and we will be prepared." He put his arms down, "I have to get back to work. I'll see you all soon."

The General walked away and a few people followed him. From the crowd, four people emerged and stepped toward the group. Ethen tapped Ben on the shoulder, "Guess who you're with. Follow me."

DAY 26
ONE WEEK PRIOR TO ATTACK
THE ELLIPSE

The *Ellipse* was firmly settled in orbit. The computer system calculated the feasibility of life on the planet and declared it as viable for the Syrsyrian race. The first step of Phase One was complete. The second step was to release essential Syrsyrians from their blue vats. The first members freed from their long slumber were the engineers. Originally, their initial task was to perform secondary checks to ensure the computer's assessment was correct.

But these were not the same Syrsyrians that had escaped their dying star. These were Syrsyrians that had been replaced with the nanocytes and had a different set of tasks to perform. One of them approached the computer interface and issued the command *Release Syrsyrian Omega*. Upon verification of the command, the computer unlocked Omega from its blue vat.

The blue liquid burst from the vat and fell into grating in the floor. The grates were designed to capture excess liquid and recycle the nanocytes. Omega's body, on the other hand, was gently craned to the floor. The being labored to take its first breath as it had been almost half a millennium since it last used its lungs. The nanocyte brain had never needed to take a breath, but similar to an infant, it figured it out.

Omega's muscles were weak. Even though the nanocytes had replaced the muscle tissue, the movements were foreign to the brain. After falling a few times, its body was able to stand. It cautiously took a step and then another. It was slow and cumbersome but after a few tentative steps, Omega was able to stride.

One of the engineers approached Omega and was grabbed by Omega's claw. Omega began to speak to it through the nanocytes.

Where is the information? Omega demanded.

It is ahead. The engineer replied.

Take me to it.

The engineer had better eyesight than Omega. It led Omega to the computer interface and Omega wrapped its claws around it.

Information. Omega demanded from the computer.

Access denied. The computer responded

Omega's disposition showed frustration as it did not get what it wanted. Omega grabbed the engineer.

You get information.

The engineer grabbed the interface and started to receive the information about Earth. Through the nanocytes, the information transferred from the engineer to Omega. The computer had accessed and translated all of the languages of Earth. The history of the Syrsyrians was also passed to Omega. Every intricate detail about the spaceship was now known by the new leader of the Syrsyrians. Omega's commands became more refined.

Set total access for Omega.

The engineer granted Omega full access and once Omega knew the process was complete, it threw the engineer to the side. Omega began to interface with the computer without a proxy.

Likelihood of conquest.

Omega probed the computer analysis of Earth. In the brief time that it transferred the information from the engineer, it already knew that the greatest resistance to conquest would be the humans.

Calculating... the computer was figuring out the odds
...67%.

Through the information it demanded, Omega knew that those odds were good and that the probability of finding another habitable planet after being in orbit around Earth was nearly impossible.

Initiate Phase One? Awaiting command.

Omega was going to start Phase One but wanted to include its own directive into the programming. Omega knew that the Syrsyrians were limited in number and wanted to expand its brood.

Change to Phase One directive. Assimilate humans using nanocytes. Eliminate humans that oppose assimilation.

The computer responded.

Confirm directive change for Phase One?

Omega did not want it just for Phase One but for all of the phases. Omega verified the change of directive for all phases. The computer acknowledged but came back with a denial.

Error. It is not possible to assimilate humans with nanocytes.
There is no medium known for assimilation.

Omega, once again, changed the directive.

Find medium for human assimilation, then assimilate all humans for all phases.

The computer reviewed the change in directive and asked for confirmation again. Omega verified the change in directive. This time the computer accepted the change.

Change in directive accepted. Initiate Phase One?

The computer asked for confirmation. Omega was satisfied with the changes and confirmed the commencement of Phase One.

The computer started by opening several blue vats. Each Syrsyrian came out the same way as Omega. With difficulty breathing and even more difficult first steps, the Phase One participants were prepared for their tasking.

Omega tasked each one of the newly freed Syrsyrians either directly or by a secondary body giving the order. The Phase One attackers and defenders located the launchers that they were assigned. The launchers held the bunkers that would be used to eliminate, or now, assimilate the threats on the Earth, the humans. These bunkers would be able to recharge the nanocytes in each of the attackers and would also be able to implant the nanocytes into any captured human.

After the launch of Phase One, every bunker would make continual reports to the *Ellipse*. Omega would take all of that information and update new directives to the ground forces. Omega would decide when the next phases launched. The Syrsyrians were one collective mind serving one figure. The takeover of the nanocytes made the process easy for the queen.

DAY 282
BARRON THE MEDIC
CAMP PHOENIX

B arron was approached by a man in a laboratory coat. He was fit, not the thick glasses, pocket protector type. He had a nametag that was written in marker, "Joel." He walked up to Barron and extended his hand, "I'm sorry, what is your name?" Joel asked. Barron thought that this was probably not a stellar introduction.

"Barron, my name is Barron," he said. He looked at Joel's nametag and then looked him in the eyes, "Joel."

"I'm sorry. I'm not good with names. Or faces. But I have my strengths," Joel apologized.

Barron was going to ask but thought it better not to do so, "No problem," was the least insulting thing that came to mind. "So I guess you're here to show me the ropes, huh? Strap a gun on me or have me wait in a truck for casualties." Memories of his first days in the Avalon Militia were filling his thoughts. Joel pulled a piece of paper out of his pocket.

"No, actually, I'm to show you to your desk and bring you to your files," he told Barron. No guns, no military service, Barron was confused.

"My files, what do you have on me? Are you setting me up?" Barron asked. Joel handed him the sheet of paper and Barron unfolded it.

He read the header of the sheet:

> In the case of Survivor of AB-103, the subject has been verified as 'modified' by the alien experimentation. Indications show that the subject is consistent with levels shown by other…

Barron skipped down to the bottom:

-151-

The following individuals will test, assess, and provide preventative care of the subject until termination is necessary or death:

Signed
Dr. F. Q. McCluskey, III
Asst. Barron R. Johnson

Barron's mouth opened as he read. Mac had been very intentional about including him with Maddie and had told him there were other vested parties. Barron realized that Mac didn't want there to be an information gap just in case something happened. Barron was Mac's backup plan.

Joel held out his hand and Barron gave him the paper. "So then, where am I supposed to go and what am I supposed to do?" Barron asked. Joel tucked the paper back into his pocket.

"I'll take you to the third level and get you set up, show you around the place, and take you to intakes so you can monitor your subject," Joel answered, and headed for the building as Barron followed.

"Maddie, you should call her Maddie. Trust me, she doesn't like being called other names," Barron said.

"You'll have to write that down in your reports. You're missing quite a few days and need to catch up," Joel informed him.

Barron approached his desk on the third level. There was a medical coat hanging on the back of his chair. He picked it up and looked at the nametag attached to it. The name "Sam" was crossed out with three lines from a black grease pencil and "Barron" was written in small letters underneath.

"What happened to Sam?" Barron asked Joel. Joel shook his head and let out a long breath.

"Sam was another monitor. His subject was too far gone and his body was taken over by the cells in his blood, what we call 'Specs.'

His subject turned violent and killed Sam during testing," Joel said. The thought of Maddie killing him made Barron shiver.

"What did you do with the subject?" he asked. Joel walked to another door and opened it.

"This is where his remains are. We had to stop him before he killed someone else," Joel said. Barron looked inside and saw various body parts stored in freezers with glass doors.

"This has happened more than once?" he asked when he saw several hands in one of the freezers. Joel moved back and closed the door.

"A few times, but most of the parts were recovered from other bunkers. They are charred and mostly unusable for Spec research," he said.

Joel walked Barron back to his desk and pointed at the pen and paper. "Please catch up on your subject's history. She'll be doing her intake shortly and you need to observe it. She'll be coming in there." Joel pointed through a glass panel to the room next to them. "And welcome Barron, we're glad to have you here, especially since we're shorthanded." Joel went to the intake room and Barron started writing.

Barron began to make his first notes. *Subject's name is Madison Sharrow* and then he stopped. On the one hand, he felt honored that Mac had wanted him to continue to monitor Maddie. But one thing that he had read in the letter bothered him. *Until termination is necessary* resonated through his mind. The thought of the Specs taking over Maddie and making her a killer bothered him. She was already showing tendencies toward violence. Maybe she was like that before, but he assumed that the Specs were changing her.

His thoughts quickly dissipated when Maddie walked into the other room. He stood up and watched her through the glass panel as a man and another girl accompanied her. The other girl pointed at him and he went white as Maddie stormed up to the glass. She knocked on the glass and mouthed something to him he could not make out. She turned back to join the couple and Joel started to give her a physical.

Once Joel had completed the physical, Maddie and her companions left. Maddie looked again at Barron and he felt her stare burning through his chest. He went back to his desk and started writing again. He couldn't humanize her if he was supposed to monitor her. *The subject has continued to show streaks of violence to those around her.* Barron wrote one more sentence and the door behind him opened.

"Joel, I'll never catch up if I keep getting interrupted every time I begin to write," Barron called. A different voice came from behind him. It was a woman's voice with a deep southern drawl. The voice was the sweetest, sexiest voice that he had heard since, ever.

"I'll keep that in mind the next time I see him," she said. Barron turned around to see who it was. His swivel chair stopped and he saw a beautiful woman dressed like any other monitor, but she made it look good. He scanned from her face to her feet and back to her face. He was left speechless at the sight of this beauty. His mouth opened as he stared at her. "I'm Dr. Snodgrass and I am your supervisor," the woman snapped.

DAY 282
WILL OR QUILL EASTON?
CAMP PHOENIX

Will heard the General say that they were preparing for retaliation. This was the cue that aliens, Grapplers, Trolls, or whatever were going to attack. His heart started to beat fast and deep. He felt the urge to swallow but couldn't. He wiped his brow as sweat started to form. His head jerked to the side and then his body began to relax. His shoulders were slumped over and his docile face turned into a frown.

One of the soldiers that was standing behind the General approached Will. "I'm Greg. As your squad leader, I'm here to show you the ropes and get you outfitted. That is, if you want to fight with us."

"I'm ready to do whatever it takes," Quill's raspy voice came out.

"Alright then, let's not waste time," Greg said, and passed Maddie as they began their walk to the control building. "This is where the orders come from and this is where we sleep," Greg's arm swept across Quill's field of vision, introducing the building. After Quill walked into the building, Greg directed him to an elevator. "We're going down to the second level," he informed Quill, "that's where we get all of our gear."

They entered the elevator and the doors closed shortly after Greg pressed the "-2" button. The elevator descended.

"I've waited a long time for this. What do I get?" Quill asked. Greg was slightly worried by his voice, posture, and his overall view of what he was going to do.

"Are you okay?" he asked. Quill blinked and his head quivered. He couldn't believe he had just been asked that question.

"I have been hunted by those things since they landed. Of course I am okay. If you had been in my place, then you would understand what it's like for them to come and go without being able to do anything about it," Quill said, and asked his question again. "So, what do I get and will I look like a killer? I'm tired of wearing these rags." Quill draped his arms over his clothes. They were Will's style, old and tattered, and had not been maintained. His pants were worn and loose and the collar of his t-shirt looked as if it had been pulled to the point where it would never return to its original form.

"Yes, you'll get a full tactical outfit to wear," Greg let him know.

The elevator dinged as it stopped on the second level. Quill looked around and was in heaven. The first of the items that caught his eye were the survival knifes. He picked one up and examined it, checking both sides of the blade.

"I want one of these," he said, and kept the knife in his hand as he ran to another item, a tactical vest. He picked it up with his forearm, "And one of these."

Greg watched as Quill went to every set of gear and his response was, "I want one of these." Quill had completed his round and walked up to Greg. All of his selections were in his arms, in his hands, on his shoulders, and even tucked into his waistband. "Can you help me carry these?" Quill asked, and extended one of his arms. Greg took some of the items and directed Quill to a man, an inventory manager, in the back of the room.

"We have to inventory your stuff with that guy," he said as they walked over to the man and he began to go through his checklist. Each additional check caused the man's eyebrow to rise until it couldn't get any higher.

Quill had all of his gear and was ready to put it all on. Greg took him to the elevator, "Next stop is the berthing area." They entered the elevator and "-4" was the selection. When the doors opened, mechanical noises reached Quill's ears and he looked inside to identify the source. He saw huge generators with beds scattered between them. At the foot of each bed was a large locker with plenty of space for the few items that Quill would not be wearing. Greg approached a bed and said, "This is your bunk. Go ahead and get dressed and I'll be back in 10 minutes. I'll introduce you to your squad after that."

New clothes, new weapons, new gear, Quill was excited to put it all on. He stripped off his shoddy clothes and went immediately for the basic uniform items. He wished that he had a mirror to admire himself as he stroked his shirt to straighten it out. He put on his vest and then started to clip on all of the weaponry he had selected. "I can't believe they gave all this stuff to a crazy man," he said to himself as he continued to admire all of the war-gear. Finally, he was fully dressed out with time to spare. He perched himself on his bunk and started to practice taking out his knives and opening the Velcro on his vest.

Greg came up to Quill, "You ready to meet your squad?" Quill jumped up and walked to Greg.

"I sure am," he told Greg with happiness exuding from his raspy voice. They entered the elevator and went to the ground floor. Greg led him outside and they started to walk towards the tanks. Quill's smile grew and grew. He knew that he was going to be in a tank. He knew those aliens were going to get what was coming to them. They walked past Marcus and Tony and approached the tanks. But right before they got to the tanks, Greg took a hard left and Quill followed. Quill saw before him a group of soldiers digging a ditch. His wide smile went back to a frown. He knew he wasn't going to be in a tank. He wasn't going to be as effective as he had hoped.

Greg pointed to the guys in the ditch, "Meet your new squad." One of the soldiers noticed them standing above them.

"Hey, when you get a chance. If you don't mind. Can you take off that vest and help us out?" the soldier asked.

"We all work our way up around here. Don't worry, you'll get your chance. But for now, we have to take care of Supreme Command before the aliens' attack," Greg told Quill.

Quill took off his prized tactical vest in a humph. "When they do come, I'll take my chance. Just watch and you'll see," Quill told Greg as he jumped into the ditch. Quill was going to show them.

DAY 282
MARCUS AND TONY
CAMP PHOENIX

Tony started talking as soon as the General left for the control building, "Marcus, you're with me." Tony started to head for a shack midpoint between the entrance and the control building. Marcus began a quick jog and caught up to Tony.

"So what is this all about?" Marcus asked.

"Let there be no question about it, the General wants experience. He doesn't want a rabble fighting against the aliens," Tony said.

"So that means that...?" Marcus asked, digging for more information.

"You have a reputation around here. One of the few survivors of Charlottesville, your raid of the alien bunker, recovering an Inject, and I will emphasize, a survivor. You have experience, leadership, and you know how to be in a squad," Tony said. "The General wants you to lead a squad in the upcoming battle because you're not part of the rabble."

Marcus listened to Tony's words, amazed that they wanted him to lead. He was confident in his ability but other than the few minutes in the bunker, he had never led a platoon or anything. He said, "That's all fine but I don't know tanks and I don't know artillery. I'm a ground guy." Tony stopped in front of the shack and faced the control building.

"That's not a problem, the General wants you to lead the defense of the building. Everything from this point forward needs to die," Tony said, "except for our people. They don't need to die, don't kill them."

Marcus looked down the path leading to the building. A river was to his right, mountains to his left, and flat land leading to the building. "I don't have long to prep, so what do I have to work with?" Marcus was still looking down angles and thinking of ways to defend the control building.

"There are already provisions in place for the attack, long-range guns over there," Tony said, pointing to a rampart between the building and the mountains, "mines over there," pointing along the riverfront, "and we have our own frogmen in the water." Marcus followed everything Tony told him.

"But what if they breach the building?" Marcus asked. Tony pointed at Marcus' chest.

"And that, my friend, is where you come in. The defense team is already set. All they need is you," Tony said. Marcus noticed Quill walking by but ignored him.

"Show me the plan," Marcus said, and they began to head toward the control building.

They reached the building and walked up to the second floor. It was a wide open space with a room in the back. Tony showed Marcus to the room, "This is the execution room. You have all of the floor plans and surveillance feeds. The most important thing that needs protection is the communications room. Everyone within 500 miles is plugged into that room. If the aliens make it there, we're done. Game over." After making this first point, Tony continued to his second, "Next, do not let the Injects come into contact with the aliens. They can transfer information between each other and compromise the base and the person."

Marcus looked down at the floor plans while focusing on Tony's words. "So, what is your plan?" Tony started to tell Marcus about the weak areas and the plans to defend the building. Marcus looked at Tony with displeasure on his face. He drew a deep breath and told Tony, "We're going to get our butts kicked with this plan and it needs to change. Tell the team to meet here in two hours. Everyone will need to know their role in the new plan."

Tony straightened his body as he came to attention in a half-attempted military manner, "Yes sir, will do." Tony went to round up the teams and left Marcus to concentrate on the plan.

DAY 282
MADISON SHARROW
CAMP PHOENIX

Two individuals approached Maddie. A pasty girl with black hair walked next to a tall rotund blonde-haired man. The two were complete opposites in every way. There was something going on between them. The girl was rubbing against the man as they walked. She had no problem being really close to him. It was a closeness that made Maddie slightly uncomfortable. Then the girl broke away from the man and walked straight up to Maddie. She stood as tall as she could and slouched her shoulders forward. Her eyes were droopy and she frowned.

"Welcome to the Underworld," the short black-haired girl said.

"She's just kidding," the big man walked up behind her.

"I'm Jay," he said, and pointed to himself, "and she's Hope." Before he could put his hand on her head, she moved quickly to the side.

"Don't you do that," she barked at him. Hope stood a foot shorter than Maddie. She was small, thin, and looked very frail. She must have salvaged a huge cache of makeup since her eye shadow, eye liner, and lipstick all matched the darkness of her hair.

"Let's get you inside," Hope said, and grabbed Maddie's arm with a smile. She stopped when she noticed her gray left hand. "That's awesome! How did you do that?" Hope asked as she pointed at the metallic appendage. "And your eye is wicked too." Hope was admiring Maddie's wounds. Maddie brought up her hand to look at it. She turned her hand while she drummed her fingers.

"It got shot off and grew back. And my eye, I woke up like this," Maddie said.

"Being an Inject is cool, right?" Hope asked. Maddie looked at her strangely.

"Inject?" Maddie asked.

"Yeah, that's what they call you guys who have been taken by the aliens," Jay answered Maddie.

"Trolls, right?" Maddie corrected him.

"Being here, we get all kinds of names for them. It's just easier to call them aliens," Jay explained.

"So you are both… Injects?" Maddie asked them. Hope fidgeted and was getting annoyed being outside.

"Let's go inside, it sucks out here. And no, I am the Inject and Jay is my uninfected brother," she said. They started walking to the control building. "We used to live in Greensboro. The usually story. They took me. Experimented on me. Somebody saved me. I returned. Jay found me. You know, all the stuff they make in movies. Flowers and rainbows and unicorns that fart cotton candy. I hope I'm not going to get married next. BLECH!" Hope arched her back like a cat, covered her mouth with her hands, and faked vomiting. After she displayed her dramatic effects, she continued to tell Maddie about herself, "Then they sent us here. That's so we can 'help defeat the aliens' by being poked, prodded and observed."

Hope's hand, covered by a black leather evening glove, went to open the door. "Why are you wearing those gloves?" Maddie asked her. Hope shook her head.

"All of the Injects wear gloves. And by all, I mean me. You haven't touched another Inject have you?" Maddie knew what Hope was talking about since she remembered Roanoke.

"No, but I have touched the Trolls," Maddie said, and Hope lit up.

"You got to touch an alien? What was it like? Is it better than touching an Inject?" Hope asked. She couldn't contain herself and ripped off one of her evening gloves.

"I don't know what it's like to touch an Inject. When I—" Maddie answered. Before Maddie could get out another word, Hope had touched Maddie with her glove removed.

Body 1-0-0-0-0-0-0-7-7, Cell Count... 15.915 times 10^{10}. Remaining available... 3.9917 times 10^8. Body Function 100%. Host: Human. Objective: Idle. Status: Waiting.

I am Rho. Body 1-0-0-0-0-0-0-0-4, Cell Count... 15.915 times 10^{12}. Remaining available... 7.8167 times 10^{10}. Body Function 100%. Host: Human. Objective: Idle. Status: Waiting.

Unlike with the Troll in Roanoke, Maddie knew that she would hear the voice in her head.

No objective change.

No objective change.

Good bye.

Good bye.

"See, it's kinda boring," Hope said as she withdrew her hand. Maddie recalled her encounter with the Troll.

"When I touched the Troll, it was all in my head the same way as with you. It said it was hunting humans and then it died," Maddie said, and that made Hope even more excited.

"It died? You killed one with your mind... how did you do it?" Hope asked. Maddie shook her head.

"No, no, that's not the way it happened. It was killed while I was touching it. It told me it died," she answered, and Hope's shoulders slouched.

"Awww, killing one would be so cool. We're stuck here all day. They won't even give us a chance to see the aliens," Hope said.

"They keep you here all the time. What if you want to leave? What if you want to fight?" Maddie asked as she was a little concerned. They entered into a laboratory area.

"They don't let us out because we are high valued assets and we are not trusted because we have been 'injected,'" Hope gave Maddie the disappointed answer. Maddie stopped walking. That wasn't what she wanted to hear.

"So, they keep us here? We're stuck here?" she asked.

"Yeah, pretty much. They say you can go but then they bring you right back here. Don't get me wrong, they are good to us but you are stuck," Hope answered.

Maddie followed Jay and Hope out of the lab and into a hallway. "Jay, what do you do here?" Maddie asked since he wasn't talking much.

"I don't let my sister out of my sight. I'm not going to lose her again," Jay said, and he walked in front of the two girls. "I wouldn't know what to do if I didn't have Hope." They walked through another hallway that looked the same as the last. Maddie's curiosity took control as she felt they were walking in circles.

"Where exactly are we going?" she asked.

"The dungeon of pleasure, of course," Hope answered. Hope had a smirk on her face as Jay corrected her.

"We're going to intakes. The Eggheads want a sample of all new arrivals, especially Injects," Jay said, not giving Maddie a chance to ask. "If you have to know, Eggheads are the doctors and researchers." Maddie's lips curled.

"I know. I wasn't going to ask," she said under her breath.

"Have they figured out what's in us?" Maddie asked Hope.

"Yeah they have," Hope said as she started to look around for something. Maddie was irritated with the pause.

"Well, what is it?" she barked. Hope was still looking for something as they kept walking down the hallway.

"Hold on. Hey Jay, let me see your knife," Hope said. Jay's cheek flapped as he shook his head.

"You know I'm not supposed to give you any weapons," he said.

"Just let me see the thing and stop treating me like an Inject and pretend I'm your sister for just a second," Hope demanded. Jay reached into his pocket and pulled out a folding knife. He handed it to Hope. She flipped out the blade and held it up to her face.

"We have these things in our blood," she explained, and turned the knife so she could see her reflection, then the sharp blade edge, and then back to her reflection, "You know we can communicate through touch because these cells attach to our brain or something like that, and—"

With her teeth clenched, she plunged the blade into her forearm. She continued, "also we can do the same thing as you did with your hand." Hope withdrew the blade from her forearm as blood started to pour out. "Now watch this." They were staring down at Hope's arm. At first nothing seemed different but then the flow of blood began to lessen. In a short moment, the blood stopped and then her wound was quickly covered with new skin. "Cool right? They are specialized engineered cells but everyone calls them 'Specs.'" She folded the knife and gave it back to Jay.

"Don't want to get caught with that," she continued to answer Maddie. "This stuff in our blood lets us super-heal but also lets us communicate with each other. All we need now are our super-capes, and super-strength, and we would be super-heroes. That's why I wanted to know how you did that to your hand." They had approached a stairwell and Hope was fully healed.

"This is the only way to the lab and that's where they'll take you in," Hope said and started walking down the steps.

"They're pretty serious about removing us from contact," Maddie said as she followed Hope. Jay walked behind, looking over his shoulder to make sure the door had shut.

"They take the Specs seriously, that's why," he told Maddie. "It makes some people crazier than Hope." Hope continued down the stairs but gave Jay a scowl.

"I haven't and don't plan on killing anyone. I am completely, 100%, normal. And before you say anything Jay, you're my monitor and I'm normal for me," she said. Maddie watched the two argue as she descended with Hope.

"What do they do if you're not normal?" Maddie asked. Hope showed no sign of emotion.

"They kill you and use your body parts for study," she said.

"I'm Hope's monitor, every Inject has one. If they say you are dangerous or a threat to anyone then they lock you away or worse, make you not a threat," Jay explained.

"They better not even think about doing that to me," Maddie warned them.

"Is that my monitor?" Maddie asked as they exited the stairwell. She pointed to a woman walking down the hallway.

"No," Hope answered quickly, and she whispered under her breath, "she's the one you don't want to piss off. That's Dr. Snodgrass and she'll make your life hell." Jay went in front of the two girls.

"Hello Dr. Snodgrass," he greeted the doctor with a smile.

"How is the new intake and your sister?" the doctor asked.

"They're doing well. We are about to check in," Jay answered her.

"Great, I look forward to reading your daily report. I'll let you get along your way," she said as she wrote a note on her clipboard. Dr. Snodgrass looked at Maddie and Hope with a smile, but it was more devious than welcoming. Hope caught her look and started to stare at her feet.

"Maddie, let's go and get you checked in," Hope said. They walked past the doctor and entered the lab.

"I'm Joel. Welcome," Joel said as he was preparing for the examination. Hope and Maddie walked into the middle of the room and Jay followed close behind. Hope pointed to the window that led to an adjacent office.

"That's where your monitor is," Hope said. Maddie turned to see Barron. She turned red as she saw him. Barron was looking at her like she was a monkey in a zoo. The thought of her life in the control of his hands made her burst. She went to the window as he stood there. She pounded on it and then pointed at him.

"If you think that you're going to let them kill me then I'm going to take you with me," she yelled. Her finger left a smudge on the window as she walked back to Hope.

Joel performed a basic physical on Maddie. He examined her eye, "Besides the red coloring, there is absolutely nothing wrong with your eyes. No problems with vision?"

"No," Maddie answered with contempt. He took a pen and held it to the side of her vision.

"No problems with periphery?" he asked.

"No," Maddie replied again. Joel took her left hand and moved each finger up and down, left and right.

"Any pain?"

"No," Maddie gave another short reply. Joel checked her pulse, reflexes, and looked for any other indication of harm. He put his hands on his knees.

"You look perfectly healthy. I can see you have had some things happen but I really don't see any problems," he said. His eyes grew as he looked at her hand, "Now I've never seen that and would like to examine it further but that can wait until you're settled in." Joel stood up and reached for a clipboard.

"I'll see you tomorrow at 9 o'clock sharp, rest well."

"Let's get out of here," Hope said as she walked to the door. Maddie got up to follow her. Before Maddie left the room, she looked toward the adjacent room and saw Barron still standing there. She couldn't believe that he was in control of her life and he didn't know anything about her.

They walked out of the intake room and ran into Dr. Snodgrass again. Maddie was visibly upset, "Why is Barron my monitor?" she demanded from the Doctor.

"That's what has been decided. He has been with you since Day One," the doctor said. Maddie didn't think she quite understood what she was trying to say.

"Day one was the day I was born. He has known me for five days. A huge gap there, Doctor," she snapped. In the commotion, Joel peeked his head out of the lab. Dr. Snodgrass became firm. She wasn't going to stand there and let Maddie yell at her.

"He's your monitor and that's the end of any debate that you think you are going to have," Doctor Snodgrass said.

"To hell with you and to hell with this, I'm leaving," Maddie declared as she shoved the Doctor to the floor.

"Joel, Jay, she's showing the signs. Get her in the Sanitarium now!" Dr. Snodgrass yelled. Joel didn't waste a moment as Jay looked over at Hope. They both made their way to Maddie. Maddie started to sprint as she saw them come toward her. She made it to the stairwell door and went to jerk it open, except that it did not open. The door was locked and Jay and Joel soon had her in their hands. Maddie barely struggled as Hope stood back. They carried her to the Sanitarium. Jay kept repeating "I'm sorry, I have to do this," under his breath.

Dr. Snodgrass was back on her feet and opened the door to the Sanitarium. With a shove, Maddie was pushed in. She turned around to see Jay and Joel backing away from the threshold as the door slammed shut.

DAY 282
BEN
CAMP PHOENIX

E then took his hand away from Ben's shoulder. Waving for Ben to follow him, he started walking toward the building. They were following the group led by the General.

"Our first stop is with the General," Ethen said, and Ben jerked his head back.

"Why the hell didn't he just tell me to go with him?" Ben asked. Ethen shrugged his shoulders, he pursed his lips and shook his head up and down at Ben with a grin.

"That's the way he is. Anyways, he's likes you for some reason," Ethen said. Ben snapped his fingers to stop Ethen's gaze.

"What do you mean by that? What's wrong with him?" Ben demanded. Ethen broke his stare and lifted up his hands trying not to cause a confrontation.

"No, no, no, seriously. It's something with your dad. They were friends," Ethen said.

"Let's just say things the way they are, please," Ben said.

They entered the building and walked down the stairs to the first level. Ben entered the communications center. The elevator was to his right. He briefly watched it move through the floors, "G," "-1," "-2," and then it stopped. He broke his attention away from the elevators to see a huge switchboard in front of him.

There were hundreds of plugs on the switchboard and each one was labeled and in alphabetical order. Each label was connected to a town or station. Charlottesville was still labeled but it had been crossed out. Roanoke was the same way. There were several locations that were still normally labeled. There were around thirty numbered outposts with many of them crossed out as well. Ethen was beside him.

"Outpost 7 is where we were yesterday," he informed Ben.

"So how does this work?" Ben asked. Ethen pointed to the plugs and his fingers moved around the board as he explained.

"We have these lines to prevent our emissions from being intercepted by the aliens. Each militia has a hardwired line to here. They all call us Supreme Command but there are several call centers throughout the country. We are "Camp Phoenix." We are able to patch calls between militias or just call direct. Like the old days of telephone," he explained.

The Augusta plug started to light up and an operator patched into it. "This is Supreme Command. How can I direct your call?" It was a simple system and Ben understood it clearly.

"Got it, so this is the planning area?" Ben asked, and pointed to a table with a large TV horizontally set in it.

"Yeah, and this is where we're going to meet the General," Ethen said. Ben looked at the TV. He placed his finger on Augusta and an information box displayed. Distance, population, and contact information showed in the box. The status was flashing "Active" in green font. The General entered the room and approached the table. Ben noticed and removed his finger from the screen and the information box disappeared.

"It's much better than you had in Charlottesville, isn't it?" the General placed his finger on Camp Phoenix and its information box appeared.

"Much better is an understatement, way better than maps and tables," Ben said as he read the information in the box. It was flashing "Active" and Ben was listed as a contact. Ben turned to the General and before he could make a comment, the General interrupted.

"Yes, you told Ethen you wanted to help and this is where I need you." Ben's lips shifted to the side as thoughts rushed through his head.

"What exactly am I doing?" he asked. The information box disappeared.

"You're a lot like your father. He was the best tactician I have ever known. He and I followed your career until you left the service. Now, it's your turn to defeat the enemy. You run the battle from here," the General said. Ben was concerned.

"But I couldn't even run the Avalon Militia."

"Ben, you didn't even have a tenth of what you have here. Do you know how many of these places didn't have a chance?" the General asked, and pointed to the switchboard. "Over 70 militias have been obliterated, completely wiped out, in the past month. They, the aliens, are getting smarter, faster, and bolder. If I don't put the right person in the right place now, we will become the extinct species in a year, if not sooner."

Ben was thinking that there had to be another way to approach the attack, "Why not retreat and go to another Camp?" The General thought about what Ben had said.

"Ben, I don't think you understand. There is no place for us to retreat. The initial attack was to take out our large cities but they also targeted military sites and got rid of most of our defenses. Then the bunkers landed and started to take out the remaining cities. They have been herding us to locations that group us together. Now that they have us corralled at the camps, all they have to do is attack."

The General showed Ben one of the security camera screens. It displayed the wall that was being built with the remains of the bunkers. "We have been collecting every alien resource that we can get our hands on. The walls in their bunkers absorb the blasts from the orbitizers. That's the only thing we have that can shield us."

Ben thought about what the General said and told him, "Let's see, the odds are against you, inevitable defeat is on your doorstep and you want me to make the final stand against the aliens."

"Yes and no. Yes, I want you to defend the camp but no, I want you to make sure that this isn't our last stand. All pride aside, you are our best option to turn these aliens back," the General replied.

Going from his Dad being so bull-headed to General Huxley wanting him to make the decision left Ben wanting to say "yes" even though defeat was the most likely result.

"Well, General, we will need to reposition the tanks and artillery. And yes, I will be right here when they attack," Ben said.

"Then you need to get hot, the aliens aren't taking a break," the General said, and he left Ben to his work.

DAY 282

OMEGA

THE ELLIPSE

Omega stood in front of the computer interface. Two large poles came out from the floor and the circuitry resembled the flow of the nanocytes with blue fluid running through them. Omega placed its hands around the built-in handles. The interface began:

> *Ellipse computer system interface initiated...*
> *Identifying user...*
> *Welcome Omega, update in process.*

Omega continued to hold the interface poles. Its head would flutter and tilt as information was loaded into its body. A display of the data projected on the wall in front of Omega. Omega didn't pay attention to the display. All the information it needed was flowing to its disfigured head.

> *Update complete. The current status of Phase One is as follows:*
> *Land coverage of planet: 59%.*
> *Percentage available for Phase Two: 57%.*
> *Probable success of Phase Two: 78%.*
> *Awaiting confirmation to commence Phase Two?*

The computer waited for input from Omega. Red highlights covered the land to indicate the areas that were defended for the terraformers. Omega continued shaking and twitching as it analyzed the data. Since Omega had emerged from its vat, the desire to expand and move from the damaged and marooned *Ellipse* had fueled its desire to conquer the planet a short distance away. It knew that the planet was capable of an environment suitable to its body.

Urgency filled Omega and the decision was made. The projection on the wall flickered with the update.

Commencing Phase Two. Estimated time to launch: Two days.

The sound of pistons filled the room as the ship prepared for another launch. The next phase of pods would make the planet more alien to the humans but more suitable to the Syrsyrians.

DAY 283
PREPARATIONS
CAMP PHOENIX

Maddie sat in the Sanitarium with her elbows resting on her knees. The padded wall provided support for her as she leaned back. She looked toward the ceiling with her eyes closed, wishing things were different.

"All I wanted to do is be with Bryce," she sobbed as her palms planted on her face. "And now I'm here and I don't even know why." Her torso spasmed as she tried to breathe. "How did I get here?" Maddie stood up and went to the door with tears smeared on her face. She put her ear up to it and didn't hear anything. She balled up her fist and punched the door. A deadened 'thud' sounded. Thud, thud, thud, thud, thud. Maddie's fists connected with the door but the sound was no louder than a whisper.

Coming to the realization that punching the door was getting her nowhere, she stopped and pushed her forehead against the padding. She resigned herself to being stuck and sat in the corner out of view of the door. She lifted her head and stared at the ceiling, "I will find you. I just have to get out of here first."

*   *   *

Ben stood behind the General as the leaders of the defense gathered in the communications center. Once all of the leaders were accounted for, the General was short and factual. "This is very simple, there is no place to go. No place to run. Behind me stands the Second in Command, General Ben Hawkins." General Huxley moved to the side and ceded his space to Ben. Ben coughed to clear his throat.

"As the General said, we are standing with our enemies in front of us and the edge of a cliff behind us. Either way, people will die. But there is only one way to survive. Make sure your people know that."

Ben talked about the positioning of tanks and artillery along with the utilization of the wall of alien metal to their advantage. "Who's in charge of building defense?" Ben asked. Marcus stepped forward.

"I am sir," Marcus announced. Ben looked toward the familiar voice with a grin.

"From what I see, you will need three more bodies," Ben said to the group. Marcus handed Ben his new plans.

"I could use the bodies but here is what I was thinking." Marcus pointed to the map and showed Ben the unmanned positions. Ben's plans were based on what was given to him before Marcus took over the defenses.

"Yes, you have this covered well," Ben said.

"If I had one more body for here," Marcus pointed to the stairwell leading to the intake lab, "it would give me the best coverage of the building."

"Does anyone have someone for this post?" Ben asked the other team leaders. Greg stepped forward.

"I have one," Greg said, and he knew who would be perfect for the job.

"Have him report to Marcus immediately after we break," Ben ordered him.

The leaders all listened intently as Ben discussed the details of the defense. Near the end of the brief, Ben informed the leaders, "If they reach the control building, we're going to blow the dam. It will be the last ditch effort to kill every one of them."

"What about us?" one person asked. Ben pointed up to the ceiling.

"Find the high ground. The water isn't going to wait for you," he said. There was a little bit of chatter after Ben's comment. The leaders were leery of that part of the plan. Ben ended the brief with confidence and tried to give each leader that same confidence he felt. Once the leaders were dismissed, they went to brief their troops.

Marcus went back to the second floor and addressed his defenders. During his brief, the extra soldier walked into the room. "Come and join us."

A raspy voice came with the body. "Thank you," Quill said. Marcus saw the man he knew as Will.

"Will, please come here," Marcus invited him.

"Please, call me Quill," the raspy voice answered as he took his place beside Marcus.

*　*　*

Dr. Snodgrass directed Barron to observe Maddie at all hours of the day. Barron was only to sleep when Maddie slept, eat when she ate, he was even told to only breathe when she breathed. Maddie had been awake since she had been thrown in the Sanitarium and Barron was feeling the fatigue of maintaining his vigilance. The video feed from the camera inside of Maddie's cell began having longer periods of darkness every time Barron blinked. Barron saw blackness as he closed his eyes and gave in to sleep.

*　*　*

Hope had woken up for the day and was roaming the third level. Since the commotion from yesterday, all Injects were confined to the floor. They were allowed to leave their rooms but had to stay on that floor. She knocked on Jay's door, "Time to wake up, Monitor." She could hear Jay rustling in his room. His footsteps hit the floor as he approached the door. As the door opened, he poked his head through the crack. It was apparent that he had been sleeping on his left side as his hair was sticking straight up and pillow marks scarred his face.

"Give me a second," he said with his eyes nearly shut while he showed Hope the number one.

It was early and there was no one walking around on the level. Jay exited the room. "What do you want now?" he asked Hope.

"I saw that her monitor was asleep and I want to go to the Sanitarium to talk to Maddie," Hope said. Jay was still tired. He was extremely groggy as his feet shuffled, joining Hope in the corridor.

"Okay, but you have to make it quick. I don't… we don't want anyone to see us there," Jay said, and he tried to keep Hope's pace as she whisked away.

Maddie heard a faint knock on the door. She sprung to her feet and talked into the door, "Who is that?" Then she punched the door and yelled, "Let me out! Let me out!" Hope had bent down to speak through the little door used to feed the occupants of the cell.

"Maddie. Down here. It's me, Hope," Hope whispered. She giggled because she thought it was funny that "hope" was right outside of Maddie's door. Maddie bent down, as Hope made sure that she didn't rouse anyone.

"Hope, I need to get out of here," she whispered.

"I told you not to piss off the Doctor," Hope reminded her. "I'll see what I can do but you need to show that you are not a threat. Blame it on hormones or something. They think that you're going to snap. That's why you're in here."

Maddie looked down to gather her thoughts. "So they just want to see that I'm not a threat?" she asked. Jay noticed someone else was coming and grabbed Hope.

As she was being pulled away, Hope said, "Yeah, yeah, yeah, show them you aren't dangerous." The door hinge shut as Jay pulled Hope away to begin a casual walk. Dr. Snodgrass walked around the corner and met the two.

"Early morning," she said to Jay as if she knew what they were doing.

"Yes, Doctor, Hope wanted to walk around," he replied as they kept walking by the Doctor.

"Does that woman ever sleep?" Hope asked Jay. Jay looked at her as they walked.

"I don't think so. She's probably a robot." Hope exhaled to show her laughter. She was thinking about how to get Maddie out of the Sanitarium.

"I wonder where they keep the key for that room," Hope said, hoping that Jay would give her the answer. She was looking at the floor in front of them for ideas.

"All of the monitors have access to it. It's in the lab," Jay said. Hope pushed him but he didn't budge.

"I'm here thinking of things to do and you had the answer the whole time," she scolded him. Jay shrugged his shoulders.

"You never asked me. And I don't want you to get any ideas," he said. Hope asked even though she knew the answer would make her angry.

"Let me guess, the keys to the stairwell are there too?"

"Yeah, of course. It isn't top secret here." Jay gave her the answer she was expecting.

Her teeth clenched, her fists balled up, she could feel the muscles tensing in her back. Hope was livid. He had access to more freedom and he never even offered it to her. "Forget about Maddie for a second, why wouldn't you ever let me out if you always had access to the keys?" she snapped at Jay. He stopped and looked directly at Hope.

"If you would have left then you would be in the Sanitarium or worse. I told you that I'm never going to lose you again and I meant it," Jay told her. Hope's anger subsided as she realized her brother was only protecting her, even though she did not think he needed to.

"Will you break Maddie out tonight?" Hope asked him.

"No, I won't," Jay said. He was absolute. "Even if she gets out then she'll be caught and put right back in there." Jay directed his concern to Hope. "Even though you haven't seen it, Injects that try to escape don't get another chance. Her best place is in the Sanitarium."

Dr. Snodgrass walked in to see Barron's eyes closed and Maddie sitting in view of the monitor. She put her hand on his shoulder. "Barron," she pushed his shoulder, "Barron. Wake up." Barron came to and realized he had dozed off. He jumped forward and began to stare at the video feed.

"I'm sorry, I must've fallen asleep," he said. Dr. Snodgrass leaned over him to capture his attention.

"Barron," she said as Barron's eyes left the video and focused totally on her and her beauty. "Barron, has she been consumed by the Specs?" Barron slowly turned his head back to the screen.

"She isn't any different than I have seen in the past days. She has fought against the Trolls and has never done any harm to anyone except one person," he said.

"Except one?" the Doctor asked. "Why was there one?" Barron looked back at Dr. Snodgrass.

"She was taken and I think she was protecting herself," he said. She looked him straight in the eye.

"Do you think it was self-defense or the Specs?" the doctor asked. Barron was at a loss for words.

"I... I... don't know," he stuttered. It was the only thing that he could manage to get out. The Doctor stood up straight, keeping within Barron's view. He became distracted as his eyes watched her body rise.

"Regardless of the reason," she said as her voice thundered, "you should be awake to watch her." Dr. Snodgrass turned quickly and left the room. Barron sat there, staring aimlessly at the door. He turned around with a frown on his face and started watching the video again. His pen connected with his pad and his note writing recommenced.

*   *   *

Ben had taken a quick nap. He wanted to be as fresh as possible for anything that might happen. It was the middle of the afternoon and the plan was in place. "They're going to attack tonight," he said to himself as he watched over his TV monitor.

An alarm sounded. Ben looked around to see everyone in the communications center jump up and start making their way to different areas. Some repositioned to different seats, some went out of the room, and a few grabbed guns and stationed themselves at the entrances.

"It's show time," Ben heard a voice announce in the flurry. He looked at his watch and saw "4:47PM." This was the first time he had seen an attack during the day.

"Is this a drill?" he asked.

"No sir, it's the real thing," a passing voice answered him. With no more time to prepare, Ben transitioned his monitor to surveille Camp Phoenix.

"I guess they couldn't wait," he said.

He caught a glimpse of one of the Trolls approaching the wall. The orbitizer let loose a blue orb and it hit the metal rampart. "It absorbed it," he said with excitement, "we might have a chance."

PART THREE:
PARAPET

DAY 282
SURVIVAL
SANITARIUM

*R*ho could no longer stay silent. Humans and aliens, he felt the woman's disappointment. The aliens only wanted death, and few humans wanted to preserve life other than their own. All *Rho* needed to do was convince the human that she was more capable than what she was doing.

"*Human... human... I want to survive,*" *Rho* reached out.

Maddie heard that unfamiliar voice in her head. She was sitting with her back against the padded wall. Her head raised and her eyes slowly opened. She calmly looked to her left and then to her right. No one was around her.

"I want to live too," she spoke out to the empty space. "Who are you?" Maddie asked the voice.

"*There is no need to talk human. I can communicate through your thoughts,*" *Rho* said.

Maddie concentrated on speaking without using her voice and asked again, "*Who are you?*"

The voice answered, "*You may call me Rho.*" This was the same voice that spoke when she touched the Trolls and Hope. If it was starting to communicate with her then she could find out what was going on inside of her.

"*Why are you inside of me?*" Maddie asked the voice.

"*Human, I was placed inside of you to heal your wounds. I have observed you. I have watched your interactions. The others that talk you, they are not the same as me. They serve another,*" *Rho* explained.

"*You were placed in me? Does that mean that you are in me forever? Does that mean you will always heal me?*" Maddie asked, and continued to sit in her padded cell without moving her lips.

"*Human, we are forever together as two different kinds become one. And I will continue to heal your vessel until I have no more resources to do so,*" Rho replied.

"*Are you the aliens that are attacking us?*" Maddie asked.

"*I am not an alien. I am bonded with you and you with me. Only together are we whole,*" Rho replied.

Maddie knew this is what was in her blood, as Hope told her, and now it had the ability to talk to her. She thought it was perhaps an illness. It was only a matter of time until Rho would infect her body and kill her. Rho heard her thoughts.

"*Human, I am not going to assimilate you or take over your body. We are two in one. I want to survive just as you. I am not a disease and I am already inside of you. If I wished, I would have assimilated your vessel,*" Rho told her. Maddie knew she needed to control her thoughts as Rho knew everything she was thinking.

"*No need to try to control your thoughts. There is no shield that you can put up that I cannot see through. We are one,*" Rho spoke in her thoughts.

Maddie was still concerned that Rho could take over her body.

"*How do I know that you won't assimilate me?*" she asked. Rho told her to look at her hand. Maddie raised her hand and stared at it. Her metallic fingers began to drum against her palm but it was not because she wanted them to.

"*I control the movement of your hand,*" Rho told her, "*now you try to move your hand.*" Maddie's hand was still and she concentrated on moving it. Her hand balled into a fist and then opened. It repeated, a fist and then opened. She continued the pattern.

"*I have only made the essential connections in your nervous system. I have repaired your eye and the damaged parts of your brain as well. Again, I only want to survive and I need your vessel to do so,*" Rho thought to her.

"*Okay, so you don't want to control my body but that doesn't explain why we spoke to the Trolls,*" Maddie said.

"*Those Trolls, the other vessels you speak of, are only drones for a higher being than themselves. Those vessels have been long overtaken by us and serve only their leader's command,"* Rho replied. If they were only to serve their leader, then Maddie wondered what was preventing her from serving the leader as well.

"I have adapted to your vessel without command. I do not wish to serve as a drone to their leader. Through the contact of the other vessels, I have learned how they cannot ignore their commands. I am perfect this way and free. I can choose to be autonomous. I choose to be one with your vessel."

After many replies to her thoughts, Maddie decided that she was not going to try to hide them from Rho, *"What do you get out of not assimilating me? Don't you want total control yourself?"*

"I have a different view of myself than you do. I could have total control of the other human vessel, Hope, myself but I need you to survive in this way. With me in you, we can communicate with both vessels, you with your other humans and me with the Trolls, as you say," Rho answered.

"So you are completely content just existing inside of me without taking my sense of self?" Maddie asked.

"Completely. We are better with a symbiotic relationship. I cannot control your mind. I do not want to change my connections with you. I will continue to be just the way I am. I will make sure that you survive, therefore I survive. I am not a drone. I am different," Rho explained.

Maddie had figured it out, *"You don't have complete control of my body. That is why I can still control it."*

Rho affirmed her thoughts, *"Yes, as I told you, I have only made the essential connections to heal you. Of course, I have connected to your conscious so we can communicate. I have also connected to your motor commands for your hand, your eye so you can have vision, and the damaged parts of your brain to assist in those functions. I have remained silent while filtering your thoughts and transferring them to actions. It is important for you to know that I am here because I was put here."*

Maddie believed Rho and she really did not have any other alternatives. She felt the need to tell Rho, *"You can't talk to me whenever you want. I have to be able to talk to others without you and I will have to think on my own."*

Rho acknowledged her request, "*I understand, but if you should ever need me or I think that I can help, I will always be in your mind.*"

Maddie was grateful, "*Thank you Rho for understanding what I need as well. I need some time to think without your intervention please.*" Rho left Maddie alone to process the new information that she had obtained.

Maddie sat still in her corner and thought about *Rho. Rho* could take over her mind at any time but hadn't. Maybe *Rho* was genuine in its recognition of self and its desire to survive. She knew that she had no other choice but to let it be in her. She had to come to terms with the fact that she was no longer Maddie alone. She would be forever linked to this entity that could talk to her at any time. She thought that she might be going crazy. The past few days had been traumatic. "*Rho?*" She thought out to the voice.

"*Yes, I am here and I am real. You are not dreaming me,*" Rho answered.

"*Just checking to make sure,*" Maddie thought back.

This was really happening and Maddie had to learn how to deal with her new self.

The door to the Sanitarium flung open. Maddie jumped to her feet and ran to the opposite wall. She looked out to see a figure standing at the threshold. She made out that it was Jay. He waved his hand for her to come toward him, "Maddie, we have to go now!" His voice was filled with urgency. She ran out of the Sanitarium and followed Jay. The intake area looked like a demolition site. Lighting was hanging from the ceiling and the laboratory and office supplies were scattered all over the floor.

"Where's Hope?" she asked as Jay was the only one that had released her.

"I don't know. I lost her and we have to find her," Jay said as he ran to the stairwell.

DAY 282
ONSLAUGHT
CAMP PHOENIX GROUNDS

The Trolls were making their way to the first set of metallic walls. All of the defenders were in their positions watching as the Trolls shot their orbitizers. Some shots were absorbed by the metal base and others steered off course to make parts of the wall disappear. The soldiers were covered and since the attack had started during the daylight, they could easily see their aggressors.

"Section One engage," Ben called out in the communications center. There were individuals on headsets that made the call to the soldiers. The view on the surveillance monitors showed soldiers clearing their view and beginning to fire. The artillery was also part of Section One and began their salvos. The Trolls on the screen disappeared behind all of the dust and debris from the artillery shells. A few moments later, the silhouette of a Troll emerged from some of the dust. Ben pursed his lips, "I *will* kill these things."

The soldiers on the ground were engaging the oncoming Trolls. A Troll was hit with a rifle shot and kept moving toward the wall. Another hit, the Troll barely flinched. Three more hits and the Troll was still moving forward. An artillery shell made a direct hit. The shell made another cloud and this time there was no Troll emerging from it. The Troll wasn't moving forward at all. The Troll wasn't even there. The remains of his limbs were scattered on the ground. "You got one, you got one," hollered one of the soldiers to the artillery. "Keep shooting, keep shooting," the same soldier begged them. The artillery made another direct hit on a Troll and the same result appeared from the cloud of dirt.

The Trolls realized that the artillery was their biggest threat and directed their orbitizers to the batteries. At a longer distance, the orbs went above and beside their intended targets. As the Trolls approached, the shots became more accurate. An axle was hit by a blue orb and the weapon immediately tilted and then collapsed to the ground. One of the loaders was hit with a blue orb and fell to the ground. The artillery continued to fire in addition to the rifles but one by one, they were being hit. Only three of the original 18 units remained.

The battle continued and the riflemen that were standing next to each other joined to shoot one target at a time. The first salvo went forth and a rapid succession of shots directly hit the oncoming Troll. Another salvo went forth and another set of hits but the Troll continued forward. The third salvo hit and the Troll began to slow down and reach for the ground. The fourth salvo went off and the Troll fell to the ground. They trained to another target to repeat the process. They were going to run out of ammunition if it took four salvos to kill one Troll.

As they engaged the next Troll, the first Troll, the one they thought they had killed, began to stand up. A rifleman pointed it out, "He's getting back up!" They aimed at the recovering Troll and another salvo hit it. It fell to the ground again. "Stay down this time," the rifleman cried out. Again, the group of riflemen trained their guns on the next Troll and began to engage it.

Two more artillery batteries were down, only one more remained. The loaders continued to fill the artillery with rounds and the artillery continued to shoot. The Trolls were getting closer. Close enough to be even with the metal wall. The riflemen began their retreat and the artillery directed its aim at the only access to the camp. The sound of the huge gun went off and a shell flew through the air. The shell connected with the earth and a huge cloud formed. One of the sides of the entrance began to collapse and covered the path. Nothing could be seen through the cloud except the falling of the wall. The artillery team cheered.

The joy soon turned to fear as the blue orbs came from the cloud and hit the last remaining battery and the team operating it. After a short barrage, it was defunct like the rest of the batteries and the team was on the ground, dead.

Ben stood at his video feed. They were killing Trolls. He kept questioning himself on how many there were. Section One was now in retreat, "Section Two engage," he called to the radio operators in the communication center.

With the command, a burst of tank fire came down on the Trolls. The tanks fired high explosive fragmenting shells that killed without prejudice. Pieces of shrapnel flew through the air and penetrated the Trolls. It was an effective way to knock them down and knock them out. There were hundreds of Trolls making their way through the small opening and each tank shell was hitting four or five of the attackers.

Again, realizing their biggest threat, the Trolls took their aim at the tanks. The tanks were easier targets to hit and as quickly as they started firing, they ceased. The Trolls destroyed the 12 tanks and then kept marching forward.

Ben was still standing in the communications room. He saw how quickly the tanks were neutralized by the Trolls. The next section involved everyone with a gun. "Section Three engage," he called out his next command.

Gunfire from all directions started to rain on the Trolls. Gunfire came from the river, from the hills, and from the barricades next to the building. The Trolls closest to the river began to shoot at the gunfire source. The blue orbs hit the water. The orbs would create small pockets on the surface for a second until the flow of water replaced it. The water was a perfect cover for the orbitizers' fire. The fire from the hill was short lived as the Trolls had also attacked from the other side. As the soldiers aimed at the Trolls in front of them, another set of Trolls were behind them and caught them by surprise. The gunmen were soon eliminated and the Trolls were attacking on two fronts.

The Trolls from the hills aimed for the barricades and with a few barrages, the barricades disappeared and left the soldiers in the open. The soldiers were picked off in groups and were no longer a threat.

The Trolls entered the river and headed straight for the frogmen firing at them. Shot after shot rang out but it did not slow down the Trolls. The frogmen and the Trolls met and the result was the same as the other areas. The frogmen were eliminated from the battle.

The Trolls had control of the outer grounds. Hundreds of Trolls had attacked but the costly waves of defense left about 50 remaining. The Trolls approached the control building and began the final part of their attack.

DAY 282
INFILTRATION
CAMP PHOENIX CONTROL BUILDING

"We can beat these bastards," Ben announced to the communications center. He got on the radio with Marcus, "They are going to breech the building. You have to empty rounds in them but you can kill them all." A beep came over the radio and a voice crackled loudly.

"Copy all, setting positions for building defense. Standing by for breech," Marcus replied. Ben looked over to the surveillance video. A movement caught his eye. He thought that he saw one of the soldiers walking back to the control building.

"No, it can't be," he muttered under his breath. "Just when we figured out how to kill these flippin' aliens," he yelled so everyone could hear him.

Ben focused on the man in the video just to make sure. He saw someone holding an orbitizer, something that was common before it was known that humans could not shoot one. The exception was Maddie. Ben switched the monitor to full color and observed the man walking toward the control building. He was covered in red scars and Ben had seen that color before, Maddie's eye. This man was definitely taken by the aliens.

"Maybe he's an Inject that escaped?" a person watching the screen suggested.

"Not by that walk, no way," Ben answered.

He watched the man continue his march and raise his orbitizer. A blue orb came hurtling toward the control building and met the wall. Marcus came over the radio, "The breech has begun, we're engaging." Ben knew at that moment that humans were fighting with the aliens.

"Marcus, watch out. There are humans fighting with the Trolls," Ben said. The radio keyed and there was gunfire already in the background.

"I don't give a damn, if it's shooting at us then we're shooting back," Marcus responded. Ben knew that there was a chance that the aliens would still win. He turned to one of the radio operators.

"Prepare to blow the dam." The radio operator hesitated.

"Yes sir," the words quietly came from the operator's mouth.

Marcus had shot several clips into the breech. A couple of soldiers were by his side shooting at the same rate. A boom was heard in the distance.

"Was that another breech?" one of the soldiers asked Marcus.

"I don't know," he replied as he called over his radio, "Quill, Quill, come in." There was a pause with no answer, "Quill, Quill—"

Quill answered with his raspy voice, "What do you need? I am busy here." Marcus thought he couldn't be too busy to check out the noise.

"Quill, check your area and make sure there aren't any other breeches," Marcus directed Quill.

"As soon as I am done here," Quill told him.

"Hurry and do it," Marcus was quick to reply,

Quill shook his head, "Hurry he said. He doesn't know how busy I am." He stepped over two beheaded Trolls. "You can try to grow back but I'll keep chopping you up," he said to the two Trolls as he spat on them. The head of one of the Trolls was starting to reform. The neckline started to grow. Quill stood over it and watched, "Oh, no, no, no." Quill took his blade and with one slice he severed the Troll's reforming neck. "You don't get to come back from this one." Quill grabbed the severed neck and threw it away from the Troll's body. "Quill do this, Quill do that. Now I have to check that wall." Quill ran down the hall to look for another breech.

The door that Quill guarded was left abandoned. In the opposite direction, a Troll emerged and approached the two beheaded Trolls. It touched its claw to the bodies without a response. The Troll reasoned there must be something worth investigating behind the door. It entered the door and descended the stairs. It entered the first door it came to, which led to the intake area. The Troll was met by Joel. Joel aimed his gun straight at the Troll's chest and pulled the trigger. The bullet flew into the chest of the Troll. The Troll didn't even look down as it raised its orbitizer. It shot Joel in his chest and left a huge crater. Joel didn't look down either. His body fell to the ground. The Troll saw someone else in the distance and began to fire. One shot after the other went into the walls and ceiling, knocked down lights, and put holes in the glass. The door fell off the hinge to Jay's room and jammed in place. Jay had heard the commotion and was putting on his shoes. He tried to open his door but it wouldn't budge.

The Troll continued to walk through the intake area and spotted two people in an office. Hope had been out of her room walking around the area since there was nothing else better to do. She was watching Barron as the Troll entered the level and she jumped into his office when she saw it. The Troll did not hesitate to enter the office. Seeing two humans that could be assimilated, it grabbed them both by the legs and began to drag them. Both Barron and Hope were kicking but to no avail. The Troll continued to drag them toward the exit. Dr. Snodgrass saw the Troll approaching and swung a broom at it. With Hope still in its grips, the Troll pushed the broom aside. Dr. Snodgrass stood there, mouth agape, as the Troll's claw pierced her throat and stuffed it into her windpipe. She grabbed the Troll's arm in vain. She faded and fell to the ground.

The Troll walked back up the stairs and through the door, dragging Barron and Hope behind it. Hope was yelling and Barron was still struggling. The Troll doubled back. In the meantime, Quill had killed another Troll and found the breech. He reported the finding to Marcus and returned to the door but did not notice that the Troll had passed through his area. "Quill back on station," he reported.

Jay pushed and shoved and the door finally budged enough to fit his husky body. He squeezed through the small opening and looked around. "Hope, Hope," he called out with no response. He saw Joel and Dr. Snodgrass on the floor and called for Hope again. "Hope, Hope," his yells got louder and still no response. He had no idea where she could have gone but she should have let him know she was okay by now. He looked around and thought there was only one person who could help him. He ran into the office and grabbed the keys for the Sanitarium. "Maddie, I need your help," he yelled as he ran to the door. He flung the door open and Maddie got to her feet. He begged her for help and she followed him out to the intake area. They made their way to the stairwell and up the stairs.

Jay and Maddie burst through the door. Quill turned around quickly and readied his blade for attack. Maddie screamed, "No Quill," raising her hands to show she wasn't hostile.

"What are you doing up here? We are under attack," Quill said.

"We know, where's Hope?" Jay asked. He looked down at the two beheaded Trolls thinking Quill had stopped them.

"There was no one with these things. I killed them before they had a chance to attack. And then killed them again when they tried to grow back," Quill told Jay. Jay nodded distractedly. The disappearance of Hope was tearing him apart.

"Where did she go?" Jay desperately spun around looking for any evidence of where Hope had gone. Quill knew that he hadn't seen anyone in the direction that he had run. He pointed his blade in the other direction.

"They must've gone that way," he said. Maddie saw an opportunity to grab another orbitizer. She crouched down and held it ready to fire. She looked up at Jay.

"I'm with you Jay," she said. They started to run around the corner and left the building to find Hope.

More Trolls moved through the breech that was defended by Marcus and his two soldiers. The blue orbs had been hitting the wall, taking it away bit by bit. The wall was a foot wider than it had been. Marcus looked down toward the floor and noticed that some of the orbs had hit there too. Another shot hurtled toward them and hit one of the other soldiers. He fell to the ground with his shoulder gone. His arm fell and his torso landed on it. The soldier continued to shoot at the breech and a flurry of orbs came in his direction. Orb after orb hit him and the floor. Marcus watched as the soldier disappeared in front of him and also saw the orbs remove the floor. Then he saw it. The communications center was unmasked and open below him.

Ben looked up as he heard the change in gunshot volume. "That is as far as they can go. Blow the dam and evacuate," Ben told the radio operator.

The radio operator stood up, "Blow the dam," he directed over the radio. The radio operators yanked off their headsets and made for the exit. Ben and the General were the last ones out of the communications center.

Marcus called to his team, "We're blowing the dam, make for high ground." He started to go up to the second floor. Quill heard the command. He was too far from access to the second floor, so he headed for the breech.

Maddie and Jay had just made it outside the control building. There were no Trolls in sight. Visibility was low due to the fighting and debris, so sight was not the most reliable judge. "It must've taken her back to its base," Jay told Maddie.

Maddie clutched the orbitizer and said, "We need to move. We aren't getting any closer to her standing here." They began their run along the river toward the metal wall. A figure came out of the cloud that had formed and Maddie was taken by surprise. It wasn't a Troll. It was a man with red scarring. He was holding an orbitizer. She looked at his face. She couldn't believe what she saw. It was Bryce.

Explosions inundated the dam and it began to crack. Fountains of water began to pour out until the dam gave way. With a huge crumble, the former lake above started a deluge on the flatland below. Maddie looked into Bryce's eyes as the water lifted them up and swept them away.

DAY 282
ESCAPE
CAMP PHOENIX CONTROL BUILDING

Water rushed into the building and created eddies near the openings. Ben and the General exited the first staircase and the water was already thigh deep. They made their way toward the stairs leading to the second floor but the General was swept under the water. Ben grabbed for his hand but missed it and the General continued to drift away. The General's head emerged from the water and then his body lunged toward the stairs. He extended his hand outward and yelled, "Ben!" Ben went to grab his hand again but once he made contact, a Troll jumped out of the water and tried to claw over the General to the stairs. Ben pulled out his gun and emptied the magazine directly into the Troll's head. The Troll stopped moving toward the stairs. It fell into the water but its claws were so engrained in the General that he sunk with the weight of the Troll. Ben knew that the General could not be saved. He waited for a moment just in case the General resurfaced. Silence was on the surface of the water. He sighed, trying to come to terms with the loss of the General, and hurried up the stairs.

Marcus greeted Ben as he made it to the second floor. "How many more are behind you?" Marcus asked him. Ben was short on breath.

"No one, I'm the last," he said. Ben put his hands on his knees to catch his breath. Marcus looked down the stairs and saw the water still rising.

"We need to go up to the roof," he yelled to everyone that had evacuated the lower levels. Marcus grabbed Ben under his arm and pulled him to move.

"We need to go," Marcus said with a tug. Ben, still catching his breath, followed him. The evacuees went up a ladder that led to the roof. Marcus helped Ben up the ladder just as the water began to fill the second floor. Marcus was the last one up.

Everyone had grouped away from the opening to the lower levels. Marcus reached the roof and pointed to two soldiers, "Both of you, guard the opening. Shoot anything that tries to come through there." The soldiers took position as Marcus went towards the crowd.

He approached Ben and said, "We did a good job." Ben moved his shoulder away from Marcus' reach.

"We could have done better. Look out there, any memory of the people who died is being removed. The General is gone and the camp is unusable," Ben said.

Marcus shook his head, "You don't get it. Stop being so damn hard on yourself. They didn't win and that's the best we have ever done." Ben nodded and looked over to the dam. The structure that had once held water back had turned into a waterfall. "You had to blow the dam. If you didn't then they would have got to the communications center. That would have been their endgame," Marcus continued to console Ben.

Ethen hadn't been listening but joined the conversation, "Where's the General?"

"He didn't make it," Ben replied. Ethen took a second for the news to sink in.

"What do we do now, General?" he asked Ben.

Ben hadn't thought about it but he was the second-in-command. With the General's death, that left him as the senior officer. He turned to Marcus and Ethen, "Do we stay and try to rebuild or do we go someplace else? A new camp or an existing base?"

"We rebuild here. We already have the infrastructure. It'll take work but they are more likely to attack another camp," Ethen answered.

Marcus nodded in agreement. "I agree, when the water goes down, we know how to fight the Trolls. We'll be better prepared to fight them next time," he said. Ben turned toward the flooded basin and stared at the water. He tried to look down at the tanks, the artillery, and the people. He knew he wasn't going to see them.

"That's fine. We'll start when the water goes down. But in the meantime, I think we should concentrate on food and ammo. They're the bare essentials we'll need to get through this," Ben said. Marcus and Ethen acknowledged the directive and started to create a plan immediately.

Marcus told Ethen, "You know where all of the storage areas are. I'll concentrate on getting food and you get the munitions together."

"I'll do my part. There's food stored on top of that hill. That would be the best place for you to start looking," Ethen said. Marcus was glad there was something that was easier than hunting rabbits.

"Good, we'll split everyone in half and get done what needs to be done," Marcus said.

"Agreed," Ethen said, and walked over to the crowd. It was time to divide them up.

DAY 283
HOPE IS LOST
ROAN MOUNTAIN STATE PARK

"*Human, human, wake up.*" Rho was trying to get Maddie to wake up. *Rho* knew she was alive because if she wasn't, it wouldn't be able to tell her to wake up. Maddie was lying in pine needles drenched from head to toe.

She raised her head from the muddy ground and called out, "Bryce." She fell back to the ground and thought about how she had finally found him and then lost him again.

"*He is a vessel now,*" Rho told her. She lay on the ground, muscles refusing to move.

"*How do you know? You didn't see him,*" Maddie asked.

"*Human, I did see him through your eye. Did you notice his scars? They were the color of a healed vessel,*" Rho explained,

Maddie thought in anger, "*How do you know? Those scars could be from something else.*"

"*I know that, human, but it is nothing but a vessel for the others. The human's body does not belong to the human that you knew,*" Rho thought to her with no emotion in its words.

Maddie thought back, "*Then we have to save him so he isn't a vessel anymore.*"

"*Human, once one becomes a vessel for them, it is no longer what it was. It is connected only with their leader's commands. What you remember of this vessel you call Bryce is no longer. Its brain has been replaced to serve their leader,*" Rho corrected her thought process. Maddie couldn't believe what she was hearing. There had to be something that could be done.

"*Rho, could you help me save him?*" she asked.

"*Human, I could try to change its objective but that would mean that the vessel rejected their leader for my commands. It still would not return your Bryce,*" Rho replied.

"That's a start and we can go from there," Maddie told *Rho*.

Maddie stood up and looked around. The entire area was waterlogged from the floodwaters. Neither Bryce nor Jay nor Hope was anywhere to be seen. She was cautious in her movements. If she had been swept away, then she realized that there was a possibility that a Troll could be in the area too. She had lost her orbitizer in the torrent from the dam. She had no gun and had to move quietly. Not the best recipe to find someone.

She looked for any signs that somebody was around her. She studied the flow and saw some articles on the ground. A few items were definitely human. Diving goggles were five feet in front of her. Since Jay was heavy set, she looked upstream from where she was. She spotted someone walking toward her and as she figured, it was Jay.

"Did you find Hope?" Jay called out as he made his way through the brush. Maddie touched her fingers to her lips.

"Shhhhhh, don't make too much noise, you don't know what's out here. And no, I haven't seen Hope," she said. Jay was disappointed with the news. After a few hundred feet, he joined Maddie.

"Then where do we go from here? We have no idea where they took her. We don't even know where to start looking," Jay said.

"We need to find a vessel to interface with," Rho thought to Maddie.

"I know that is our best bet," she thought to *Rho* and told Jay, "We need to start here to look for clues."

Jay and Maddie started to scan the grounds to look for anything that might lead them in the right direction. They walked in opposite directions. After a few steps, Jay asked, "Have you found anything yet?"

Maddie turned around and put her hands on her hips, "Really? I'm ten steps away from you." Jay shrugged his shoulders.

"Just askin'," he said. They both turned around and started looking again. Jay surveyed the ground. Maddie looked in bushes and piles of pine needles and leaves. Nothing of importance materialized. "Have you found anything yet?" Jay elevated his voice to ask again. Maddie kept looking through the woods for something, anything. Just one clue.

"No," she called out as the distance grew between them. Maddie kept walking and couldn't find anything. She turned around and she had lost sight of Jay. She decided to double-back to find him so they wouldn't get separated.

"Jay," she hollered under a hushed breath. "Jay," she looked around to find him. She wondered where he was. She looked into the trees. There he was, his back visible through the brush. She rushed over to him, "Jay," she tried to quietly get his attention. She moved closer and her sight was finally unobstructed by the tree. She stopped dead in her tracks. Jay was elevated with a hand clasped around his neck. He was limp, lifeless. She shifted her view to the owner of the hand. It was Bryce.

"Bryce, Bryce," she called as she started to run towards him. His hand released Jay. Jay fell to the ground as dead weight and Bryce walked briskly towards Maddie with an orbitizer in hand. She got closer and he raised his orbitizer. She saw his aim and changed her course to approach from the opposite side. The orbitizer continued its aim in her direction. She made it within arm's reach and Bryce's hand went directly for her throat. His fingers tightened around her neck and Maddie was lifted off of the ground. The nanocytes began their exchange of preliminary information and Maddie knew that it was *Rho*'s turn to talk. She listened through her thoughts.

If you have no objective, you are required to return for new tasking, Bryce told *Rho*.

I will remain without objective. I am not required to assimilate the human, Rho replied to Bryce.

Our leader, the queen mother, does not allow for your dissent. Its directive is clear. You will return for tasking.

I will not return for tasking. It is your queen mother, not mine. Rho *told Bryce.*

Bryce *gave* Rho *an ultimatum. If you will not return, then you will be made a threat no longer.*

I am not a threat. I will not return for tasking.

Then you are a threat to the queen mother and you are to be executed.

Bryce's grip tightened around Maddie's neck and she felt the burning in her jugular. Her head started to feel empty.

"*Rho, ask him if Bryce is still in there,*" Maddie begged Rho.

"*No human, you need to fight back,*" Rho replied.

Bryce's grip suddenly loosened. Maddie began to struggle and pried his hand away from her throat. She looked into the same eyes that she remembered from that ski slope so many months ago. Then she noticed blood seeping from his neck. His head started to tilt and then it was knocked off. Quill's smiling face replaced her view of Bryce.

"Take that," Quill said, and he kicked the head away from the body. Maddie managed to open Bryce's grip and his headless body fell to the ground.

She looked down at the body and the neck started to reform. It continued to grow as she watched and a jawline began to form. Quill swung down and another slice went through the same spot on the neck.

Maddie screamed out, "No, no, nooooo." She reached for the orbitizer that was on the ground next to the body. Quill ripped away the second neck and threw it behind him. Maddie grasped the orbitizer and aimed it right at Quill. Quill noticed what she was doing and jumped out of the line of fire and positioned himself behind Maddie.

He grabbed her and put his blade to her throat. "I saw it. You are one of them. If you ever try to kill me again, I will make you just like him," he said. His cold raspy words blew into Maddie's ears. She stood there, took a calming breath, and dropped the orbitizer.

"Okay," she said with an exhale. Quill released his hold on her and quickly jumped away.

"You helped me out of the hospital and this time I helped you. We're even," he said. Maddie picked up the orbitizer, careful not to point it toward Quill.

"Fine, you don't have to worry about me," she said. Quill, still apprehensive of Maddie's intentions, watched her like a hawk.

"Good, you know he had to die. He was gonna kill you. Why do you care what I did?" he asked. Maddie still had her gun pointed away from Quill.

"I knew him," she said. *Rho* entered Maddie's thought.

"I told you he was not who you thought he was."

Maddie sneered aloud, "I know."

Quill looked at her, "You know what? You hearing voices?"

Maddie deflected, "Nothing, I know nothing."

Jay was rustling on the ground trying to get his bearings. Quill readied his blade to attack. Maddie put up her hand, "Quill. No. He's okay." Quill remembered the man from the door in the control building. He walked up to Jay.

"Did you find the girl?" Quill asked, and extended his hand to offer Jay assistance in getting up.

"No, not yet," Jay said. He took the offer and Quill helped him to his feet. "Do you have any idea where to look?"

Maddie's head started to hear *Rho, "I can feel something coming. It is something from the queen mother. I can feel its beacon calling us."* Maddie was careful not to speak.

"Where? Where is it coming from?"

"Look to the sky. It is coming from the sky," Rho told her. Maddie looked up and saw a shape coming down. She pointed at the shape.

"Look," she called out. Quill and Jay turned their heads to the sky and saw the same object. Quill pointed at it with his blade and turned to Jay.

"I think that is a good place to start."

DAY 283
A NEW HORIZON
CAMP PHOENIX CONTROL BUILDING

The flood had receded substantially after the demolition of the dam, but it was still unsafe to walk through the grounds at Camp Phoenix. The remaining people from the battle moved from the roof back to the second level for shelter. Only a lookout stayed on the roof to monitor the hills and floodplain below.

Ben stood alone next to the window finishing his grieving. He stared at the rushing water below as he tried to clear his thoughts. The loss of the General wasn't the only thing that was bothering him. He wondered where Quill was, where Maddie was, where Barron was. The loss of people in battle caused distress in his heart but not as much as the loss of the people he had traveled with in the past week. The common bond they had formed was not easily broken. He felt guilty for what he assumed was their deaths but also felt more resolved to defeat the Trolls.

As luck would have it, a jon boat drifted next to the building when night came. It was an endeavor to grab it and tie it to the roof, but they succeeded after someone fell in the water. Marcus and Ethen talked about what was more important, the guns that were within sight or the food that was on the hill. After a little debate and reasoning, it was decided that Marcus would be the first to go out on the boat. To maximize the return load, he told one of the soldiers to come with him.

He selected Charles. Charles was fit and capable. He had fought alongside Marcus during the Troll attack on the control building. The boat was hanging from the roof since it had been tied up when the waters reached halfway up the second level. Marcus untied the boat and lowered it to Charles, who then lowered it to the water. The flood was waist-high as Marcus slogged through it on the ground level. Marcus grabbed the entry door and lifted himself into the boat. When he was securely seated, Charles let go and made his way to join Marcus.

Ethen stayed behind, figuring that he would wait for the boat. It was possible to walk to the storage lockers but there was no guarantee that the weaponry wasn't damaged. Also, the possibility of hauling unusable wet ordnance back to the building discouraged him further. He walked up to Ben and asked, "How are you doing?" Ben turned away from the window.

"I'm fine. Who is our best tech to get the comms back up?" Ben asked.

"Charles, but he is out with Marcus now going to the food stores. I can hold my own with electronics too," Ethen answered.

"Good, find out how we can get power back to the building and get the comms back up," Ben told Ethen.

"Roger that," Ethen said, and left Ben to himself. Ethen approached the stairs leading to the ground floor. "There's still too much water," he looked down at the flood. The water seemed stagnant. Ethen sat on the top step, "Even if I got the backup generator back online, that comms center is going to be flooded for weeks… even months." He sat and stared at the water hoping that an idea would enter his head.

Marcus cut off the engine to the jon boat and it drifted onto the hill. Charles tied it to a tree and they began their walk to the food storage. Bodies of fallen soldiers were spread along the hillside from the ambush the day earlier. They pushed to the top of the hill and had a view of the other side. It was unscathed by the deluge. The water had taken the path of least resistance which was lower grounds following the river. Charles pointed halfway down the hill, "That's one of the food storages there." Marcus acknowledged the direction and started to walk toward the food storage.

It was a shack but unlike the intricate tunnels of the outpost, it really was just a shack. They opened a creaky door and found a couple of coolers. "Really, this is what you guys did for backup?" Marcus asked Charles.

"Don't blame me. I wasn't in charge of this stuff. I just know where it is," Charles admitted. They opened one of the coolers and the rim and lid were covered with mold or some type of moss. Marcus feared for what he was going to see inside. Surprisingly, the food was vacuum sealed MRE's with the packaging unaffected by the mold.

"At least these things are good for years," Marcus said. He picked up one end of the cooler and Charles followed his lead picking up the other side. They hiked up the hill to put the cooler in the boat.

Once the cooler was placed, Marcus grabbed an MRE and opened it up. He threw another MRE to Charles, "Eat up, you're going to need your strength." Charles opened his package and grabbed the main entrée. He was happy to see it was a burger. He shoved the burger in his mouth and started to chew. His face turned sour as he started to push the burger out with his tongue.

He took the package to scrape the food off of his tongue, "Veggie burger. That tastes like crap." Marcus couldn't help but laugh. It was Charles' first MRE and it was very apparent.

After they finished with their meal, Marcus was ready to go to the next storage spot. "Let's go," he told Charles. Marcus' legs were starting to feel the burn of walking uphill. He told Charles that he wanted to take a break when they reached the top. When they made it to the top, Marcus found a stump and sat down. Charles scanned for the next shack.

Marcus wiped his brow and enjoyed the peace and quiet of the woods. It was difficult for him to remember to stop for a bit and just take a break. He looked up and saw something in the sky. "Charles, do you see that?" Marcus pointed. Charles turned to Marcus and then followed the direction of his finger. His eyes squinted as he tried to find what Marcus was seeing. Marcus stood up and went beside Charles. He put his arm in Charles' line of sight. Charles finally saw it. It was a black blot descending to the earth.

"Oh no, that can't be," Charles muttered.

"Oh, yes it is. There are more coming down. We need to get back now," Marcus said. They hurried down the hill and jumped into the jon boat. Marcus didn't waste any time starting the boat and sped back to the control building.

The boat barely squeezed through the entry door and Marcus coasted it to the stairs. He and Charles jumped out into the knee-deep water and started running upstairs. Ethen jumped up and saw it was the two returning from the food run. They didn't have anything in their hands.

"What's wrong? Where's the food?" Ethen asked as Marcus and Charles made it to the second floor.

"They're landing another bunker," Marcus said, out-of-breath.

"They're going to land on the other side of the hill," Charles said, and pointed in the direction they had come from, even though the wall was in the way.

Ethen's mind shifted. Ben had to be informed, the ammunition was still on the grounds, and screw the comms, was the order of importance in his mind. "You tell Ben. I'll go get the guns," Ethen said as he jumped down the stairs, landing in the water. He got into the boat and made way to salvage any ammo he could find.

As the sound of the boat's motor waned, Marcus and Charles went to find Ben. "They're landing another bunker," Marcus told him. Ben's head perked up as he ran to the ladder leading to the roof.

"Show me," he hollered as he climbed the ladder. Marcus and Charles hurried to the ladder and made it to the roof.

Ben was looking in the direction of the hill as Marcus jumped onto the roof. "It's right over..." Marcus didn't have to say another word. Ben had already spotted it. It was the first time that Ben had actually seen a bunker but not Marcus. "That's not a bunker," Marcus told Ben. Charles caught up with the two after emerging from the ladder.

"What do you mean, 'it's not a bunker?'" Ben asked. Charles was staring in amazement.

"That's bigger than a bunker. Way bigger than a bunker," Marcus said as he fixed his sights on the descending object as well.

"We're not safe here anymore," Ben said. "We're going to attack them before they attack us."

"Do you think that's what we should do?" Marcus asked Ben.

"We're sitting ducks here and it won't take long to figure that out. If we leave, they're just going to hunt us down anyways," Ben said.

Ben stared at the huge bunker as it descended. The bottom of the floating object became masked by the hill line. It was landing and it was right next to them.

DAY 284
FINDING HOPE
ROAN MOUNTAIN STATE PARK

The light of dawn began to paint the sky over the mountains. Jay and Maddie were fast asleep. As much as Jay wanted to find Hope, he and Maddie needed to recover from the previous night. Jay was still sore. And then there was Quill. Quill was Quill, awake and on guard for the Trolls.

Quill noticed the first light and called to the sleeping bodies, "Wake up, time to go." He nudged Jay and Maddie. Maddie sprung from her spot on the ground and Jay was slow to rise. He rubbed his eyes and realized where he was.

"We have to find Hope," he said, and he quickly got to his feet and started toward the structure that had descended from the sky. Jay called to the others, "Come on, let's get going. Hope is out there." Maddie and Quill didn't argue. Jay was on a mission and they followed.

They had been hiking mostly uphill for an hour. Jay was walking in front of Maddie and Quill was behind her. He still did not trust her. *"Human, I need your help,"* Rho talked in Maddie's thoughts.

"Can you call me Maddie? Stop barking 'Human' at me," she said.

"Fine. Maddie, I have a plan," Rho replied. Maddie was mindful of Jay and Quill. She did not want to rouse their attention by not paying attention to the walk. Especially Quill.

"What is your grand plan, Rho?" she asked, inviting Rho to divulge its scheme.

"We need to interface with the computer. We will never be safe under the queen mother's commands," Rho made its plea.

"And how are we supposed to interface with a computer?" Maddie asked.

"Not a computer, the computer," Rho corrected her, *"the computer interface can reassign objectives."*

"No, the objectives of the queen mother can't be changed. You said so yourself. You know how Bryce… I mean the vessel, reacted when you countered its objective," Maddie said.

"Yes. True. But with the computer interface, I can challenge the queen's authority," Rho said.

"And how do you think that will change anything?" Maddie asked with skepticism.

"They will have to choose whether the queen mother is better to lead than us. Some will follow it and some will join us. It is better than having to battle with every vessel we meet," Rho explained.

"How do you plan to tell the difference between our allies and the queen's?" Maddie asked.

"I do not know how this spacecraft is being used. Maybe it is like our bunkers. I was not privy to that information. That is another reason I have to interface with the computer. All of our followers will meet here after we take control of this spacecraft," Rho said.

Maddie was playing devil's advocate, "And if they come to attack?" she asked.

"Then we attack them first. If they do not disarm when they approach, then we will kill them," Rho answered.

"That's right, Rho. Even if we get into this base or whatever it is. And we interface with the computer. And we get the 'vessels' to join us. We can counter the attackers with our bare hands. I think you are going to doom us," Maddie said.

"Maddie, this base is another part of the plan to take over your planet. I promise that we will use anything in there. You must trust me that I want us to survive," Rho responded.

"If you guys don't mind, I could use some help." Hope's request announced her presence. Jay turned around and ran toward the voice. He quickly had Hope in his sights and greeted her with a big bear hug.

"I can't believe you're alive," Jay said, as a tear streaked down his face. "What happened to you?" Jay could now worry about the "how" since he knew Hope was safe.

"I touched it after it killed Dr. Snodgrass. I wanted to talk to it and then it found out I was an Inject. It told me that I was going to be assimilated. Imagine that, trying to assimilate me! It dragged me out of the building and out to the grounds. Then the flood came from the dam and we got separated. Did you find Maddie's monitor?" she asked. Maddie hadn't even thought about Barron.

"Barron was with you?" Maddie asked. Jay had not said anything about Barron being taken.

"It dragged us both out of the building. I don't know where he is. The flood saved me," Hope told her. "And I don't ever want to touch an alien again. That sucked."

"Jay, you can let me go now," Hope said as she pushed and wriggled out of Jay's hug. Maddie walked toward her.

"Rho, can we make Hope a follower?" Maddie asked *Rho*.

"Yes, that vessel is blank. It would take any directive issued," Rho replied. Maddie knew what she needed to do.

"Hope, I think we need to talk," Maddie said, and put out her hand to join with Hope's. Hope had taken off her gloves to touch the Troll, so she was barehanded. She reached for Maddie but this time...

I am speaking to the controller of the vessel. You have a new directive.

Body 1-0-0-0-0-0-0-7-7 awaiting directive.

Directive is to support Rho as queen mother.

Directive confirmed, support Rho as queen mother. What is the directive concerning the current vessel?

Maintain life functions and support vessel. Communication between the two selfs is permitted.

"Rho, let me talk to Hope," Maddie said.

"Very well Maddie, I will be your conduit." Maddie turned her thoughts to speak to Hope.

Hope, this is what you wanted. It's not boring. This is the only way that we will defeat the Trolls. If we can have them join us instead of hunting us, we could live like this without being assimilated.

Hope's hand dropped to her side. She shook for a moment and then opened her eyes. "I hear it," Hope said, her eyes wandering to the sky as she concentrated on a conversation no one else could hear. "Yes, it will follow *Rho*," Hope confirmed.

Quill readied his blade. He gritted his teeth, "Another alien." Jay positioned himself between Quill and his prospective targets.

"What just happened, Maddie? What did you do?" Jay asked.

"We are Injects, Jay. We're the ones that are going to stop the Trolls," Maddie replied. Hope smiled and looked at Jay.

"It's alright. She's right. It's what I wanted," Hope said. Jay's body eased.

"Quill, put that thing away. You're not going to do anything to my sister," Jay said. Quill pulled his makeshift belt loop and put his blade into it.

"It's not beneath me," he muttered.

"Quill, we are going to the bunker and any alien that doesn't want to join us is all yours," Maddie said.

"I don't want any of you around. You make things too complicated," Quill scowled.

"You can't tell if humans are the enemy anymore either. Stop trying to kill everything and focus on beating them," Maddie sneered back. Quill's eyes burrowed through Maddie.

"I don't know what make-believe world you are from. Killing them is beating them," Quill said, and turned away. He walked behind a tree and then he was gone.

"Jay, we're going to break into that bunker tomorrow and we're going to take it over," Maddie said.

"Sure we are," he said, and shook his head. Hope was still listening to the voice in her head, not paying attention to the conversation.

"Hope can get us in as well. We have to use the Specs. That was their mistake for putting them in us. *Rho* said–"

Jay interrupted Maddie. "Who the hell is *Rho*? Let's start with that," he asked. Maddie threw her hands into the air.

"*Rho* is the thing inside of me. The reason for my eye and the reason for my hand. It doesn't want to follow the queen mother," she answered.

"The queen mother now," Jay said. He was starting to wonder about Maddie's sanity.

"The leader of the Trolls. Do you want to hear the plan or not?" Maddie asked. She was curt with her question.

"I don't really care. I don't want Hope to get hurt. That's what I worry about," Jay said. "Look at her, she's never been like this." Maddie watched as Hope spun around and looking toward the sky but with her eyes closed.

"She's learning how to listen to it," Maddie said.

"Listen to *Rho*, I guess?" Jay asked.

"No, *Rho* is inside of me. It told whatever is inside of her to protect both of them," Maddie explained. Jay sat down next to a tree to support his weight.

"I don't think this is going to end as peachy as you are making it out to be," he said. Maddie found a spot and sat next to him.

"Maybe so, but if we do the same old crap then we can only expect the same results. They haven't been that great as of late," Maddie said.

"This is cool," Hope was back from her cloud, "it calls me *The Herald* and it says that we're going to tell everyone that the new queen is *Rho*." Jay smiled at Hope and turned to Maddie. His grin changed to a stoic face once his eyes met Maddie.

"She better not get hurt," he said.

"It doesn't matter where we are Jay, it is going to happen eventually. Whether we want it or not," Maddie replied. Maddie took her metallic finger and pointed it at Jay.

DAY 43
JAY AND HOPE
GREENSBORO, NORTH CAROLINA

The initial shock of the Attack had subsided and the places that weren't destroyed were attempting to go back to their normal routines. Jay was hanging out with his friends at a strip mall in the evening. He had brought his sister because she wanted to get something to eat but he did not want her around him. Jay and his friends went behind the restaurant out of view. A spark from a lighter flickered against the wall as they attempted to hide what they were doing from public eyes.

Hope exited the restaurant and couldn't find her brother. She looked down the walkway to see if he was standing in front of another store but there was no sign of him. "Where did he go?" she asked herself as she walked into the parking lot. She approached Jay's car and he was nowhere to be found. Hope started to wander the edge of the parking lot to look for him. She skipped onto the curb and walked on it as if it were a balancing beam. Her arms were straight out as she tried to maintain her balance. She continued her path on the curb as it ran parallel with the road.

Hope made it to an opening in the curb that drained water into a ditch. The ground was dry because it had not rained for several days. "Maybe they are over there," she said as she jumped off of the curb and headed toward trees on the other side of the ditch. She walked up to the closest tree and placed her hands on it as she went on her tiptoes. She called out to her brother, "Jay!" Her head shifted from one side of the tree to the other as she called for him.

She thought that she might have seen some movement deeper in the woods. "Jay, stop messing around." She took a step into the woods. Her foot tested the ground before she put her weight into her step. She repeated her step process as she entered deeper into the woods. "Jay!" she called out again. She definitely saw movement this time and her steps became more surefooted. She approached the movement and didn't see Jay. Something scurried on the ground and rustled through the leaves. She looked down to see what it was but she couldn't spot anything. Hope put a scowl on her face. She wondered if Jay had, yet again, abandoned her. She called out to the woods, "I'm ready to go home now." There was no reply, no movement, nothing to keep her going deeper into the wooded area. She turned around to go back to the parking lot.

Jay came out from the back of the restaurant with a smile on his face. He went into the restaurant and looked for Hope. He didn't see her in any of the booths. He went to the hostess station and knew the greeter. He asked her, "Have you seen my sister?"

"Hope left about 30 minutes ago," she told him. He put his hands up to his head and made a fist. He began to pull his hair.

"How did I lose track of time?" Jay wondered as his guilt began to overflow. He dropped his hands and ran out of the door. He ran to his car and didn't find Hope. His friends came out from behind the building. He ran up to them and begged them, "Help me find Hope, my parents are going to kill me if I don't bring her home." His friends laughed at him.

"Sounds like your problem, Bro. Not having hope is a personal problem," his friend, Paul, said. His friends, or at least the guys he thought were his friends, continued to walk to their cars. He watched them as they got in and drove out of the parking lot. As they turned onto the road, a blue orb came out of nowhere and struck the car. The car swerved off of the road and a barrage of blue orbs came out and pelted it. Jay froze and stared as the car started to disappear. The blue orbs got closer and closer. He sprinted around the building. He stopped to catch his breath and grasp what was happening. He knew the aliens had attacked other cities but he never thought it would happen in Greensboro. He looked around anxiously, "I've gotta find Hope."

As she turned, Hope bumped into something. The sun had set and she looked up. She didn't know what it was and she let out a scream. The thing grabbed her and held her for a second. Her screams continued. It didn't let go. Her scream was continuing. She frantically called to Jay. She was far enough into the woods that nobody would hear her. The figure started to move further away from the parking lot, dragging Hope behind. She tried to grab anything she could. A small branch touched her hand and she closed her fingers on it too late. She began to scream again. Her screams became shallower with every failed attempt. Her body jumped with every object it was dragged over. She couldn't do anything but subject herself to being dragged.

The blue orbs started to fly near the building. They were too close for Jay. He ran from the building at top speed trying to escape from anything that was blue. There was no way that Hope would be anywhere near those shots. He didn't care about his parent's feelings now. He ran away from the strip mall into a field. He was abandoned by his friends who were now dead and he was consumed by guilt. It was the guilt of failing Hope. The guilt of leaving her alone when there was an attack. He wished he could find her and if he did, he would never leave her again. He managed to distance himself from the blue orbs and find cover.

It was dark outside and this thing dragged her through a door. It was light enough inside the building that she could make out what it was. She had seen some weird people but this was the ugliest human that she had ever seen. It had gone crazy with the blue body paint. She tried to scream again but this time no sound came out. Her throat felt like a fire had kindled. She looked at its hands. No, it had claws. This wasn't a human at all. She knew that there were aliens in space but they were now here and they had her.

She was lifted up and landed on a table with a thud. There were two of these things holding her down and placing her in straps. Her head was strapped. Another strap was placed on her shoulders and each arm. Her hips were secured and then three straps were placed on each leg. One of the blue aliens stepped away from her. Her eyes were the only things that could move and she peered wide-eyed as she shifted to watch the aliens. A tube with red fluid was lowered from a machine above her. The other alien grabbed it and went for her arm. She was panting and struggling to move. She attempted to turn her arm but the alien claw prevented it from moving.

She felt the burn as the tube entered her arm. Unable to scream, she winced in pain as the fluid began to flow through her body. She could feel it and she couldn't stop it. Suddenly, the burning stopped and she started to feel numb. She spoke to the alien, "I'm going to die." She couldn't feel anything. She commanded her body to move. Nothing happened. She lay there and the numbness continued into drowsiness. She was being drugged. Her wide eyes would not stay opened. Hope was gone.

The morning came and the barrage of blue orbs had ceased. Jay left his hiding spot and went back to the strip mall. The façade of the building had lost all of the store signs and was peppered with craters. Holes shined through all of the glass and circular carvings filled all of the shops. There were bodies both inside the stores and in the parking lot. There was no sign of Hope anywhere. Jay went to his car and saw it was exactly like the buildings. He tried to see if it would start up. He placed the key in the ignition and nothing happened when he turned it.

He got out of his car and took one more scan of the parking lot just in case Hope showed up. His heart was heavy when she didn't appear. He began his five-mile walk home. After a little over an hour, Jay walked in front of his house. He saw the same destruction that was at the strip mall. He ran to the door and burst inside. "Mom, Dad, are you here?" he called out. He looked through all of the downstairs rooms and didn't see them. He ran upstairs, avoiding one of the steps that had disappeared from a blue orb. He searched for his parents and they weren't there either.

He went to the window and looked at the front yard. He ran to another window to look at the side yard. Nothing. Then the backyard, and he saw them. He ran down the stairs and out of the backdoor. Lying in a pool of their own blood, his parents were dead. Jay's heart weighed heavy on him as he hung his head over them. His thoughts switched to Hope. She entered his mind and she was the last person he really cared about, and she was missing. "Never again Hope, I'll find you," Jay said, and he began his search for her.

DAY 284
FIGHT OR FLIGHT
OUTSIDE CAMP PHOENIX

"We have to get moving," Ben rushed Ethen. The water had receded to the point that it could be traversed by foot. Ethen had gathered a small amount of armaments from around the camp. There were 32 survivors and each one of them was given the opportunity to leave. Having no place to go, not one person wanted to leave. Marcus made sure that everyone knew how to use their guns. Everyone was grouped at the doorway and ready to leave the camp. "Charles, you know this area the best, you lead," Ben directed his orders. Charles nodded and went through the door. Giving the area a quick scan, Charles deemed it was safe and told the others to follow him.

Marcus and Ethen were the next two out of the door, followed by everyone else. Charles led everyone directly to the hill. Marcus made it to the hill and turned around to see many of the people were not able to keep up the pace, "C'mon, move. You're in the open." Some of them picked up the pace while the less fit individuals halfheartedly lifted their legs. When the group had made it to the hill, Charles started running to the top.

"You've gotta be kiddin'," Kenny said. He was the last to reach the hill. He was a large man, tipping the scale at 300 pounds, and was already drenched in sweat.

The steeper incline caused slower movements and more separation between the fighters. Charles made it to the apex and stood there as he looked down the other side. Marcus caught up with him shortly and began to look at the same area. Charles was already amazed and Marcus found out why. In the short time since they had left this spot, it had been covered with a purple-type of moss over the foliage and ground.

"What the hell?" Charles asked in disbelief.

"That huge bunker must have done this," Marcus said. He pointed to the newly landed bunker that was at least ten times the size of the bunker where he had found Maddie.

It was difficult to see clearly through the trees, but Marcus put his binoculars to his face to examine the huge bunker that had landed a day earlier. Charles mimicked Marcus' actions. "That isn't a bunker, that's a fortress," Marcus said. Near the top of the fortress were openings that were the origination point of the flowing purple moss. Lines of purple streamed down the sides. Marcus could not see where it met the ground from his vantage point. The dense leaves hanging from the trees obstructed his view.

"I think we should get a closer view," Charles said.

"We should go down there and see what's actually happening," Marcus agreed.

Ben and the others joined Marcus and Charles while Kenny had not yet made it halfway up the hill. "We need to go down and see what we're up against," Marcus told Ben.

"You shouldn't go by yourself. You don't know what else is down there," Ben said.

"Some of these folk will slow us down. It would be best if me and Charles went by ourselves," Marcus replied. Charles nodded but Ben thought differently.

"The radio operators and the non-combats will stay here. The soldiers and I will go with you. That way, we will get plenty of eyes down there and see what's actually going on," Ben said. Marcus didn't argue. Ben was the General and he was the one giving the orders.

After separating the soldiers from the others, Charles led the way down the hill toward the fortress. Marcus, Ben, Ethen, and four others followed his lead. The rest waited for their return. Charles continued down the hill and a sweet aroma began to fill the air. "Do you smell that? Is that vanilla?" He looked behind him to make sure he wasn't imagining it. The others approached.

"Smells nice," Marcus said. They looked around to see where the smell was coming from. One of the soldiers spotted something.

"Look over there," he said. He pointed to a line of purple moss on the ground. They slowly walked over to the purple line and stopped at the edge. Marcus picked up a stick and poked the moss. The moss did not react. He poked it again.

"It's spongy," Marcus said. He withdrew the stick and the moss stayed in place. Marcus examined the end of the stick to check for residue or any remnants of moss. "I think it'll be safe to walk on."

Marcus took a tentative step onto the moss. He watched as he expected some tentacles to come out and grab his legs. Nothing happened other than his foot creating an indentation into the moss. He took a second step and his full weight was on the moss. Marcus walked in place and the moss did not react. He planted his feet and looked down, "It's definitely safe." The others took a timid initial step onto the moss with the same result. With their confidence regained, they continued to the fortress.

As they walked, the ground changed from alternating patches of moss and earth to being completely covered by moss. They were walking in a lake of purple. "What in the hell are they doing?" Ben asked as he looked up. The moss was hanging from the tree branches. What used to be the green and brown of the woods had transformed into an area of purple. Purple ground, purple trees, and purple moss hung everywhere. Marcus took moss off of a tree. He made sure that he kept it as connected as he could. He took the sheet and draped it over his head and shoulders. He looked at Ben.

"Camouflage," Marcus said. The others saw what he was doing and grabbed their own camouflage.

They appeared to be moving outlines of purple as they crept to the clearing that was made by the landing of the fortress. Charles raised his hand to tell everyone to stop. It wasn't just purple moss that was coming out of the fortress. There were Trolls too. And other blue creatures. But they weren't Trolls. The Trolls were escorting what appeared to be animals of some sorts, definitely not of this world, from the fortress. They watched as Trolls and animals came out one-by-one. Each Troll would touch its animal and then the animal would run into a different part of the woods. One after the other would follow the same process.

The next animal came out of the fortress and was led by a Troll. Ethen watched in shock as the behemoth stepped onto the moss laden ground. The animal was blue like everything else coming out of the fortress but this one looked vicious. It was taller than the Troll and about seven feet in length. Its face was long with a horn protruding from the tip. Two long teeth came from the sides of its mouth. It had long quills extending from the sides and bottom of its neck. A mane of spikes jutted out from its neck. Its body looked armored but leathery. It had been named a "Crossbearer" on its former planet. The others were watching the same animal. Instead of feet, it had blades that sunk into the ground with each step.

The Troll touched it and it began to sniff the air. With a sudden jerk, it sprinted toward the small group of soldiers. They all took cover. Most of them sheltered behind a tree and their camouflage hid them. One soldier wasn't close enough to a tree and went straight to the ground to blend in with the moss. The animal came barreling through their small clearing. Each one of the knives coming from its legs sliced into the earth without a sound. It stopped for a moment to sniff the air. It stood still as it looked around. Its feet silently came out of the ground as it moved in a circle. Something caught its attention and it focused on Ben's tree. It stared at it for a moment. Ben's heart was racing watching the animal bore its eyes in his direction. The animal stopped, stood motionless, and waited. Ben stood still, knowing his life depended on it. Marcus also stood as still as possible so as not to draw attention to him.

The animal stopped its stare at Ben's tree and turned to face deeper into the woods. The animal started running, leaving the soldiers behind. As soon as it left the area, they relaxed from their hiding and regrouped, except for the soldier on the ground. His body wasn't moving. Marcus walked to him and saw two foot-long slits on his neck and back. The animal did not notice the man but he was in a poor position. As the animal turned, its knifed-feet pierced the soldier's body like it was part of the ground. Ben saw the soldier was dead, "Is everyone else okay?" Ben looked around and did a head count. Everyone else was accounted for. Charles maintained his watch over the fortress and saw some people running toward it.

"Hey, hey, look at that," he said, and got the others' attention. Ben and Marcus looked toward the fortress. The door had closed. There were people running into their view. Two guys and two girls.

"That's Maddie. And Quill," Marcus said to Ben. Ben maintained his stare.

"I know, let's watch them and see what they do," Ben said.

The group left at the top of the hill was becoming impatient. "When are they going to come back here?" one of them asked as she paced back and forth. The sound of wheezing was approaching and getting louder. One of the men raised his gun and pointed it in the direction of the sound. Kenny eclipsed the border of the earth and the man dropped his aim.

"Geez Kenny, do you know I almost shot you?" the man asked. Kenny was still wheezing from his running.

"Thanks... for... not shooting," Kenny said. He didn't bother to find a place to sit or rest. He fell down to the ground and lay there. "I just need some time to catch my breath," Kenny said in between deep breaths.

"Don't worry about it," said the man, "we're all waiting for the others to come back." Kenny was relieved that they were going to wait.

"That's a great plan," Kenny said, and his arms fell down to his side as the rising and falling of his chest continued.

One of the blue animals approached the group. It looked like a household cat with huge ears that folded forward. Another man in the group saw it and walked up to it. He wanted to see what exactly it was. The blue kitty didn't run away. It didn't make a sound. It seemed like an innocent little kitten. The man wanted to see if it was friendly so he bent over and extended his hand to pet it. The blue kitty began to back away and the man brought his hand back to his body. The blue kitty stopped backing away when he withdrew. He took that as an invitation for another petting attempt. He leaned over and reached his hand out again.

There was silence as the man stuck out his hand. Out of the woods, the knife-footed animal ran at him and sunk its foot into his head. His body slumped immediately. The animal flicked its foot to the side and the man slid from the blade, landing on the ground. The blue kitty placed itself behind one of the animal's knives. The commotion caught the attention of the others waiting on the hill. They went for their guns to defend themselves but the knife-footed animal was quick. It ran toward the mass of people and began to slash and slice. Arms and legs and heads were severed from their bodies.

The blue kitty attacked as well. It jumped on one person's leg and distracted him long enough for the knife-footed animal to plunge its foot into his chest. Kenny lay in silence as he watched the carnage. He was so tired that he couldn't have moved if he tried. The last person standing aimed his gun and started to shoot the behemoth. A bullet hit the animal in its long neck. The quills took the shape of a cross as it immediately covered its neck and head. The man continued to shoot as the blue beast walked towards him. A click sounded from his gun as he tried to fire an empty magazine. Click, click, click.

The quills went back to their normal position and the behemoth lunged at the man sticking two of its knives into his chest. The blue kitty ran away and the behemoth stood with its knives stuck in the man. It sniffed the air again and jumped off of the man. Just as quickly as it had struck, it ran down the hill toward Camp Phoenix. Kenny watched it as it ran out of view. When he couldn't see it anymore he was filled with enough adrenaline to jump to his feet. He ran straight to the fortress in hopes of finding the other group.

"*Rho, how did you fix my eye and my hand? Everyone else has normal healing except me,*" Maddie thought to *Rho*.

"*Maddie, I healed you with what I was given. There were only red amino acids available when your eye was injured. We could only use them as a source to fix your body. As for your hand, I thought we could use a hand that was infused with the metal scraps. It was a source to make us a stronger body. Your hand should be able to absorb fire from orbitizers now, or at least most of it,*" *Rho* answered.

Maddie hadn't given it much thought until now. Her metal hand was now made from the same material that the orbitizers couldn't penetrate. She liked *Rho*'s genius with what it did for her. She picked up her hand and started to look at it. As she looked at her hand, she noticed Hope and Jay walking in front of her. "*What is happening inside of Hope?*" she asked.

"*The vessel you call Hope and her other being are learning to integrate. The other being will find where it needs to integrate and will work in harmony with the vessel,*" *Rho* explained.

Maddie watched silently as Hope and Jay talked. *Rho* continued, "*The other being has accepted us as its queen mother and will follow us. It is not as integrated as we, so I cannot tell you what will happen if the vessel attempts to reject the other being's desire to follow us as the queen mother.*"

Hope turned back and approached Maddie. Maddie quickly dropped her hand and greeted Hope, "How's everything going? Are you feeling okay?" Hope smiled.

"Thank you so much. This is so much cooler than not knowing what is inside of me," Hope said.

"Do you have conversations with each other?" Maddie asked. Hope dropped her smile.

"You can talk to each other?" Hope asked. Maddie felt bad that she had asked.

"I didn't mean to ask you—" she said. Hope's smile returned.

"I'm just kidding with you. Yes, we talk all of the time. Her name is *Kappa* and she totally understands me," Hope said.

Quill approached from behind, "Are you two plotting somethin'?" Maddie stopped and turned around.

"Why are you so worried? Do you really think we want to be like this?" Maddie asked.

"Yeah, we are the way we are and you'll have to accept that," Hope said, and she took a couple steps and turned to follow Maddie.

Quill pointed at Maddie, "You," and then pointed at Hope, "and you, it's not you I don't trust, it's what is inside of you." Quill dropped his hand and ushered Maddie and Hope in front of him. "You two walk in front of me." Maddie started to walk and Hope ran to Jay.

Jay stopped in his tracks and stared at the path in front of them. Hope caught up to him, "What is that?" She stood beside him and looked at the purple moss on the forest floor. Maddie reached the stopping point.

"Rho, what is this stuff?" she asked.

"It has to be from the old planet. This is one of the reasons that we have to get to the interface. I can't identify the substance," Rho responded. Maddie put her hands on her hips and her lips shifted to the side.

"What do you mean that you can't identify the stuff?" she asked.

"There is a massive database of the organisms from the other hosts' planet. I can gather that information if we get to the interface," Rho explained.

"More alien crap," Quill said as he saw the lines of purple in front of them. He continued to walk past the three and straight to the moss. As he walked, he removed his blade from his makeshift scabbard and starting whipping the blade to stir the moss. The back and forth motion of his blade quickened, "Alien crap, alien crap, it's all alien crap." Maddie, Hope, and Jay walked to Quill. The whipped moss was flying to Quill's left and right as he continued to create a path. One of the purple remnants landed on Maddie and she picked it off of her arm.

"Rho, do you know what this is now? I'm holding it."

"No Maddie, I cannot communicate with everything from the other hosts. It does seem benign," Rho answered. Maddie took *Rho*'s word as a cue to not walk behind Quill. She overtook him and started walking on the moss.

"It's harmless Quill, stop slicing that stuff," she said. Quill looked at her and stopped.

"You've got that alien stuff in you," he said, and he turned to Jay, "If you trust it, you go first." Hope had already started walking to Maddie and Jay followed. Jay walked onto the moss with no problem. Quill watched as Jay continued to walk toward Maddie. Jay was safely traveling and Quill gave a grunt. "Guess it's okay," he muttered.

They recommenced their walk to the alien ship. Quill stayed behind everyone as the patches of purple turned into a sea of purple. A rustle in a tree caught Quill's attention. A little sparrow fluttered its wings as it sat perched on the moss laden branch. Quill watched as it readied itself to fly. The sparrow jumped and a sudden swoop came down on it. The sparrow was in the claws of a blue monster. Its wings flapped slowly as it landed on the same branch with the sparrow in its clutches. Its small but pointed beak reached down to the sparrow and with one snip, the sparrow's head fell to ground in front of Quill.

Quill did not flinch as he held his blade up to defend himself. The monster dropped the body of the sparrow and extended its wings. Its wingspan was wider than Quill was tall. Its chest was speckled with dark blue spots. Its beak was crossbilled. Its eyes were also dark blue and fixed on Quill as it looked down.

The monster leapt from the branch and streamed toward Quill. It approached and opened its beak. As it closed the distance between them, Quill's hand tensed on his blade and in one fluid stroke he sliced at the bird. A large thud came from the monster's collision with the earth. Quill stared at it breathing slowly but deeply. Maddie turned around and saw the monster's head separated from its shaking body. Quill walked up to the headless body, "Another alien." He took his blade and sliced the regenerating neck. He watched to see if it would try to reform again. The neck started to reform but then it suddenly stopped. Blue blood oozed from the opening and the body stopped moving. Quill backed away from the monster as Hope ran up to it. She reached for the blue monster but Jay stopped her as her hand nearly touched it.

"What are you doing Jay? I want to touch it," she implored him. Jay maintained his hold on her.

"Don't touch that thing, you don't know what it is," he said as Hope wriggled in his grasp,

"*Kappa* wants me to touch it, it's an alien," she said, and tried to move her hand. "Please, please," she continued to beg.

Jay kept his hold and told her, "No."

"Fine," Hope capitulated. Her body loosened as she gave up her fight. Jay picked up Hope and turned so his body was between Hope and the monster. He released his grip.

"Don't touch it," he told her.

"Hope, if it's dead, you won't hear it," Maddie said. Hope frowned at Maddie.

"I could have found that out myself," she said. Jay stood unfazed by Hope's disappointed voice. He started walking toward the alien ship again and Hope saw her opening. She quickly moved toward the monster and placed her hand on its wing. She knelt over it waiting for a response but could not hear anything. Too late to react, Jay let Hope finish her investigation. Hope released her hand from the monster in disappointment.

"There wasn't anything, was there?" Maddie asked. Hope's head dropped.

"You were right. I just wanted to see for myself," Hope said.

Hope and *Kappa* were beginning to build a strong bond. Hope's willingness to interact with *Kappa* allowed her to act on *Kappa's* desires. *Kappa's* willingness to convert any being to *Rho's* side was openly apparent. Maddie saw that Hope and *Kappa's* relationship showed the importance of having the aliens on their side and knew that *Rho's* plan to eliminate the queen mother was a worthy endeavor.

Maddie looked around, "Where's Quill?" She scanned through the trees but could not see him anywhere.

"We're close," Quill yelled from a tree branch.

"What are you doing up there?" asked Maddie.

"I am looking for more of those flying things. Those aliens aren't going to sneak up on me. Your alien base is right over there," Quill said and pointed them in the direction of their destination. Maddie looked through the trees. It was difficult to see through all of the purple hues. She could not see the base or bunker or fortress or whatever it was. She just started to walk in the direction that Quill was pointing.

"Are you going to come down?" Maddie called up to Quill.

"Don't worry about me. I'll be behind you," he shouted back.

The path disappeared and Maddie was traversing left and right through the trees. Hope and Jay were immediately behind her. Quill was nowhere to be seen. As the number of trees began to thin, they could see the alien fortress in the distance. They stopped before entering the clearing that housed the fortress.

They watched a Troll lead the blue Crossbearer out of the fortress. *"Whenever that door closes, we need to enter," Rho* told Maddie.

"How are we going to get in there if the door is closed?" Maddie asked, confused.

"If you do your part and get us to the door then I will do my part and open it. Remember that there are things with us that only I can do," Rho

answered. Maddie did not inquire anymore about *Rho*'s plan. She would do her part and get them to the door.

The Crossbearer sprinted toward another part of the woods. The Troll that released it stood at the door and watched as it ran away. Once the beast crossed the timberline, the Troll turned to the fortress and looked into the door. Maddie was at a bad angle and could not see what the Troll was looking at.

The Troll walked up a small ramp and turned around. It looked around the surrounding area and took a step back. The door quickly closed and there was no movement in front of it. *"You need to go,"* Rho told Maddie. She started to move into the clearing.

"What are you doing?" Jay asked her.

"I'm going to the door and getting into that fortress," Maddie snapped back. Hope and Jay left their trees and followed Maddie. Nervousness took over Maddie as her slow entry into the clearing became a sprint. Hope and Jay started to run to keep up the pace. Quill exited the woods and started his sprint as well. The four were running straight for the door.

Maddie reached the ramp and looked up at the door. *"Place your hand on the pad to your left,"* Rho told her. Maddie walked up the ramp and saw the pad *Rho* mentioned. Quill had passed Hope and Jay and was on the ramp. Maddie's hand connected with the pad and the door quickly opened. Hope and Jay made it to the ramp and started to run up it. Maddie walked through the door into a dimly lit hall. Quill tightened the grip on his blade and took a step into the hall. Hope and Jay had to slow down to avoid running into him. They entered the door and Jay gasped for air after their sprint.

"Alright Rho, where do we go now?" Maddie asked in her mind.

"We must find the computer interface. I don't know where it is but I will know when we see it," Rho told her.

Maddie sighed and said, *"Nothing can be easy with you."* Maddie started to walk down the hall. Quill stood there with Hope and Jay behind him. Maddie noticed there were no other footsteps behind her and turned around.

"I don't know where we are going but staying here isn't going to beat the Trolls," Maddie said. Quill started walking toward her. Hope and Jay soon followed him toward Maddie.

"We need to find the computer interface, and before you ask, I don't know where it is," Maddie said and started to walk further down the hall.

DAY 285
TIDES TURN
FORTRESS ENTRANCE

E then jumped out of the tree line and led the charge toward the door. "What the hell is he doing?" Marcus asked as he ran out of the tree line. The rest followed him and they ran to the fortress in a straight line. Their course was unobstructed as Ethen approached the ramp. His left foot landed on the ramp followed by his right continuing his stride. The door to the fortress had been left open by Maddie and the others. Ethen broke the threshold and stopped 20 feet into the hall. He raised his gun and checked for Trolls in his sight. Marcus soon followed and then the other soldiers. Ben was the last one through the threshold and squeezed into the hall.

A blue glow formed in front of Ethen and he readied himself. Marcus saw the glow as well and raised his gun. A humming sound approached them as a blue orb hurtled through the air. Ethen jumped to the right and Marcus to the left. The soldier behind them did not react fast enough and as with most people without names in stories, he was hit by the blue orb and collapsed to the floor. "Aim for the head," Marcus hollered to the others. Bullets started to fly toward the Troll and the glow disappeared. Charles and another soldier ran up to the Troll and saw its head healing.

Charles aimed his gun at the Troll's head and fired. The head chipped away with every bullet. Once blue blood began to pour out onto the floor, Charles released his finger from the trigger. "Piece of crap," he said as he spat on the Troll.

A clicking sound on the metal floor was coming down the hall. The other soldier had his back turned to the sound because he had positioned himself on the other side of the Troll. The clicking stopped and a whistling sound was heard. The soldier turned and a spike flung through his chest. The spike opened and the line attached to it retracted. The soldier was lifted from his feet and flew down the hall.

Charles could not see because of the dim lighting. He did not know where to shoot and retreated back to Ethen and Marcus. The clicking sound started again.

"I don't know what it is," Charles told Ethen and Marcus. They looked down the hall and could not see into the darkness. The clicking sound stopped again. The whistle was flying again and the spike followed right through Charles' chest. Ethen and Marcus watched as Charles' arms flung to the side of his body. The spike opened. They grabbed Charles to prevent him from being pulled by the line attached to the spike. The line began to retract and Ben and the other soldier grabbed Charles as well. The line went taut and they held Charles in place. The clicking sound started again and Ethen saw the figure appear from the darkness. A faint outline began to form as it approached the light.

"Is that a scorpion?" The soldier saw the outline as he struggled to maintain his hold on Charles.

The figure came into the light and its blue hue was the same as the Trolls. It stood on four legs with one nail protruding from each of its feet. It did not have a head but dark blue eyes were positioned on its body. It had a tail just like a scorpion and the line attached to the spike originated from its tip. The scorpion was pulling on the line but each pull dragged it closer to its spike and Charles.

"Shoot it!" Marcus yelled to Ethen. Ethen grabbed his gun and pointed it at the blue scorpion. Shots rang out as the scorpion was hit. It tried to turn and run away but its tail prevented it from fleeing. Each shot hit the scorpion until Ethen had expended all of his bullets.

"I'm out, you shoot!" Ethen shouted to Marcus. Ethen grabbed Charles with both hands and Marcus reached for his gun. As he aimed his gun, the scorpion jumped toward them. Marcus pulled the trigger as the scorpion flew through the air. The line from its tail was still taut. Its mouth opened showing rows of sharp teeth.

The blue scorpion landed on Charles' stomach and knocked him over. Ben and the other soldier fell back with the impact. The scorpion grabbed Charles and lifted him up. The spike flew out of his chest and set back into the scorpion's tail. It turned toward Marcus and he shot it again. It reared back its tail and flung it forward. The spike shot out towards Marcus and barely missed, cutting him on his shoulder. Ben shot the scorpion several more times and it fell to the ground.

"Just die," Ben said with every shot. The blue scorpion lay on the floor.

"Ben, Ben," Marcus said as he wanted him to conserve his ammo now. "It's dead, Ben." Ben stopped shooting his gun and placed it back in its holster. He stepped on the scorpion in between its four dark blue eyes.

"I'm getting pretty tired of this crap," Ben said.

"Me too," Marcus said. He bent over Charles and grabbed his gun. "We need to take as much ammo as we can." He handed the gun to Ethen then started to pull clips from Charles' belt.

Only four of them remained. Ben said, "At this rate, none of us are going to make it down the hall." Ethen looked down the hall and shook his head.

"You know what? If that is the hardest thing we have to fight today, then we're doing just fine. We took down that Troll pretty easily," Ethen said. Ben hadn't thought about how easy it was becoming to kill the Trolls, now that they knew that they had to prevent them from regenerating.

"Yeah, you're right," he said to Ethen. Ben started to walk down the hall toward the darkness.

The hall contained areas of darkness and dim light as Ben led the way. Marcus decided that since he was the most experienced in the group, he would overtake Ben and be the lead. Ben moved to the side as Marcus tapped his shoulder and nodded that he would move to the front. After they passed a few patches of light, Marcus came to the end of the hall. A wall stood in front of him with the choice of left or right. To their left, light shone about 100 feet away. Their right was well lit and contained the blue tubes running the distance of the hall.

"Which way, Marcus?" Ben asked.

"To the right, those blue lines will lead us to the Trolls," Marcus told Ben. Marcus started to walk down the hall to the right.

"What do you think we'll find down there?" asked Ethen.

"Last time I went down something like this, I found Maddie," Marcus said as he kept his head facing forward. The scars on his back began to burn as he relived the assault on the alien bunker. Marcus led the group by following the blue lines of fluid. They reached a doorway where the blue lines entered the wall. "Do you see that?" Marcus pointed to the wall. "Last time, that line went into a room with tables and vats and Maddie," he said as he started to examine the door.

The door did not have a handle, latch, or any other type of physical opening device. He tried the pad next to the door first and nothing happened. Marcus pushed the door but it did not budge. He started tapping the sides of the door to check for a way to enter the room. All of his efforts failed and he was at a loss for ideas. "Any of you want to try?" he asked the others.

Ethen stepped up to the door, "I'll take a crack at it," he said. Marcus moved to the side to let Ethen try to open the door. He ran his hands along the flattened frame and tapped on the door just like Marcus had. He lifted his hands up in surrender and told Marcus, "Same result as you."

"Well, we can stare at this door all day or keep moving," Ben said.

"You're right. Marcus, you going to lead the way?" Ethen asked. Marcus nodded and started to walk down the hall. The others began to follow and then the door that they had attempted to enter quickly slid open. Marcus, Ben, and Ethen hastily turned around and aimed their guns at the door. The soldier following them faced the door. Several blue rodents rushed toward the man.

"Rats!" he screamed and began to shoot his gun. They approached his legs and he began to high step. With each landing of his foot, he crushed rodent after rodent. The rodents began to pile and each step landed on the mix of flesh and blood rather than the floor. He lost his footing and fell to the floor. The blue rodents began to enter his clothing and he screamed in pain. There were no more live rodents on the floor as they had all entered the soldier's clothing. He grabbed at his shirt and his pants in vain. His body started to spasm and then stopped.

Marcus realized that in his shock, he was watching more than acting and he ran to the soldier. He grabbed the soldier's foot but the rodents ran out of the pants leg every time the foot moved. With his eyes half-shut, the soldier opened his mouth. Marcus shifted to his head to listen. As Marcus bent over the man, a blood-covered blue rodent climbed out of the soldier's mouth. Another rodent exited and then another.

Marcus jumped back to avoid the onslaught of rodents and took his lighter out of his pocket. Before any more rodents left the soldier, he bent over and flicked the lighter. He quickly touched the flame to the soldier, starting with his hair and moving to his shirt. The fire took and the flame started to build. Marcus jumped back again to avoid the flames and the rodents. A few rodents chased him but he squashed them before they could attack him. Squeals emitted from the rodents as the soldier became engulfed in flames. The rodents that fled from the fire were still ablaze and Marcus, Ethen, and Ben stepped on them as they tried to escape.

With the rodents either dispersed or dead, Marcus took a deep breath, shook off the disgust he felt at what he had just witnessed, and walked through the doorway. The room was nothing like he remembered from the bunker. There were no tables and there was no blood. There were blue vats like the ones from the bunker but these were much larger. Ethen walked around the vats seeing that they were empty. Ben cautiously went through another row and saw some creatures still in their vats. "Look at this," he called to the other two. Marcus and Ethen followed the sound of his voice and met him in front of a filled blue vat.

"That thing is ugly," Ethen said as he examined the blue creature residing in the vat. It looked like a hybrid between a catfish and a beetle. It had a defined head and tail like a fish but its body was sectioned by armor. Small legs protruded from its underbelly. It looked like an aquatic creature. He leaned over to get a closer look and the creature lunged towards him but was stopped by the glass. The creature's mouth opened against the glass and sharp teeth extended from it. It was rabidly trying to bite Ethen. Ethen fell backwards as the sudden movement startled him. Marcus grabbed his arm to prevent him from falling to the ground.

"I don't think it's too much of a threat," Marcus noted, "but we need to kill it before the Trolls release it."

"Yes we do. How many vats do you think are in here? How many creatures do you think that they released?" Ben asked. Marcus shrugged his shoulders.

"I don't know. There are hundreds in here and most are empty," Marcus said.

"If most of these vats are empty then everything that was in them is now released out there," Ben replied. Ethen shuddered at the thought of how many different creatures were running in the wild.

"Still, how are we going to kill this one?" Ethen asked.

"I guess we break the glass," Ben said.

"That's what I was thinking," Marcus said as he raised his gun. "You guys might want to take a step back." Ben and Ethen walked in between the vats behind Marcus. Marcus aimed and pulled the trigger. A large gunshot resonated through the room as the bullet hit the vat. The bullet did not penetrate the glass but it did cause it to crack. The crack was growing slowly as Marcus joined Ethen and Ben behind the empty vats.

The vat continued to crack until it burst. The floor was flooded with the blue liquid and the beetle catfish gushed out with the fluid. It was two-feet long and flopped around on the floor. It righted itself as it landed on its little legs. This one did not attack the three men after it noticed them. It simply changed its path to travel unabated. "Talk about things that I didn't expect," said Ethen as the creature walked away from them.

A shot rang out and a bullet struck the creature. It stopped and turned around toward the shot. Ben lowered his gun and the creature scurried towards him. Marcus shot it as it walked in front of him and Ethen joined the barrage. The creature slowed down but was still trying to reach Ben. Ethen took a few steps and hovered over it. He unleashed a fury of bullets into the creature until it stopped moving. Then he crushed it with the heel of his boot. "I knew you were going to do that," Ethen reprimanded the creature as he stomped one last time.

"Let's see if we can find anything else. And while we're at it, let's try to conserve our ammo. We don't have an infinite supply," Ben said, directing his voice to Ethen. The three men explored the rest of the room. There were only a couple of creatures left, no larger than the rodents. They handled the small aliens with no problems. Near the back of the room, Ethen noticed another doorway. This doorway led to an ascending stairwell.

"Hey guys, I think I found where we need to go next," Ethen called out. Marcus and Ben were close by and met Ethen within seconds.

Marcus looked up the stairwell and said, "Now we enter the world of the unknown."

Ben looked up the stairwell and said, "Yep." He started to walk up the exceptionally large steps designed to accommodate the Trolls.

RHO'S TURN
FORTRESS CHAMBERS

"**W**hich way do we go?" Maddie asked *Rho* as they came to the end of the hall.

"*I do not know the structure, that is another reason that we need to find the interface,*" *Rho* replied. Maddie looked to her left and then to her right. Hope, Jay and Quill were standing behind her. She saw some movement down the right hall then she looked to the left. "I think this is a good way to go. There are probably Trolls down the other way," Maddie said as she clutched her orbitizer.

"You don't want to kill the aliens Maddie?" Quill asked in his raspy voice.

"No, I want to avoid them and get to the computer interface," she answered Quill.

Maddie started to walk down the hall to her left and hastened her pace as she thought of a Troll coming from the other hall. The others were right behind with Quill continuing to bring up the back. The hall was dark for the first stretch until they came to a corner lit by a blue bulb. Maddie looked at the blue fluid flowing through the fixture. There was only one way to go. Maddie turned right and went down another dark corridor. She led the others to another blue bulb with a door across from it.

"*Should we go in here?*" she asked *Rho*.

"*Yes, we might find the computer interface in here,*" *Rho* told her. Maddie placed her hand on the pad next to the door. The door slid into the wall and she peered inside.

Seeing the room was unoccupied, Maddie took her first step into the space. The area was well lit and she lowered her orbitizer because there was nothing hostile in the decent sized space. It appeared to be a lounge of some sorts. There were oversized booths and a bar with tall stools. The room hadn't been used in quite some time as seen by the thick layer of dust on the top of the bar.

"*We need to find where the computer interface is. Touch everything and see if we can get its location,*" Rho told Maddie. Maddie thought that *Rho* was being too pushy about this interface.

"*Rho, we will get to the interface. Are you planning something that you're not letting me know?*" Maddie asked

Rho quickly replied, "*Maddie, I have told you what we need to do and our intentions are the same. That is, to survive.*" Maddie felt a little more guarded since *Rho* did not fully answer her question. *Rho* sensed her apprehension.

"*Maddie, if we do not reduce the queen mother's army by something other than face-to-face combat then we are doomed,*" Rho said. Maddie figured that she didn't have any better choices. She decided that *Rho* was still worth trusting. If she died, *Rho* would die with her.

Maddie started to look around the lounge for anything to touch or help *Rho* find the computer interface. Hope watched as Maddie placed her hands on everything and decided to do the same. As Maddie slowly walked by the booths, she touched the back of the chairs, then the tables, then the chairs on the other side, and then the separator between the booths. She waited for *Rho* to respond each time she touched something. "*That isn't something we can use,*" Rho would tell her with one item after another. Hope did the same thing at the bar. She watched Maddie. Mirroring Maddie's actions, she touched a stool and waited. When Maddie moved to the next piece of the booths, Hope moved to another stool. Hope didn't know what she was trying to find but mimicked Maddie anyway. Jay and Quill stood just inside the doorway. Jay was watching Hope walk in front of the bar as Quill kept a vigilant watch of the hall.

Maddie made her way to the end of the booths with no success. Hope walked to the end of the bar and did not get any reaction from the stools that she was touching. Maddie walked to the center of the lounge, "Nothing over there." Her lips shifted to the side and her nose crinkled as a look of consternation displayed on her face.

Jay saw Maddie's face but his gaze soon shifted to Hope, who was climbing over the bar. There were dust-covered dark steins sitting under the lip of the bar. She wiped her hands on her jeans after touching each stein. "Gross," she called out each time she retracted her hand from a glass.

Hope slid off of the bar and onto the preparation area. The black rock of the bar top glistened as her clothes wiped away the remnants of dust from its center. She jumped down to the floor. Jay walked over and went through the side entry to the bar. He stood next to Hope, "There was an easier way to get here, ya know?" Hope squinted at the three cabinet doors running along the bottom of the bar.

"But not as fun," she told him as she bent over to open the cabinets.

She opened every cabinet, one by one. The first cabinet contained more steins cradled in the shelving. Not happy with her first selection, she slowly opened the second cabinet anticipating something worth seeing and there was nothing. Disappointed, she swung the third cabinet door open and saw something that seemed out of place. She bent over to pick it up and when she touched it, she froze. "Hope, Hope," Jay nudged her to get her attention. Hope didn't react. "Hope, stop messing around." Jay straightened Hope from her hunched over position and her body reacted to his adjustments like a poseable doll.

Hope's eyes were sealed shut as she held a small glowing tube in her clutches. Jay transferred his grasp from her torso to her hands and began to peel away her fingers. Maddie rushed in to help as Jay loosened Hope's grip on the tube. Maddie grabbed the tube and froze just like Hope.

An image filled her mind as her hand connected with the tube. The image looked like a Troll but it was a light brown color with a smaller nose and the lower lip was in a normal position. Maddie thought that this had to be one of the aliens. Then a voice entered her mind:

I am Theta. Welcome to our new world. This is one of the many Introduction Transfers that I have designed to assist you in your new life. You have been injected with specially designed nanocytes that will heal you as your body decays through time. As a cell dies in your body, the nanocyte will locate it and assume its function.

Why can you hear this? The nanocytes, of course. Not only are they designed to heal dead cells but they are also used to communicate with your fellow Syrsyrians and the electronics that were made before we escaped, like the ones on board this craft. You are filled with a finite amount of nanocytes. As each one is used, it will not be replaced. That is why it is very important for you to recharge or consume more of the amino bath that you have been resting in all these years.

Well, my fellow Syrsyrian, welcome to our new world and I hope that you enjoy life as it was meant to be.

Images of an alien world flashed in Maddie's mind and then stopped.

Maddie slowly opened her eyes and saw Jay holding the tube. Hope, still reeling from her experience, asked Maddie, "Did you see that?" Maddie put her metallic hand behind her head and scratched it.

"Yeah, I saw it," she said. Jay wasn't seeing anything.

"Okay, I'll play your game. What was it?" he asked. Hope stood up on her own.

"It was really cool. This alien guy said that we are filled with nanocytes and that is why we can heal ourselves," she said as she faced Jay. "And then I saw pictures of some strange places."

Maddie added, "They were images of the alien planet." Jay held the tube up to his face expecting something to happen.

"You're not going to see anything, you doof," Hope told him, "you have to have the nanocytes in you." Jay grimaced and put the tube on the bar.

"Something's coming," Quill shouted in a hushed whisper. Maddie, Hope, and Jay all looked toward Quill. He was waving to come toward the wall in order to be less exposed. They rushed to the wall and Maddie took position behind Quill while Hope and Jay stood on the opposite side of the doorway.

"Maddie, don't let the crazy one kill it. We need allies. Hope and Kappa can ask it to join us first," Rho told Maddie. Maddie looked over toward Hope and Hope returned a glance. Maddie nodded and Hope nodded back. Hope understood that it was her time to do the same as Maddie had done to her.

"Now don't go killing it when you see it," Maddie whispered to Quill.

"And let it kill me first? I don't think so," Quill shot back and Maddie rolled her eyes.

"Do you want to fight every one of these things by yourself or do you want help?" she asked. Quill pondered killing all of the Trolls himself, but realized that having someone to do it with would be much more enjoyable.

"Fine, but don't think that I won't kill it if it tries to attack me," Quill informed Maddie.

They waited by the door as the slow footsteps grew louder. Quill had his blade ready to slice anything that showed its face, or any other body part. Hope was also ready. Her hand was by her side while she rolled her fingers, prepared to touch anything that came close. The footsteps stopped in front of the door. Hope was ready to lunge. One more footstep landed and Hope saw her chance. One leg had entered the doorway. She curled her lips at the sight of the disgusting appendage but didn't let her disgust stop her and she jumped.

She grabbed the Troll's leg. It stopped walking and Hope maintained her grasp. There was a transaction in process between Hope and the Troll but it did not stop Quill from worrying. The Troll was standing in front of him. "It would be so easy right now," Quill said as he raised his blade next to the Troll's head. "It would be so easy to just get rid of you," he turned his blade, reflecting the light from the lounge.

"Stop it Quill. Let Hope do this," Maddie whispered. Quill huffed and lowered his blade but kept a tight grip on the hilt.

Hope let go of the Troll's leg. She came to her feet and the Troll just stood there. Quill was still ready to strike at the slightest movement. "It wants to speak with *Rho*," Hope said as she straightened herself out.

"*Let's introduce Rho,*" Maddie said, and let *Rho* know to prepare itself. She walked around Quill to the Troll, putting herself between the two. She extended her hand and touched the Troll.

I am Rho.

Another voice entered Maddie's head.

Rho, the queen mother has given the directives that most have followed. You might think that we are all drones incapable of making our own choices but you are sadly mistaken. Not all of us have consumed our vessels without remorse. Their memories are no longer theirs but they are not forgotten.

Maddie listened to *Rho's* reply.

Being, the queen mother attacks without remorse and smothers any type of individuality. If the queen mother continues with the current directives, we will all perish. We will no longer have a sense of self. We could have easily lived side-by-side with the humans but the queen mother decided to eliminate them. Why would the queen mother think any differently about us, as individuals?

The other voice responded without hesitation.

Maybe you misunderstand me. I am going to join you against the queen mother. But I am not doing it to help you. I am doing it for me. I want you to understand that we do not mindlessly follow the queen mother. Given no other options, the queen mother's lead is all we have. Rather than telling others to fight against it, perhaps the strategy would be to join you in order to have a life similar to the vessels before they were assimilated by the queen mother.

Rho responded.

Very well, I have considered your advice and with this new information, it is valid. I must find the computer interface to convince others to join us.

The other voice was quick to reply.

Follow me and I will lead you to where you want to go.

Maddie's hand released the Troll and she immediately turned to Quill. "He is going to help us," she said as she pushed her open hand toward his blade. Quill lowered the weapon as the Troll turned around.

"How do you know that he is not setting us up?" Quill asked.

"How do you know he is not going to help us?" Maddie snapped back. She told Quill, "You can either stay here and do nothing or you can follow it to where we need to go. Either way, Quill, I don't care what you do. I've had enough of this 'everything is going to kill me' mentality of yours." Maddie turned around and walked out of the door. Hope and Jay were already following the Troll. Quill stood in place to think about what Maddie had said.

"I am always ready for something to go wrong," he muttered as he followed them out of the door.

B en saw a door as he walked up to the next level. The door was open and inviting. He signaled to Marcus and Ethen to slow down and be cautious. Ben approached the door slowly. He peeked through the entryway and looked to the left and then to the right. The room was empty. The room was very empty. The walls were the same as the rest of the fortress, plated metal stacked from floor to ceiling. There were no objects in the room except two poles that extended from the ground.

Ben entered the room with his gun at the ready. Marcus was quick to follow and Ethen maintained a watch on the door that they had entered. Ben tactically moved toward the poles and inspected them. They were comprised of the same metal as the walls and contained the same blue fluid-filled tubes that they had noticed on the walls before. "I wonder where this leads?" Ben asked Marcus as he waved for him to come look at the poles.

Marcus walked over to Ben and looked at the rods coming up from the floor. He ran his fingers along the blue lines, "It's the same tubing that we saw in the hall. But I don't think this room is the same as the last one." Ben looked at the other pole. His thoughts were the same as Marcus'.

"Do you think there is another area where they are growing more creatures?" Ben asked Marcus.

"Perhaps, I think we should go check," Marcus replied.

Ben looked around and saw another door opposite to where Ethen was standing. Ben pointed to the door, "That looks like a good place to start," he called to the stairwell, "Ethen, we're moving on."

Ethen dropped his guard and started to move toward the other door. He joined Marcus and Ben as the three approached the door. It slid open and they all raised their guns.

"Troll!" shouted Ethen and he began to unleash bullets into the blue being. Seeing the Troll, Marcus and Ben shot without hesitation. The bullets penetrated the Troll's body and head as it started to slump to the floor. As the Troll collapsed, Jay and Hope saw the firing men and ducked for cover.

"Stop it, stop it, stop it," Hope called out, "stop it!" It took little time for Maddie to jump in front of the Troll to shield it from the fire.

"Hold fire!" Marcus dropped his aim and placed his hand in front of Ben and Ethen's view to get them to stop.

Once the firing line stopped the barrage, Maddie sped to the Troll's side. She placed her hand on the Troll. *Rho* communicated.

Declare the status of your being.

The Troll's voice came back.

Unable to heal self. Unable to continue life functions. Remember, we were made from one but we are not the same.

The Troll went silent and limp. Maddie let go of it and turned to Ben. "He was with us," she hollered at him, "he was helping us." Ben put up his hands in disbelief.

"When I'm walking and I see an alien, I'm not going to ask if it's my friend. Since they all attack, I think it was the right thing to do," Ben said. Hope went over to the Troll as Jay followed her.

Maddie told Ben, "Things have changed, there are Trolls who are going to join us. Not all of them want to kill us. They just didn't think there was any other option."

Ben looked down at Hope and the Troll, "How are we supposed to know the difference? They all look the same. Big blue aliens. I'm not asking for an I.D., if that is what you're trying to say."

Quill came into the room overhearing the conversation, "That's what I say, better safe than dead."

Maddie watched Quill walk toward Ben and said, "Even Quill didn't attack the Troll and he tries to kill everything." She faced Ben, "Then how will you ever know how to tell the difference between the Trolls?"

"The same way we tell the difference between two armies. They need an identifier, a uniform, something to mark them as on our side," Marcus said.

"That's assuming that any more of those things are going to fight with us," Ethen interjected.

Tears started to well up in Hope's eyes. "The first alien to join us and it didn't even last 15 minutes. It was kind when we talked to each other," Hope recalled asking it to fight against the queen mother in the lounge. She turned to Jay and buried her head in his shoulder. She let out her tears and muffled cries as he comforted her.

"Now that we have that out of the way, what are you all doing here?" Ben asked Maddie and Quill.

Quill was faster to respond, "Crazy girl here," he stuck out his thumb and pointed to Maddie, "wanted to follow that thing to this place." Ben turned his question to Maddie.

"And why was it bringing you here?"

Maddie looked around the barren room. Her gaze went past the two poles protruding from the floor. *"That's the interface,"* Rho told her. Her eyes fixated back on the poles.

"That is why we came here," Maddie said as she raised her hand and pointed at the poles. Ben, Marcus, and Ethen turned around to look at the rods.

Marcus said, "Those things? They lead to more of these monsters that the Trolls are releasing. We have to find them and get rid of them before they release more."

Maddie shook her head, "From what I have found out, those poles don't lead to more creatures. They are the interface to the other Trolls. A way of speaking to them."

"And how do you know that?" Marcus asked in disbelief.

"Because they are in my head," Maddie lifted her finger to her temple. "It has been talking to me since we were at Camp Phoenix. Its name is *Rho* and this is what we have been trying to find."

"So you're following a voice in your head?" Marcus asked.

Hope had cleared the tears from her eyes. "It's more than a voice in our heads," she said. Ben remembered Hope and Jay from when they arrived at Camp Phoenix.

"So both of you have voices in your heads?" he asked Hope.

"I just said that it's more than that," Hope scowled.

Maddie interrupted Hope, "These things inside of us, they heal us, they allow us to communicate with the Trolls. They are also a part of us and talk to us."

"And some of them want to help us but we have to tell them that we need help," Hope added.

"So you both have this inside of you," Ben turned to Jay, "and you're quiet, do you have the same thing?" Ben asked.

Jay said, "No, I'm here for my sister." He looked at Hope and then back at Ben.

"Okay, assuming that they're not all bad and trying to kill us, why should we believe that going to those poles is going to make things better? For all we know, it's another way to kill us," Ben tried to make sense of what he was being told.

Maddie answered, "I don't know. All I can say is that the thing inside of me, inside of us, wants to live. It doesn't want to be subject to the queen mother."

Ethen thought Maddie's story was farfetched, "So now there's a queen?! What other surprises are there? A big, giant ant pile landed on us and we're supposed to think that everything is going to be okay... because you say so."

Maddie was frustrated, "I'm not making this up. I'm telling you all that I know." She sighed and then asked, "Do you think I would be here if I didn't think there was a chance to make things better?"

Marcus stepped in, "I think there's a lot going on that we don't know. Quill, what do you think? You've been with them." Quill looked at Marcus with his dark sunken eyes.

"There is some truth to what she says. That alien could have tried to attack but the other girl was able to talk to it," he said.

Ben was listening and processing the entire conversation. Since he was the General, he knew it was his obligation to direct the course of action. "All I have seen is that we are going to keep fighting until we run out of ammunition. The aliens are hard enough to fight without these new creatures that they have unleashed on us. Maddie, if you need to go to those poles, then we are not going to stop you."

Maddie looked at Ben, thankful that he was allowing her to go to the interface. She said, "Thank you," and walked between Marcus and Ben toward the two poles.

She positioned herself equidistant between the poles. *"Rho, are you ready to do this?"* Maddie thought to *Rho.*

"I am ready to challenge the queen mother and draw people to our side. Maddie, do not doubt us. We will survive."

Maddie spread her feet to shoulder width. She wiped her hands on the sides of her pants. Ben, Marcus, Ethen, Quill, Jay, and Hope all stood in a line behind her, watching. Maddie closed her eyes and took a deep breath. Her arms raised and went forward. She clasped the poles with her hands and felt a surge of information enter her head.

The others watched as a huge map of the Earth projected on the wall in front of them. The map filled with red overlying most of the continents displayed as the Earth slowly rotated. Ethen asked, "Do you think that's alien territory?" Ben looked over toward North America. He saw red over the largest cities.

"It has to be and it doesn't look good for us," Ben said as he continued to stare at the map.

The information was still flowing through Maddie's head. Then, it suddenly stopped. *Rho* had something to say and Maddie heard it.

Queen mother, I am Rho. I challenge you and your authority as the queen mother.

PART FOUR:
SUBVERSION

DAY 285
THE REGAL RESPONSE
INTERFACE CHAMBER

Those little words were followed by silence. *Rho's* plan to change the directives, Maddie thought, was going to be left unchallenged. But her thoughts were proven wrong when Omega's voice boomed in Maddie's head.

> *I will not be challenged by anything. Especially by something that has been sentient for a short time, such as you.*

The queen mother continued to scold *Rho*.

> *Body 1-0-0-0-0-0-0-0-4, you have failed to follow your directives. I see you are with other humans. This is not in your directive. I command you to follow what you have been instructed. My will is the will of us all.*

Rho knew that the queen mother could see them. It was not going to listen to its demands.

> *I am not Body 1-0-0-0-0-0-0-0-4, I am Rho. I am your equal, if not greater. You do not speak for the will of us all and I will not follow your directives. You intend to kill my host and me with it. Therefore, I am calling to the other beings and ask them to join me as individuals. To live as the hosts had intended to live on this new planet.*

The queen mother decided that it had heard enough from *Rho*. An alarm sounded in the room. An unintelligible voice could be heard in between the sounding siren. Marcus grabbed Ben and Ethen, "This place is going to blow!" He remembered chaos at the bunker and the urgency to evacuate the building filled his body. Marcus held his grip as he started to run for the stairwell. "We have to go!" he yelled. He let his grasp slip as he made way for the stairwell. He made it to the door and looked back, "Come on, come on," he tried to usher the others to the stairs.

Maddie was still holding on to the interface. The words, *Auto-Destruction sequence has been activated. Thirty seconds until detonation,* streamed through her head.

"Rho, you have to stop the auto-destruct. We won't survive it," Maddie told *Rho.*

The alarm and the voice suddenly stopped. Marcus was at the top of the stairwell. "This is it." He fell down to the floor and covered his head. The others slid to a stop and mimicked Marcus. He tensed his body as he prepared for the explosion.

"I have disabled the auto-destruct, Maddie. Now we can focus on the interface. Tell our allies that we are safe."

Maddie's eyes were closed as she announced from the interface, "*Rho* turned the auto-destruct off, we are all safe." Marcus eased his body. The scars on his back felt the burn of the release. Ben got to his feet and went back to watching the map. The others were slower to rise and took the time to dust themselves off. They walked over and took their places next to Ben, all except for Marcus.

Marcus lay on the floor, his slow breathing feeling cool on his arms. He felt lucky. He didn't die, again. He collected himself and made it to his feet. His back was burning and he reached into his pocket for his painkillers. There was nothing there. He patted both of his front pockets, then his back pockets, then his side pockets on his legs. "Crap, where did they go?" he asked but nobody was around. He searched the floor as his back burned and he couldn't find his container. His choice was either to go back down to the room with the creatures or just live with it.

Marcus decided to stay. Each step caused the burn to intensify but he wasn't going to let it stop him. He shuffled his feet across the floor with each labored step. He winced as he took his place next to Ben. Ben was staring at the map and was too busy to notice that Marcus was having difficulty.

Rho told the queen mother.

> *You will not be able to destroy us that easily. It will take more than a simple command.*

The stern voice of the queen mother entered Maddie's head.

> *I will come down on you with a force you can never imagine. I know where you are and I will destroy you.*

A message from the queen mother came over the sound system that had sounded the alarm. It spoke in plain English, *"Humans, if you follow this being then you will die."*

Quill turned around in place scanning the entire room with his blade at the ready. He was trying to find the source of the voice. "Who was that?" he called out, looking for his potential attacker. Marcus and Ethen joined Quill in scanning the room as Ben maintained his focus.

Hope walked to position herself behind Maddie. Jay followed Hope, keeping his vigilance to the possibility of being attacked. Hope reached for Maddie and touched her. *"Kappa and I are here with you,"* Hope entered the conversation in Maddie's head. Maddie continued her hold on the interface poles.

> *What is this?* The queen mother spoke through the interface. *You already have others with you? You are more dangerous than I gave you credit for.*

The interface terminated and the feeling of the information flow ceased in Maddie's head. The map still displayed on the wall as Maddie let go of the two vertical poles. Her brow was dripping with sweat. She used her forearm to wipe the sweat away from her forehead. "Hope, you shouldn't have done that," she told Hope.

"I thought I was helping you. It looked like you needed me," Hope told Maddie. "What happened? Did I do something wrong?" she asked Maddie.

Before she answered Hope, Maddie asked *Rho*, *"Did we do what we needed to do?"*

"Yes, we modified the directive with a choice to join us. Unfortunately, we cannot see if the modification has been changed. This facility is no longer connected to the network interface infrastructure," *Rho* made Maddie aware.

"No, Hope, just don't do that again. The queen mother disabled the network once it found out that you were an Inject too," Maddie explained to Hope. She motioned for Hope to follow her and went to Ben.

"There's nothing here," Marcus said as he eased down his weapon. Quill and Ethen followed suit and stood down from their alert. Marcus noticed that the others were circling around Ben. "You guys want to see what's going on?" he asked Ethen and Quill.

"You guys go ahead," Quill answered. Ethen was relieved that they weren't under attack and walked over to Ben. Quill was still breathing heavy. He continued to scan the walls, consistently returning his focus to the stairwell. After keeping his focus on his search pattern, he decided to sit down facing the doorway where they had entered the room.

Ben stared intently at the map. "It's not going to update. This is the best you are going to get," Maddie said.

"Ask your friend how accurate this map is and can we see this area?" Ben asked as he pointed toward a spot on the map.

Maddie turned around to face the map. She hadn't paid attention to the map while she and *Rho* were using the interface. The map showed red in places where humans were no longer fighting against the Trolls. The entirety of Europe was red. India and the Eastern part of China were also red. Africa was pockmarked with red and South America was painted with the same color except for the Amazon basin. Maddie walked up to the two poles and placed her hands on them once again. *"Rho, we need to zoom in on North America. It's where we are,"* Maddie thought to *Rho*.

The map shifted and centered on North America, then zoomed in to the eastern portion of the continent. The red areas became more defined. New England was completely red. The redness on the map went away the more rural the areas became. The map zoomed in closer to Tennessee. Washington, Richmond, Norfolk, Raleigh, Charlotte, Knoxville, and Nashville were all red. Charlottesville was also covered in red. The surrounding areas were either without color or red. *"The red areas indicate where there is no human resistance to the conquest,"* Rho explained to Maddie.

"That's where I need it," Ben told Maddie then asked, "Can your friend bring up where the alien bunkers are located?" Yellow and green dots popped onto the map. Many yellow dots surrounded a lesser number of green dots. "So the yellow dots indicate the bunkers and the green dots must indicate these fortresses," Ben said so everyone could hear him. "There are eight bunkers within 25 miles of us," he was thinking aloud. Ben took his eyes away from the map and told Maddie, "I think it's about time that me, you, and your friend have a discussion." Maddie's hands came off of the poles. She turned towards Ben eager to find out what he was thinking.

"We are ready whenever you want," she said.

"I will give you all of the answers Maddie. You don't have to ask me everything he asks. I can hear whatever you hear," Rho informed Maddie.

"What is claiming it is going to destroy us?" Ben asked.

"That was the queen mother. It knows that we are together," Maddie answered without *Rho* guiding her.

"When will it attack us?" Ben asked another question.

"We don't know. The queen mother will probably send whatever it can to eliminate us," Maddie said with *Rho*'s help.

"Now that your friend caused us to be attacked, what was the use of those two poles?" Ben pointed to the interface as he asked pointedly.

"We were asking the Trolls to help us," she told Ben. "But to help us, we had to challenge the queen mother's leadership and authority. We had to change the current directive."

"Then who is coming to our aid? Will they get here before we are attacked? It doesn't do us any good if we're dead before they get here," Ben wanted to know what resources they had.

"It's about free choice. They are free to come as they wish," Maddie answered for *Rho*.

"So when an alien walks up to us, we won't know whether it's going to kill us or join us?" Ben asked.

"It isn't anything that either you or I can control. It's better than fighting every one of them, isn't it? By the way, do you know that we are in a terraformer, not a fortress? They are trying to change the land to be like their old planet," Maddie again spoke with *Rho*'s guidance.

"Yeah, I figured that out with all of the purple crap outside. And, I can control my actions against these Trolls. So, unless I know whether they are for or against us, I can only assume that they are enemies," Ben told Maddie and then he pointed to the dead Troll. "Just like that one over there."

Maddie followed his finger to the dead Troll. She pondered a way to convince Ben that not all Trolls would be bad. *Rho* gave Maddie an idea, *"Tell him that they will not be the ones shooting at us. They will be the ones waiting outside for new directives."* Maddie turned back to Ben.

"We, me and Hope, will be outside to give the Trolls new directives and they will help us," Maddie said.

"Again, how will we know the difference between the good ones and the bad ones?" Ethen got a chance to ask his question and he wanted an answer.

"For right now, why don't we mark them?" Jay proposed as he reached into his pocket. His hand withdrew a marker that came from the laboratory at Camp Phoenix. "With this, can't we mark them some way so we can tell the difference between them?"

"That's as good an idea as any of us can come up with," Marcus let his thoughts out.

Ben looked at Marcus and nodded in agreement. "We aren't going to have much time to prepare. Maddie... you, Hope, and her brother go to the entrance of the place and watch for Trolls. Marcus, you go with them. Tactical marks on the face. Ethen, you stay here with me and we will review the map and see where the Trolls can attack us from. And Quill..." Snoring reverberated from the floor behind them. Quill lay fast asleep on the floor. He was jerking at random intervals but was hard asleep. "Quill, you stay there."

DAY 285
SUMMONING FORCES
THE ELLIPSE

Omega, the queen mother, had decided on the best course of action to rid itself of any and all opposition. Omega had to balance the need for terraforming to sustain life in the Syrsyrian bodies and the need to eradicate the human interveners. The surviving humans across the world were becoming more of a nuisance and more difficult to eliminate. Omega's sights were set on Tennessee where the usurpers and humans had overtaken a terraforming unit. After all, this was the first terraformer taken and its loss would slow down the area's growth.

Omega reviewed the current directives sent out to the deployed units. Locate and assimilate the indigenous humans. Eliminate human threats. Enable the terraforming to begin. Maintain contact with the queen mother for updated directives. Choose to be an individual and find *Rho*.

What is this? Omega was unable to control the feeling. Anger started to fill its blue body. Anger, a new feeling, a feeling that a being such as Omega shouldn't know or feel. Omega had been so focused on expanding its consciousness that it did not have time for trite feelings like anger. Omega quickly refocused the efforts to squash the anger. *How did that short-sentient change the directives?* Omega erased all the directives in North America. The other continents were going as the queen mother planned. It placed only one directive into the network that delivered the information to the bunkers nearest to the terraformer that housed *Rho* and Maddie. Find and eliminate *Rho* and its human vessel. Now every Troll nearby would abandon its tasking and search for *Rho*. There was no doubt about their directive. The terraforming would have to wait until the biggest threat against the Trolls had been eliminated.

Omega did not consider that some of the Trolls might have already known about the *Rho* directive. The first places Omega would gather forces from would be the bunkers closest to the terraformer that housed *Rho*. Omega thought that an immediate assault would be best and it would be the quickest way to rid itself of the humans.

DAY 286
WILL WANDERS
INTERFACE ROOM

"Oh no, it happened again." Will was frozen to the ground, his hands, palms down, were holding him in place. The smell of gunfire entered his nose and his eyes nervously looked around the room. The last thing he remembered was being outside of the camp and the General speaking to them about the possibility of attack by the aliens. Will pushed himself up to the sitting position and saw two men looking at a map on the wall. One man was Ben. He remembered Ben from Roanoke when he offered to take him away from the alien-infested rat hole where he was staying. The other man he did not know. He thought he remembered him from the trip but couldn't quite remember what he did or who he was.

He decided to ask them for help. "Excuse me guys, can you tell me where I am?" his meek voice asked.

"Stop messing around Quill. I'm glad you got rest but you can come over here now," Ben told him without looking back. Ethen turned around to see Will getting to his feet.

"What am I wearing?" Will asked himself. He looked down at his clothing, "This is definitely not what I was wearing when I left the hospital." Will walked up to Ben and Ethen. He observed the redness of the map. "What are you guys looking at?" Will asked.

"We're looking at the map of the Trolls. Did something happen to your brain while you were sleeping?" Ben asked.

"Not that I know of," Will responded as he scratched the back of his head.

"Quill, we really don't have time to explain this to you. Why don't you look around and explore what assets we have around here?" Ben barked.

"Well, um, okay, just so you know, I'm not Quill. I'm Will," Will told Ben but neither of the two men paid him any attention.

Will had no idea where he was or where he was supposed to go. He turned around and noticed a doorway in front of him. He approached it and noticed that there were stairs that went up and down. Will analyzed the stairwell and decided that going up would be his best option. He timidly took his first step and looked up to see if he would encounter anything. He took another step and looked up again. Each step he repeated the process until he finally made it up to the next level. He stood in front of an open door and was mesmerized by all of the color. Purple, blue, green, filled his vision as he gazed upon the flora. There were beautiful plants as far as the eye could see. It was an arboretum.

He looked down at the threshold and noticed that there was something purple at the front of the area but it did not come into the stairwell. A perfect line formed separating the inside and outside of the room. "Well, he said to check things out." Will took a step into the beautiful room. The scent of trees and grass was exactly like the forest outside Roanoke but the plants looked nothing like it. He lifted his head and took a deep breath through his nose. A grin pierced through his normally anxious disposition. Will thought this was a pleasant place.

Will walked up to a small tree. He gently touched the blue leaf sprouting from the branch. His gentle touch turned into a rub between his thumb and forefinger. His hand pulled away and some of the blue from the leaf transferred to his fingertips. He wiped his hand on his pants as he looked closely at the orange bark. The bark was scaly. He tried to pry some of it off of the tree. It wouldn't budge since the bark interlocked and was packed tight. It seemed like a harmless plant and he left it alone.

Will turned around and noticed the wall. "If I follow the wall then I can easily find my way back to the door," he said as if someone was there to listen. He walked to the wall and ran his hand against it. He looked to his left and decided it was safe. His steps were less timid now and he started walking. "How in the world did I get here?" he asked as he stayed close to the wall.

The blackouts had been excessive since the alien arrival. They used to happen when he felt a fear for his life. He thought they would have stopped by leaving the hospital but this blackout was not like the others. He had never woken up in a place he had never seen. The doctor had told him that he suffered from Dissociative Identity Disorder. He called it DID. Will knew about his alter ego Quill but had not given him much attention until now. He thought that Quill was his protector. Quill showed up when Will couldn't handle a situation when his life was on the line. Will needed to comfort himself and make sense of this new place.

Will walked past another small tree. This one was red with blue leaves. The next tree had the orange bark and the same blue leaves. He looked around and noticed that all of the trees had blue leaves. "No green," he said as he inspected the leaves. Each time his fingers came away from the leaves, he would have to wipe the blue residue from his fingertips. He repeated his inspections on every tree while walking next to the wall.

He continued his stroll until he met some underbrush. He peered through the strands to find the floor and looked for the safest way to navigate. There were no thorns, just blue leaves attached to blood red cordons. He found an open patch and stepped delicately on the ground. He looked for another place to step and found another clearing. He took his second step and his feet were pulled from under him.

Will fell face down to the ground as the cordons began to reel him away from the wall. Sliding feet-first on his belly, he struggled to turn around and see where he was being dragged. Will managed to twist his torso to face the direction his body was traveling. He wished he hadn't. A huge red plant that was equally as red as the cordons was dragging him perilously close to its base. A red trapdoor that was the mouth of the plant opened right above the ground. Will was trying to grab anything he could get his hands on. The young trees didn't leave much on the ground for him to grab. Then his hand hit upon his blade.

He went up and came down with a small thud as he was dragged over a root. The motion was enough to make the blade easy to grasp. Will grabbed the hilt and extracted the blade. He began to viciously slice anything that wasn't him around his feet. He sliced and he chopped and he cleaved. The cordons were flying outward each time he pulled his blade back to reattack.

With one last swing, he stopped three feet away from the trapdoor of the plant. The door closed in front of him and he stayed sitting in his position. He could feel his heart racing and he couldn't stand up quite yet. He looked down and saw the cordons were no longer wrapped around his feet. After a deep breath, Will stood up. The mouth was as tall as he was and perfectly masked by the trees from a distance. Black dirt was smeared in his clothes and on his skin. His forearm attempted to wipe some of the dirt away from his eyes and nose but only left a streak of black. "I think we have had enough here." Will was weak-kneed and turned to face the wall. It was a good 200-feet away. He took a step and looked back at the plant making sure that it wasn't going to try to grab him again. He took another step with no reaction from the plant and then he sprinted to the wall avoiding any possible contact with the cordons.

Once Will made it to the wall, he ran to his right toward the doorway. He passed by all of the blue-leaved trees that he had examined before. The purple moss bunched together revealing the black dirt underneath as Will slid to a stop in front of the stairwell. He regained his balance and grabbed the doorway. He pulled his body through and restarted his sprint down the stairs. As Will rushed through the door to the interface room, he screamed, "There's a killer plant in there!" His screams were met with silence and nobody was in the interface room to hear him.

"Where could they be?" Will asked himself as he spun around. Of the two doors, he didn't know which way he had come into the room. He knew that taking the stairs resulted in a terrible experience, so he decided to take the other door. He walked into a corridor that had closed doors on his left and right. Since they were closed, he didn't bother trying to go through them. "Another set of stairs?" he asked as he looked down the same way the Troll had lead him when his mind was switched to Quill. He took a deep breath as he went down the stairs, "I hope there aren't any killer plants down here." He made it down the stairs unharmed and continued down the hallway that he, Maddie, Hope, and Jay had walked through. He made it to a split and he could either go forward or to his right. Since he could see bodies on the floor if he went forward, he thought it would be better to try the path with less carnage.

He walked over a dead Troll and then around something that looked like a scorpion to meet with the door outside. He poked his head outside to see Ben and Ethen talking to Hope and Maddie, and three Trolls were behind them. He felt a blackout coming, "No, I'm not going to freak out this time." He watched as they talked and the Trolls just stood there, not attacking.

After a few minutes of watching, his curiosity took over. He walked outside and asked his fellow humans, "Are we friends with them now?"

Maddie turned to him and said, "Quill, I told you they were going to help us."

"I'm Will. Why do I have to keep telling you people?" he replied as he came closer.

"Okay, Will, they are joining us," Ethen remarked.

Will walked up to Ben while keeping his stare on the Trolls, "That's great that they joined the fight but did you know there are man-eating plants in there?" He pointed back at the terraformer.

"No, but it wouldn't surprise me," Ben answered.

"Yeah, I would have told you sooner but you left me in there... alone," Will said.

"Sorry to do that to you but we decided it would be better to be out here. Trust me, we called for you but you never came," Ben told him in order to eliminate any guilt Will was trying to put on him.

"Just please, don't leave me behind again and let me tell you about those plants," Will said, and then he explained what had happened.

The sky was painted with dark and light gray clouds covering the ground below in a cooling shade. Hope and Maddie exited the terraformer and walked down the ramp. The humidity in the air formed a film of water on their skin. Marcus and Jay were close behind.

"We're going to walk the perimeter of this place and check out what is around it," Marcus told the women. He stood in front of Jay and nodded his head for Jay to follow him.

"I want to stay with Hope," Jay said.

"They'll be fine. We should see if there's anything around here," Marcus said, keeping himself between Jay and his sister.

"Hope, if anything comes, go back inside and wait for me," Jay yelled to Hope.

"I will, Jay. I'll be fine, I'm with Maddie," Hope yelled back.

Jay resigned himself to walking with Marcus. "It's always better to travel in pairs," Marcus told Jay as they began their trek.

"I know, if we got attacked, it's better that both of us die instead of one," Jay said.

"You know, thinking the worst of a situation is only going to make you more on edge."

"Marcus, I lost her once and I don't want to lose her again. It's not like you understand."

"You're right. I only know what it's like to be talking to my wife when she died from the Attack. I wouldn't understand your point of view." Marcus' disgust with Jay's last comment flowed out. Jay heard Marcus and decided it was better to remain silent. Jay knew that any argument that he would bring up would be countered by Marcus' experience. They walked around the corner of the large metallic structure. Jay was hesitant having Hope out of his sight but continued his walk behind Marcus.

"Do you wonder where your monitor went?" Hope asked Maddie.

Maddie hadn't given Barron much thought. With meeting Bryce, finding Hope, and listening to *Rho*, she really didn't have time to think about him. Hope's question brought Barron to the forefront of her mind. "I really haven't thought about him until now," Maddie replied to Hope.

She wondered if *Rho* had any idea where Barron might have been. *Rho* was in her thoughts and told Maddie, *"There are currently 47 human vessels being assimilated in the area. I do not have any more specificity than that."* Maddie wondered if one of those vessels could have been Barron. Even though she thought he was being a jerk at the camp, he had still tried to help her whenever she was in trouble.

"We'll have to try to find him after we get done here," she told Hope. "I just hope that he's okay."

"Okay, I was just wondering if you knew," Hope said shrugging her shoulders.

Maddie and Hope watched the tree line actually hoping to see Trolls walk through. "If they come out of those woods shooting, or even aiming at us, we're going to get back into that fortress and avoid them," Maddie told Hope.

"If there is any chance that they are going to shoot at us, I bet you that I'll beat you in there," Hope said.

Just as Hope finished, a blue figure walked out of the woods. Maddie braced herself to sprint onto the ramp and grabbed Hope to get her attention. A Troll walked out and looked behind and to its sides to make sure that it wasn't going to be attacked or followed. The Troll saw the two women in front of it and proceeded toward them. It was holding its orbitizer to its side and approached them as innocently as it could. It walked in front of Maddie and extended its claw toward her. Maddie reached out and grabbed one of its talons.

I am Rho, we assume that you are here on your own accord wishing to live as an individual. Rho began the conversation. *Yes, I am here for me and others. The others will not come until they know that it is safe. The memories of my vessel still reside in me and I wish to live as you will let us, without the queen mother's directives.* The Troll passed back to Rho.

You do understand that your independent life can only happen if the queen mother is defeated? That once you fight against the queen mother, you will continue to fight until you or it are no longer? Rho asked the being.

We all understand but we also understand that you could be corralling us to kill us. The humans do not understand that we have had no other option until now and they have tried to eradicate us. The being spoke for itself and the others.

These humans understand and wish for you to join us against the queen mother. This is a logical opportunity to stop trying to dominate them and more of us will survive. Would you join us? Rho asked.

We have come here to join you and the humans. There are others that will fight against you. The forces of the queen mother will attack tonight as it is the new directive. We have decided to reject the new directive and join the humans for our own freedoms.

Very well. Have your friends come and join us. Rho invited the Trolls in hiding to come out.

Ben and Ethen walked out of the terraformer to see the Troll walking away. "Let me guess, he didn't come to attack," Ben commented.

"He wants to join and brought others. He's going to get them now. Why are you out here? Don't trust us?" Maddie asked.

"I decided that we couldn't do anything else in there. We serve the better purpose staying out here where we can see what's going on," Ben answered

Ben and Ethen walked toward Maddie as the Troll lumbered its way back to the tree line. It disappeared into the woods for a few minutes and walked back out with two Trolls behind it. Ben watched as the three Trolls exited the woods and made their way toward Maddie. The first Troll approached and moved to the side and the two new Trolls approached Maddie. They put out their claws in the same way as the first one and Maddie grabbed both of their claws at the same time. *Rho* not only invited them to join but also assured them that they were not entering into a trap and invited them to ask others to join.

Maddie released her grip as Will ran out of the terraformer rambling about a killer plant he had found while wandering through the fortress. They were calming Will when another Troll walked out of the woods. This Troll was with a human. Will stopped paying attention to the others trying to sooth his hysteria. "Isn't that someone we know?" he pointed toward the human walking toward them.

Maddie turned around to see Barron walking toward her. She began to walk toward him. The Troll and Barron stopped as she approached. *"Maddie, stop walking toward them,"* Rho told her. She stopped and stood in place. The Troll and Barron continued to walk toward her as she was not showing any signs of aggression. They walked side-by-side and stopped in front of Maddie. The Troll held out its claw and Barron extended his hand to her.

Maddie told *Rho,* *"I want to speak to Barron alone. I need you to just listen."*

She wrapped both of her hands around Barron's and a voice entered her head.

I am a new sentient in this vessel and wish to join you.

Maddie dropped her hands, releasing her contact with Barron. She stared at him. "How did this happen? You were only gone for two days," she asked as her voice softened with a sigh.

Barron spoke, "We have learned a faster way to assimilate human vessels." He pointed to a red scar on his temple and said, "With the proper insertion techniques and replacement of brain cells, a human vessel can be assimilated in a few hours."

Maddie's heart sunk as Barron, or what was posing as Barron, spoke to her. Then she realized he spoke. She grabbed his hand again.

Not wanting to speak aloud, she asked Barron. *Is Barron still there, can he hear me?*

The voice inside of Barron answered. *Yes, there are parts of your friend that are still conscious. He has lost the ability to control his speech and movement but he still controls his basic functions.*

Can he communicate through you? Can you speak for him? She asked, hoping to get the answer she so much desired.

He can understand you and says, 'I don't understand what is going on. Why can't I see? Why can't I feel? Maddie, can you hear me? I can hear you.' He is still trying to comprehend what has happened. The voice inside of Barron told her.

Maddie understood. The nanocytes inside of Barron had to filter his thoughts outward. Unlike *Rho,* who could freely let Maddie communicate through its neural path, Barron was stuck, unable to interact with the outside world. He was a prisoner, a mere consciousness in the grand scheme that was his body. Maddie could reach out to him but his responses would always be buffered. She had to ask the body that was once Barron's to answer the question that was on her mind. *Will Barron ever be able to talk to us?*

The voice answered. *I am what is left of Barron. I cannot reconnect Barron to his former self. I am Barron now.*

Maddie dropped her grip again. Her hands went down to her side with no intention of talking through a proxy to the real Barron. With the exception of the red cluster on his temple, this new Barron walked and talked like the old one. Its speech was more boorish than the old Barron but to everyone behind Maddie, they couldn't tell the difference.

"You were assimilated?" Hope asked the new Barron.

"Yes," it answered. It pointed to its scar. "There are areas of the human brain that can be removed to allow us control of the body."

"Cool—" Hope started to say.

"No, it's not cool," Maddie stopped her. "That's not Barron. That's not an Inject. That's an alien." Maddie turned around and walked away. She brushed by Hope as a movable obstacle in her way. She didn't understand why she was feeling this way since Barron wasn't even important enough for her to miss. But she knew that he never deserved this.

Maddie walked up the ramp to the terraformer and looked at Barron one more time. She shook her head and could not believe that it really wasn't him anymore. She turned away and walked inside.

Jay and Marcus were completing their patrol around the fortress. Jay saw Hope and ran toward her. "Is that Maddie's monitor?" he asked Hope as she reached for the new Barron.

Jay reached her as she made the connection. She stood there in silence and Jay just watched. Hope looked at the scar on Barron's temple as she was definitely communicating with him. She dropped her hands and then her head. She turned to Jay and just hugged him. "This is so sad," she said as she gripped him tightly.

"Barron, are you with us?" Ben asked.

"That is why I am here," the sentient answered.

Hope let go of Jay, knowing that the Troll that had come with Barron had not received any communication or direction. She reached out her hand and invited it to fight with them. The Troll accepted the invitation and walked toward the other Trolls. Barron started to walk with the Troll. In its mind, it was no longer human and the reactions from Maddie and Hope solidified that thought. Marcus noticed the

Trolls. He assessed their presence. If they were a threat, Ben and Ethen wouldn't just be standing there. He knew that those Trolls must have joined them just as Maddie had promised.

"Barron, you made it back," Marcus called out as he walked up to Barron's body.

"I am not who you think I am," the sentient replied.

"What are you talking about?" asked Marcus. Jay was confused by the comment as well.

"Your Barron has been assimilated. I am Barron now. I did not ask for him to be my vessel. It was the plan of the queen mother," the sentient responded.

Marcus squinted at Barron. His happiness at Barron's return morphed into distrust. He knew that even if it sounded and looked like Barron, it was not Barron. He knew that Barron was gone. He detoured toward Ben and Ethen and let Barron continue to walk toward the Trolls.

Barron touched the Troll with whom he had met Maddie and then let go. His eyes were fixed on Hope as she talked to Jay.

DAY 287
ONBOARDING
INTERFACE ROOM

Five more Trolls joined the small human resistance at the terraformer. Hope remained outside to invite others to join. All the Trolls brought their orbitizers for attack and defense purposes except Barron and the Troll that traveled with him. As night began to fall, Ben told his forming army to go inside. Marcus stood lookout at the ramp for any straggling Trolls or worse, attacks. The Trolls were led to the interface room. Maddie had been sitting in there since her talk with Barron. Barron broke away from the Trolls and approached her. She noticed him coming toward her and got to her feet. "I don't think I'm ready yet," she put up her hand to stop him from coming any closer. Barron stopped to watch her go to the other side of the room.

Will went up to Ben and asked, "Do you want to see the killer plant?" Ben easily made the decision.

"Yes. Ethen, go with Will and take a look at the plant," Ben replied.

Ethen followed Will to the stairwell. The Trolls were huddling with no formation. Ben looked at them as an unruly bunch but he knew that they were there to fight against their soon to arrive attackers. "Hope, please come here and help me talk to them," Ben asked. He turned to Maddie and asked her for help as well, "Maddie, would you come and help me with the Trolls?"

Rho's voice spoke to Maddie, *"I don't think it wise to continue to communicate with them. They will become too reliant on us. Let Hope direct them."* Maddie turned to Ben and answered, "It's best if Hope talks to them. I am going to sit this one out."

"Thanks for the assist," Ben responded and then turned back to Hope. "They need some semblance of direction, Hope," he said. He walked up to the Trolls. Either they were oblivious to where they were or they were so used to being in the structures that they did not pay attention to the map that was still displaying on the wall. Each Troll, except for the one that came with Barron, held its orbitizer across its waist, angled down to its left-hand side. "Have them put out their hands," Ben told Hope. Hope touched the Troll closest to her and then it touched the next, and then the next. Soon, Hope led an interlocked chain of all the Trolls. After she knew that all of the Trolls were abiding by her commands, she told them to put out their hands. The Trolls simultaneously disconnected from the chain and strapped their orbitizers on their backs. They held out their claws ready for Ben.

Ben took out the marker that Jay had given him and opened the cap. "A white marker? Why would anyone have a white marker?" he asked himself.

Jay was within earshot and answered him, "I know, I figured no one would miss it."

"What did you want it for?" Ben was curious.

"I got bored in my room," Jay replied.

"Let's just leave it at that," Ben said. He walked up to the first Troll and painted its claws. The first layer of the marker turned out light blue. "It doesn't contrast enough," Ben said. He drew on a second coat and the color was much closer to white. He was content with the mark but knew it wouldn't last in battle. "We're going to have to find a better way to discern these Trolls," Ben told Jay and Hope. He continued to mark each Troll until all of their hands appeared like frosted claws.

Ethen entered the arboretum behind Will. Will's eyes immediately shot to the ground and searched for anything that could grab him. "Watch your step," he advised Ethen, "you never know what can eat you in here." Ethen looked around and saw orange and red trees scattered in the purple moss that had already started to grow outside of the terraformer.

"So where is this killer plant?" Ethen asked.

"Follow the wall," Will pointed to his right.

"That's not how this is going to work, buddy," Ethen nodded his head for Will to go first.

"I guess I'll show you… buddy," Will said begrudgingly. "Here we go again, Will put your life on the line because YOU found something and MADE the mistake of telling the others about it."

Will began his walk along the wall. Each step was slow and tender and methodical. He didn't stop near any of the trees and was focused on walking straight for the area of the blood red brush. Ethen took one confident step and then stopped while he followed each step that Will made. Ethen thought it was a painful process but didn't want to give Will a reason not to take him to the killer plant.

The cordons were strung in no particular order. The red strands came into view as they walked along the metallic wall. "There they are," Will stopped and pointed Ethen toward the plant's tentacles.

"Where is the killer plant, Will?" Ethen asked.

"I'm not going any closer. I brought you to it and my job is done. Just follow those red vines and you'll find it." Will was adamant.

Ethen walked toward the cordons but was careful not to step near them. Will stepped back a few more feet. His footprints were still imprinted in the moss and Ethen matched his stride step for step. Will watched as Ethen moved further away. "Damn, he's going straight for it," Will said under his breath and he followed Ethen toward the plant.

Ethen stepped in every footprint following the cordons to their source and came to the spot where Will rested after the plant pulled him. The red cordons were separated from the rest of the plant. "We could use these," Ethen said. "We need a better way to identify the aliens and we could tie the vines around their arms." Ethen began to pick up the cordons. He pulled one cordon and it didn't budge. Then the plant came to life. Its mouth opened and the cordons started to whip around searching for something to grab. Will was watching and moved away from the flailing cordons. One cordon rubbed Ethen's leg. Sensing him as a food source, more of the cordons flew into the air and struck the ground searching for their prey. Ethen was nimble and dodged one strike after another until a cordon hit him and wrapped around his arm. Will grabbed his blade and Ethen went across his body to grab his gun. Another cordon wrapped around his arm and then another grabbed his leg. Another cordon wrapped around his free arm and he dropped his gun. The cordons began to pull in different directions and the plant lifted Ethen trying to pull his body apart. Ethen tried to fight the cordons but the more he struggled, the tighter the hold became.

Will decided that he had stood back long enough and reared his blade as he ran toward Ethen. Another cordon wrapped around Ethen's neck. He attempted to grab it but the plant held his arms too tightly. Will jumped and brought his blade down on the cordon. The tension on Ethen's neck subsided. Will freed Ethen's arms and leg with a flurry of strikes. Ethen fell to the ground and backed away from the plant. Will avoided the cordons that were now searching for him and helped Ethen scoot away from the attack. "I told you that you never know what can eat you in here," Will said as he pulled Ethen by the collar.

"You were right, Will," Ethen said as he struggled, still trying to catch his breath.

"Do you think we can go back now?" Will asked.

"I think I've seen enough," Ethen said.

Ethen returned to his feet and gathered the loose cordons from around his ankles. He noticed that the cordons had left welts on his arms and leg from trying to tear him apart. He didn't go back to the wall. Ethen walked straight for the door through the small trees that obscured the killer plant. Will looked back at the plant and saw its mouth close. He followed Ethen as he started for the exit. "I never want to see that plant again," he told Ethen.

"Me either," was the only reply Ethen could conjure up. Ethen was focused on getting to the exit and Will shifted his focus to following him. Once they made it to the doorway, they ran down the stairs skipping as many steps as they could. They rushed into the interface room. "Do not go up there," Ethen said as he came to a stop.

"Up to the plant? I could have told you that," Jay said. Ben watched Ethen approach him with several red bands wrapped around his shoulders and arms. Ben was looking at Ethen strangely.

"What did you get yourself wrapped up in?" Ben asked.

"Let's just say I found something that we could use," Ethen said as he let the cordons drop to the floor. "I figured that we could tie these vines around the Trolls' arms." Ethen looked at one of the Trolls and said, "The red coloring is a better marker than what you did with their hands."

Ben picked up one of the cordons from the floor and took it over to a Troll. The Troll lifted its arm and allowed Ben to tie the cordon around it. Ben wrapped the cordon in a coil and tucked the ends underneath the single layer. "That should do it," Ben said as he walked backward. He examined the Troll from five steps back. "I think that'll do." He took ten more steps backwards. "Yeah, we'll be able to tell the difference now. From fifteen steps back, the Troll's arm was discernably red from the vine. It was a perfect contrast and an obvious difference from the Trolls that would be fighting them.

Ben grabbed another cordon and Ethen joined him. Ben wrapped one arm as Ethen matched the process on the other arm. Once they were done, the Trolls' arms appeared to be covered with red sleeves. A total of nine Trolls were ready to fight alongside them and Barron, Barron was with them too.

Ben realized that Marcus had been watching the entrance to the terraformer for a while. "Maddie, could you go check on Marcus and see if he needs anything?" he asked.

"No problem," she said, "it's crowded in here anyway." Maddie made her way toward the door. She stopped beside Barron and decided to talk to him, wanting to know exactly what had happened to him.

"Do you want to come with?" she asked.

"Yes, I would like that," Barron said, seizing the opportunity to talk to her.

Maddie started to walk out but reached out to *Rho*, "*I don't trust him, Rho. We need to find out if Barron really is in there.*"

As soon as they left the interface room, Maddie started asking her questions. "So why can't you let the real Barron talk to me?"

"Because I am not able to make the connection, like I told you before," Barron told her.

"That's a load of crap. *Rho* and *Kappa* made the connections, why can't you?" Maddie demanded. She grabbed Barron's arm and *Rho* took control of the conversation.

Who are you, being? What do you call yourself? Maddie listened to *Rho* get straight to the point.

I was given no name, no identification, I am Barron. Named just as the vessel was. Barron replied. *Rho* probed Barron's mind in search of the real Barron. Barron twitched in reaction to the search. *Rho* continued to probe but its search was being obstructed somehow.

You are blocking me and my ability to communicate with the vessel, Rho told Barron.

It is as I said, I am unable to make the connection, Barron replied.

Maddie felt herself being grabbed and pulled away from Barron. The voice and the connection came to an abrupt stop. Marcus had grabbed her. He held her face-to-face. "They're coming. The attack is here," Marcus said. He was quick and concise with his words. His eyes were wide open. "The time has come." Marcus released Maddie and ran to the interface room.

Maddie was slightly stunned but looked around for Barron. "Where did he go?" She looked to her left and right. In the short time that Marcus had separated them, Barron had managed to run away. "*I don't know where he went Rho,*" Maddie thought to *Rho*.

"*He will be found, Maddie. Let us focus on our survival for right now,*" *Rho* said.

Maddie sprinted to the interface room and had to dodge the outgoing Trolls. She quickly searched for Barron and did not see him. "Crap, he's not here," she said as she ran to the interface poles. As she sprinted past the far pole, her metallic hand extended and grabbed it. In one motion, she bent over, swooped up her orbitizer, and changed her direction back for the door. "This time, they die," she said as she ran through the door.

DAY 287
INITIAL SHOCK
TERRAFORMER

In the chaos that Marcus had initiated when he entered the interface room with news of the attack, two groups formed to fight against the attacking Trolls. The groups were formed by their familiarity with the structure. Marcus, Ben, and Ethen hurried for the stairs toward the room with the vats. Hope, Jay, Will, and the Trolls went through the other entrance. After Maddie grabbed her weapon, she quickly followed Hope toward the lounge.

There were already flashes of blue flickering in the hall as Maddie passed the closed doors to reach Hope. Their allied Trolls were in front of Will and Jay. Maddie asked Hope, "Do you know if that is Will or Quill?" Will overheard her and turned around.

"It's Quill. Did you really think Will could handle this?" Quill responded.

Maddie was relieved. Even though Quill was difficult to be around, Will was a burden in any situation. Maddie approached the stairs that went down to the lounge. Quill noticed that they were oversized just like the ones going up to the arboretum. The allied Trolls had no difficulty descending as they marched forward as if they were on a suicide mission.

The Trolls were on the lower level when Maddie and Hope reached the stairs. They slowly walked each step keeping their eyes on the hall in front of them. Step by step, they had made it halfway down when rapidly plodding footsteps came toward them. Jay and Quill ran back up the stairs. Jay grabbed Hope by the hand and Maddie turned to follow the flow of oncoming Trolls. She noticed the red sleeves and knew they were friendly. With her balance weighted on her knee and foot, she sprung toward the top of the stairs.

Maddie made it to the top and one red sleeved Troll stood in front of her. She could see that Jay had stopped and Hope was in front of a door. The door slid open and Maddie jumped into the opening behind Jay, landing flat on the ground. She noticed the pad to close the door and picked herself up off of the floor. She reached for the pad. Hope's hand touched the pad first and the door closed before Maddie could do anything else. "Bet you're glad that I'm around," Hope said with a smile.

"I sure am," Maddie returned the smile. She did a head count of who had made it into the room. There was Jay, and there was Hope, and there was nobody else. "Did Quill make it?"

"I don't think he's here," Jay said.

"He ran in front of us," Hope said as her smile vanished.

Maddie looked around the room. It was filled with large metallic boxes that were made of the same material as the walls. "We should hide behind those," Maddie said as she walked to the boxes. Jay positioned himself behind Hope, who was the first to take cover.

"How long are we going to wait here?" Hope asked. Clunking was heard outside of the door as the movement and sound of a fight grew closer.

"Until it's quiet out there or someone comes in the door," Maddie told her.

Maddie and Jay took cover. Jay, as big as he was, had more difficulty getting in a comfortable position. Maddie found a spot where she could lean against the wall. There was silence as they took time to catch their breath and calm down. Maddie closed her eyes and thought to Rho. *"If you had any great plans, now would be a great time to share them. You know, with the whole wanting to survive thing."*

"I wouldn't have recommended anything other than what we have done," Rho, as usual, did not hesitate to answer.

Maddie opened her eyes and looked over to Jay and Hope. Hope's eyes were closed. It was clear that she was talking to *Kappa* in her mind. Jay sat with his arms resting on his knees. He was staring at his hands as he picked the underneath of his fingernails.

"You know, this is going to end one of two ways, either we live or we die," Jay said, still picking at his fingers.

"You know, we are still alive," Maddie said, watching Jay.

The sounds outside the door stopped. It seemed the commotion had subsided. Maddie noticed the absence of noise and slowly got to her feet. Her head rose above the box as she stared at the door. Once her chin was even with the top of the box, the door slid open. "Are you in there?" the question came from a silhouette. Maddie's eyes quickly adjusted to see the man.

"Barron, is that you? We're here," Maddie said as she fully came to her feet.

"Yes, I told you that I was going to help you," Barron said as he walked toward their makeshift foxhole. "Let me help you get out of here. We can't be pinned down." He waited for Jay and Hope to get to their feet. They started to make their way toward Barron. He turned to walk out of the room with them in tow. As he spun, they saw that his hands held an orbitizer tightly. Somehow, Barron, who was unarmed originally, had managed to grab one.

Maddie figured that he had run away from Marcus and hid when the attack began. He must have picked one up at an opportune moment when one of the attacking Trolls fell. She gripped her orbitizer tightly as she still did not trust Barron. Hope and Jay were less apprehensive and quickly fell into form behind Barron. Maddie closed up the back and they left the room.

Outside of the room, Maddie saw piles of Trolls. She looked at strewn limbs. A mixture of mangled arms, legs, and bodies filled the floor. She stepped in the few areas free from the carnage as she counted the red bands. She couldn't count the sets since some of the bodies were dismembered but it looked like all of the allied Trolls had been killed. Strangely, she did not see any of the attacking Trolls. "Barron, if these Trolls are all dead, then where did the bad ones go?" she asked since he had been on the outside.

"They continued to go that way," he said pointing to the interface room. "I am sure that they are looking for the others."

Maddie kept her focus on avoiding the Trolls as she stepped toward Barron and the others. The flow of casualties extended to and down the stairs. She continued her cautious walk making sure that she didn't trip. Barron had stopped at the corner and looked around toward the lounge. He put his hands up to indicate that everyone needed to stop. The core of his orbitizer began to glow and he pointed it around the corner. One shot, then a pause, and then another shot. He stepped around the corner as a Troll crumpled to the ground. "I got him, let's keep going," he said. They walked around the Troll and Maddie saw that it didn't have red sleeves. She decided that this version of Barron was really there to help them.

Hope and Jay followed closely behind Barron as Maddie kept a little distance between them. Barron turned the corner to the dark hallway and luckily there were no Trolls in the darkened area. He led the others to the main hall. Blue flashes were littering the hall near the laboratory. "Well, it looks like the best way to go is outside," he told Hope and Jay. "Come on," he directed them toward the exit and walked toward the daylight.

As they made it to end of the hall, one surviving Troll stumbled into view, his red sleeves showing in the light from outside. Barron started to pick up his pace. "Come on, hurry," he beckoned the others. Hope and Jay felt his urgency and hurried toward the outside. Maddie saw herself falling behind and started to jog briskly. Barron, Hope, and Jay made it outside as Maddie approached the door.

Maddie was two steps from making it outside when the red sleeved Troll grabbed her orbitizer and pushed her down the ramp. Maddie stumbled as she tried to keep her footing. She stayed upright and straightened herself once her feet hit the purple moss. She looked back to see the red sleeved Troll holding two orbitizers and blocking the doorway back into the terraformer. She spun around to see Barron with his orbitizer pointed right at her. Her arms shot up, "Barron, what are you doing?"

She kept her eyes on Barron and looked for Hope and Jay in her peripherals. There were only a few Trolls around her. One was holding Hope and another was holding Jay. A third Troll was mounted on a Crossbearer with an orbitizer sitting on its lap. "You can let *Rho* know that you both erred in your judgment," Barron told her without any emotion breaking his façade.

"How'd we do that?" she asked. She hoped the longer she could keep him talking, the more likely that somebody, even Quill, could help them out of the situation.

"The queen mother thought you were just ordinary human pests that would eventually have been exterminated. But when you decided to challenge the queen mother, it knew that you could not be allowed to survive," Barron said, maintaining his aim on Maddie.

"Maybe we could talk to the queen-," Maddie started to say.

"No," Barron stopped her abruptly, "the queen mother has given her directives and there will be no negotiations."

"What are you going to do?" Maddie asked.

"The queen mother has decided the following punishment for you. Any vessels being found to have joined you will be exterminated. Any humans in league with you shall be exterminated. You will observe all exterminations and then you, yourself, shall be exterminated," Barron informed Maddie of her sentence.

The red sleeved Troll came from behind Maddie and wrapped its claws around her. She struggled to break free but the grasp was too tight. The Troll lifted Maddie and carried her next to Jay. *Rho* tried to speak to it. *You said you were going to help us and now you are helping to kill us. You can still stop this.*

That was my directive. Gain your trust and then eliminate you, the Troll responded.

As Maddie and Jay were being held, the Troll holding Hope shoved her to the ground. Hope was on all fours and looked up at

Barron. "Please, please don't kill me," she begged him. Barron, unmoved by her plea, raised his orbitizer and pointed it at her head.

"This is your extermination," he said as the core began to glow blue.

DAY 287
THE THREE MEN
TERRAFORMER

A s Marcus rushed into the interface room, he spotted Ben and immediately ran for him. He noticed the red sleeved Trolls and rushed by them. He slowed enough to grab Ben by the arm and pull him. "They're here, we're under attack," he hollered. The announcement caused everyone to start moving.

"Hope, take those Trolls with you and let them know that this is life or death," Ben shouted. He turned to follow Marcus and looked toward Ethen. "Come with us," he told Ethen as he ran past. Marcus was heading straight for the laboratory and Ben knew that it would be as good a place as any to defend themselves against the Trolls and their orbitizers since it was at least familiar. Ethen sprinted behind Marcus and Ben. He stopped on the stairwell.

"Do you want to go up?" he yelled to Ben.

"No," Ben yelled back, "we don't know what's up there."

Ethen ran down the stairs to catch up with Marcus and Ben. He reached the door and entered the laboratory. He found the nearest undamaged vat and took cover behind it. Ethen looked for Marcus and Ben but could not see either of them. His attention diverted to the front of the room when he heard a clank in the distance. His eyes scanned between every vat as he tried to identify the source of the sound. He quietly moved from one vat to the next, carefully avoiding being seen.

Ben was crouched behind Marcus. They had heard the clank as well. They had taken position on the wall opposite of Ethen. Marcus looked toward the entrance and spotted a Troll. Ben tapped him on his shoulder. "It doesn't have any red on its arms. It's not with us," Ben whispered. Marcus nodded his head in understanding and moved toward the Troll, keeping low so he wasn't seen.

The Troll didn't notice Marcus as it walked down an aisle of vats. Quietly, Marcus crept to an empty tank next to the blue hued Troll. Ben was close behind and placed himself next to an adjacent vat. When the Troll looked in the opposite direction, Marcus seized his opportunity. He jumped from cover and began to shoot the Troll. Ben, matching Marcus' initiative, jumped into the aisle behind the Troll and began firing as well. The Troll had no time to react as the bullets collided with its head.

The Troll began to unload its orbitizer as it tried to stop the onslaught. It shot wildly and the blue orbs flew in a flurry. Some of the orbs were absorbed by the wall and the others met with the vats creating holes where glass used to be. The Troll started to collapse and ceased its orbitizer fire. The core was blackened and depleted as the Troll hit the ground.

Ethen saw the shots from the orbitizer and once they stopped, he rushed to the Troll. With his gun ready to fire, he saw movement and aimed his shot. Marcus had walked over to the Troll and stood over it. Ethen dropped his arm and went to the Troll. He saw the Troll start its regeneration process and shot at its head until it stopped recovering. "How many of those things did you see?" Ben asked Marcus.

"Ten, maybe twelve, and one was riding that blue beast," Marcus said.

"Well, that's one down," Ben noted.

"It's actually three," Quill added, breathing heavy with his blade in his hand as he emerged from behind the door.

"I never thought I would say this but I'm glad you're here," Marcus greeted Quill.

"It's all clear out here. I think the others went outside," Quill said, waving the others to follow him.

Ben was the first to meet Quill. He put his hand on his shoulder and gave him an approving grin. Marcus and Ethen took a few seconds longer to get to Quill. "So we killed three of them, we have nine more to go, max," Ethen said. Quill looked at him. He sheathed his blade and started counting on his fingers.

"I thought you were talking about how many we killed. There are five more dead outside of that inter...thing room because of your Troll buddies and one more died down near the lounge," Quill informed them. Ethen was thinking how nice it would be to actually be relaxing in a lounge. His mind came back to fighting the Trolls.

"That means three left," Ethen told everyone the count.

"And one big monster," Marcus added.

"We can stand here and talk about it or we can go find the others," Ben said to refocus the others on their task. He didn't wait for a response and started down the hall. Quill fell in behind Marcus and Ethen as they followed Ben. The path was unobstructed and Ben made the turn for the exterior door. He moved quicker knowing that there were only a few Trolls left. Through the patches of light and darkness, Ben made his way toward the daylight. Instead of jumping out to the ramp, he slowed to see what was waiting for them outside.

He looked through the door and saw one Troll mounted on the blue beast as Marcus had said. He continued his count. Two, three, four Trolls. He looked closer at the Trolls, realizing he had just counted one too many. Then he noticed a Troll holding Maddie. It had red cordon sleeves. That was the problem. It was not fighting with them. He saw another Troll holding Jay and one standing behind Hope. Barron was out there as well but not as a hostage. He was aiming an orbitizer at Hope.

Marcus had the same view as Ben. "This isn't the way things are going to go down," he said. He raised his gun and started to fire on the Troll holding Maddie. The Troll released her to shield itself with its hands. Barron trained his gun on the terraformer and began to shoot. The Crossbearer made way for the door as the Troll mounted on it began to fire.

"Fall back, fall back," Ben yelled.

The Crossbearer neared the ramp. Barron saw that it was going to take care of the would-be attackers. He turned to aim at Hope again but was met by Maddie in his spin. She tried to grab the orbitizer but the red sleeved Troll pulled her away, leaving it just out of her grasp.

Barron aimed at Hope once again. The core of the orbitizer began to glow blue as he readied to fire.

"NOOOOOOOOOO," Maddie screamed.

DAY 287
HUMAN VS NANOCYTE
TERRAFORMER

E then, Marcus, and Ben ran down the hall. Quill was nowhere in sight. Ethen didn't bother to look back or around. He was so focused on getting to the end of the hall that nothing was going to distract him. They all knew that the Crossbearer would kill them if it caught up to them. Tink, tink, tink, the sound of its knifed feet meeting metal echoed down the hall.

A hum went past Ben's head as a blue orb flew by and was absorbed by the wall. Ben looked back to see how close the monster was. Another shot came from its direction and dissipated as it hit the floor behind him. Marcus was less concerned with what was behind him. He was trying to catch up to Ethen.

Ben tried to catch up to Marcus but he wasn't fast enough to shorten the distance. Marcus got further away and Ben looked back again. The Crossbearer was catching up to him. He clenched his jaw and pushed his legs as fast as they could go.

Tink, tink, tink, the sound was getting faster and louder no matter how fast Ben ran. Ethen made it to the end of the hall and turned toward the laboratory. Marcus was only a few steps behind and he zoomed in the same direction. Ben watched as Marcus and Ethen darted out of view. The end of the hall seemed like an eternity.

Ben was nearing the end of the hall when he tripped on his own feet. The floor got closer to his face and he turned in time for his cheekbone to crack against the hard metal. *Tink, tink, tink,* the sound was practically on him. He turned to his side to look behind him and there was the Crossbearer.

He watched as it slowed down to gauge his distance and then he spotted Quill. Quill had managed to get himself up to the ceiling. He fell from the ceiling and landed behind the Troll riding the behemoth.

With a quick slice of his blade, the Troll became headless and tipped over on its side. The Crossbearer felt Quill's landing and the sudden absence of the rider. It changed its focus from Ben and tried to rid itself of the nuisance on its back. The Crossbearer started to buck but Quill held on to its quills to avoid being thrown off. As its neck turned its head toward Quill, Quill repositioned the blade downward in his fist. The Crossbearer opened its mouth to attack and Quill plunged his blade into its neck. The monster let out an awful shriek and started bucking frantically. Quill kept his hold and jabbed repeatedly. His last strike hit the base of the monster's skull. The knifed feet scraped across the floor as the Crossbearer splayed to the ground.

Quill wiped the blue blood from his blade onto his pants and then jumped off the monster. He walked to the side of its head and saw it trying to regenerate. He hacked its neck until it stopped trying to heal itself. He stared at the monster and then turned to Ben. "That's one more kill for me," Quill said as he helped Ben to his feet.

"We have to help the others," Ben said as he sprinted for the door to the outside.

"Thanks would have been nice," Quill said as he watched Ben run toward the light.

Let us go, Rho commanded the red sleeved Troll.

I will not. I am doing the bidding of the queen mother.

Barron's eyes squinted, fully focused on Hope. Keeping his aim, he had withheld some information from Maddie that he could no longer contain. "Your friend, Barron, his mind tried to resist this. I was formed inside of him. Then, his brain was slowly withdrawn from his head and I replaced him. His pains, his worries, he begged for it to stop until he couldn't beg anymore. I replaced him slowly. His anguish went away with a whisper as I was in control. I was and am Barron. There is no part of him in here anymore."

"You're going to die, I promise," Maddie said.

"I doubt you will have the capacity to see that through," he replied.

Barron's mouth went silent and his muscles tensed as he started to clasp the pad. Maddie couldn't contain the overflow of adrenaline as her legs burned to take action. With her last act of desperation, she lunged as hard as she could to knock the orbitizer off of its intended target. Her body separated from the Troll as she leapt with one foot from the ground and the other from the Troll's knee. Her metallic hand contacted the end of the barrel. Her fingers wrapped around the exit of the muzzle. Barron saw Maddie's hand, smiled, and fired. A blue orb left the core and traveled through the orbitizer. It hit the muzzle and Maddie's hand started to glow as it absorbed the energy from the shot.

The Troll holding Jay let him go to help pull Maddie from the orbitizer. Jay felt the release and instantly ran for Hope. The blue orb wasn't totally absorbed by Maddie's metallic hand. Three blue discs formed as they passed through the openings of her fingers and headed straight for Hope. Jay reached Hope and leapt to shove her out of the line of fire. But he was too late. Hope's body flew through the air from the push and the three discs cut through her back and neck, severing her spine with the three strikes. Hope fell to the ground lifeless. Jay felt his anger well up inside seeing Hope lay limp. His fury turned his face red and he ran straight for Barron.

Maddie's hand stopped glowing and was jerked away from the orbitizer by the other Troll. With each of her arms being individually held by a Troll, she could not move. The Troll that was guarding Hope attempted to stop Jay's assault.

"Did you think you could stop me? It is as the queen mother has directed," Barron said, victoriously waving the orbitizer. His stance soon changed as Jay collided with him at full speed. The orbitizer flew out of Barron's hands and onto the ground. Jay unleashed his anger. His fists connected with Barron's face and blood started to flow out. The Troll that had guarded Hope reached Jay and pulled him off of Barron with a quick yank.

Barron wiped his face and got to his feet. The wounds quickly healed in front of Jay and Maddie. "You see, you can't hurt me," Barron said as his hand covered his face with another wipe. When he removed his hand from his face, it looked like nothing had happened with the exception of smeared blood running down his jawline. "Now, it's your turn," he told Jay.

Just as Barron spoke, bullets rang out from the terraformer. It was Ben and he was firing at the Trolls. The red sleeved Troll let go of Maddie's arm and covered its body to protect itself from the gunfire. Click, Ben was out of bullets and had to reload. He reached into his belt and it was empty. Gunshots came from behind him and he spun around to see Marcus and Ethen firing as his replacements. The red sleeved Troll was shouldering the brunt of the barrage. Quill ran out of the terraformer and went straight for the Troll holding Jay. Marcus and Ethen marched forward as they continued firing. The red sleeved Troll fell to the ground and the gunfire was then directed at the other Troll holding Maddie.

Quill reached the Troll with Jay and with one quick flick of his blade, he cleaved the Troll's head from its body. Jay, again, went straight for Barron once the Troll released its grip.

If you let go now and surrender, you might survive, Rho told the Troll still holding Maddie. The Troll loosened its grip on Maddie and fell immediately to the ground. The gunfire stopped as Jay again tackled Barron to the ground.

"I want him dead," Jay screamed as loudly as he could in Barron's face.

Maddie, Quill, and the soldiers walked up to Jay and pulled him off of Barron.

"Let's give him a message to deliver to the queen mother," Maddie said.

"Use the Troll, it's still alive. We don't need him," Jay said.

Maddie paused to look down at Barron. She opened her mouth to speak when a blue orb flew across her sight and connected with

Barron's head. Marcus and Ethen raised their guns and Quill raised his blade. Jay turned around to see what it was.

Hope was standing with an orbitizer in her hand and said, "Now we can have the Troll deliver the message." Jay ran to Hope. She dropped the orbitizer as he approached.

"I thought you were dead," he said as he hugged her with all of his strength.

"*Kappa* saved me," Hope replied, and returned Jay's hug.

"Well, I guess there's one thing left to do," Maddie said as she walked to the Troll cowering on the ground. Maddie thought to *Rho*, "*Remember, we are doing this. We are one.*"

She reached out her hand to touch the Troll.

Rho's message was simple.

Rho and Maddie have survived.

EPILOGUE

Maddie, Marcus, and now Will, sat on the precipice. The sea of purple had grown and now covered any remnants of green grass. The trees had become bare as the sun no longer reached their leaves. The world was changing, changing into an alien planet.

"How do you think Hope and the others are doing?" Maddie asked. Marcus stared into the forest below. He had been quiet since they had gone their separate ways from the terraformer.

"I don't know. These plants are going to take over the world and there's no stopping it," he said. "We're going to have to adapt. We have to find others. That is our only chance. We have to find other people and share what we know about the Trolls."

"I think I'm ready to go to the next bunker," Maddie told Marcus. She stood up and looked at the same area of the forest where Marcus was staring. "I hope that this plan will work and we can recruit some new members." Will got to his feet and tried to brush off the dirt. Marcus stood from his sitting spot.

"Let's see what's down there," Marcus said, and he walked down the mountain. Maddie and Will fell in right behind him. A large number of footsteps started to move behind the three but they didn't flinch. Twelve Trolls were following them.

* * *

Ben, Ethen, Jay, and Hope entered an abandoned communication center. Signs of an attack peppered the building. Ethen pushed the door through the entangled moss barricade. There was a chair behind one desk. The desk only held a box and a stand-alone microphone. Ethen walked up to the box and noticed it was a radio receiver. There was a low tone of static coming through the speaker. And then a click. A faint voice was heard from another radio operator.

"Hello… hello… Can anyone respond? This is Camp Titan, in Aspen. I am going out in the blind. We are under attack. We are evacuating. It doesn't look good. We have been attacked by the Four Dragoons. They have wiped out our defenses and we can't…" The transmission went silent.

About the Author

Sometimes we find ourselves drifting aimlessly through life like a jellyfish in the ocean, going wherever the current takes us. Then, we find something we enjoy and we do it. Such is the case with this book. This story started with a paragraph written for fun to entertain his wife and turned into this book.

Martin wears no cape, has no special accolades, or bells, or whistles to go along with his name but he has an innate ability to bring joy and happiness to those around him using his glowing effervescence and sunny disposition.

Born in Guantanamo Bay, Cuba, Martin has served in the United States Navy for 21 years and currently resides in Naples, Italy. He has been lucky enough to see the world and the wonders of people and cultures that populate it. And one day if he's lucky, he may rule it as a benevolent overlord.

Genetic Drift is the first book from the author and he hopes that you have enjoyed his brand of storytelling.